See what critics are
Readers Favorite™ A
Love on the Bac
A Tasty Romantic Comedy

Scintillating and refreshingly original....there is more to this romcom than meets the eye as Oliverio cannily entwines the joys of cooking and love with the sustenance found in the sanctuary of family.

Bookviral.com

...all the ingredients for the perfect romcom...fascinating characters who spring from the page with their energy... interesting settings that are clearly depicted for us... lots of fun, dollops of anguish, and a well thought out and executed plot.

Readers Favorite

...a wealth of fantastic and hilarious characters...

Novelgrounds

This was a good first book from the author, and to top it off we got some authentic recipes provided in the back.

Mrs. B's Books

...just the thing to take my mind off the wet, windy, wintry weather raging outside my windows last weekend.

BondiBookGirl

It's nice to read a book that can leave you weak in the knees from just a few well-timed kisses...(and) the best part of Love on the Back Burner *is the food!!*

Window on the World.

Great debut. Barbara Oliverio thrills readers with a recipe of humor and a crisp storyline...I loved it, loved it.

Chicklitpad.com

...perfect for lovers of romantic comedies, and I am curious to read what will be next from this author!

A Spoonful of Happy Endings

Barbara Oliverio

Love on the Lido Deck

Love on the Lido Deck:
A Nautical Romantic Comedy

Published by Scolapasta Press™
Denver, CO
719.339.6689

info@scolapastapress.com
www.scolapastapress.com

Author Photo Copyright Cliff Lawson
Cover Art Lisa Hertzi

Library of Congress Control Number: 2014906719

Oliverio, Barbara
Love on the Lido Deck – A Nautical Romantic Comedy
Barbara Oliverio

ISBN 978-1-497586390
1. Romance
2. Comic Fiction
3. Humor

Book Design and Cover Design © 2014

This book is printed in the United States of America

Barbara Oliverio

Love on the Lido Deck

A Nautical Romantic Comedy

DEDICATION

For Darby
You'll be in my heart, always.

ACKNOWLEDGMENTS

Thank you, as always, to my parents who gave me my life, my blue-collar work ethic, and the greatest gift they could: my Catholic faith. Thank you to my big brother, John, the best remaining part of my childhood (and the only other living person who can remember all the intricate rules to the "Salvo Cinnamon" game). Thanks to the rest of my extended Italian family.

Thank you to the early readers and book clubs who took a chance on my debut novel Love on the Back Burner and showed that even in the 21st century, people still appreciate a romance that is PG rated. Thank you to everyone who tasted recipes for me as I narrowed them down for inclusion in this book.

Thanks to Nancy, Wade, and Drew for love and laughter during many great travels in planes, trains, automobiles, and cruise ships "all over the world and parts of Alabama."

Thanks to Maryanne for including my humble efforts in wordsmithing and presentation as you brought great new projects to St. Thomas More Parish, and to everyone else in my St. Thomas More family—all of you have been a great support in my writing endeavors.

Thank you to Grandma Janet, who unconditionally accepted me into the family and continues to share her best recipes with me. Thank you Nikky T. for sharing what it's like to be on the crew of a cruise ship; if I bent any facts to fit the story, it's certainly not her fault.

Appreciation once again to Susan Hindman for her deft editor's pen, to Li Hertzi for a killer cover, and to independent publishing gurus Polly Letofsky, Gail Nelson, and Andrea Costantine.

Finally, thank you to the love of my life, Darby, who didn't blink when I said we needed to go on a cruise on the largest ship sailing the ocean as research for this book. He still manages to be the hero and leading man in my life story.

PROLOGUE

"Keira, I think my job is a metaphor for my life."

That was my best friend, Alexandria, opening a phone conversation as we so often did, without so much as a "hello" or "how are you?" I couldn't keep from giggling.

"Seriously, Alex? How can that be? You know you're more organized than any three people I know."

I had been away from Denver on business for several weeks, but I had kept up with every crisis in Alex's personal and work life via phone, text, and even Skype, so I knew she was just overreacting and needed to vent.

"I don't know, Keir. I just feel like I'm not as settled as I should be."

"Do you want my true opinion?"

"You know, that always sounds like it is going to be helpful, but when people start that way, they're going to say something negative."

"Not necessarily," I offered helpfully. "Maybe they're going to say the most positive thing in the world."

"Really? Go ahead."

Uh-oh. I could tell from her tone that anything I said was going to get her blue eyes flashing and her short brown pixieish hair standing on end.

"Well, you do have a tendency to act impulsively ..."

Oops, not a good beginning. I needed to back out of that.

"But all in all, you do go about things in an orderly fashion."

I realized that was the worst non-statement statement ever, but I could explain it.

"Explain please."

"Settle down. I see you squishing your mouth up to one side and squinting your eyes."

"I am not!" she insisted, but I instinctively knew she was un-squishing and un-squinting.

I continued. "It's like after we had just one discussion about you branching out from always cooking your Italian specialties for your dates, you immediately decided that you would attempt to cook these guys the cuisines of their own families."

"Yes, but I didn't just blindly decide to—"

"Calm down, you asked for my opinion."

"Hey!"

I ignored her and continued to point out the positive side of her dating escapades not so long ago. Although ... each one had turned into an episode of *I Love Lucy*. We both laughed as I recounted them.

"Admit it, you even kind of like the drama. Life would be too boring without it."

"Oh, Keir, I'll be so glad when you get back home next week."

Oh boy. There it was. My opportunity to let my best buddy know what was going on in my life. Go ahead, Keira, tell her. She'd never believe it, though. I'm just not an impulsive person.

"Um. Actually, I'll be staying for another several weeks."

Coward.

"What? How messed up is that company? You never have to take this long to finish an installation," Alex said, referring to my job of traveling around the country doing software installations for corporations.

"Oh well, you know, things happen." There. Missed another opportunity to spill.

"Okaaay. So do you have a guess as to when you'll be back?"

I opened my mouth to say something, but she cut me off because she had reached the airport and had to concentrate on looking for her brother in the pickup area. Whew. Saved by traffic.

We closed the call, and I smoothed down my dress, checked that my long blonde hair was still tucked neatly in its professional chignon, and walked back into the office where I had been tied up in a meeting for the past hour. I had just asked for a few moments' break when Alex's call came in.

"So, Ms. Graham," said the important-looking gentleman on the other side of the imposing desk. "Are you ready to take the plunge?"

I blew out a sigh, took my lucky pen out of my purse, and glanced over the paperwork again. Then I signed my name on the line.

"Congratulations!" he said, grinning. "We're glad to have you on the team at Worldwide Event Planning. It'll be a whole new world for you!"

I shook his hand and smiled nervously. A whole new world indeed.

CHAPTER ONE

Four Years Later

"Keira Graham Events. What can we plan for you today?"

I answered the phone the same way I had since opening my own event planning company and with the same excited anticipation. Would this be a newly engaged bride eager to plan her destination wedding? Would it be the marketing manager of a software company planning the launch of its newest offering and looking for the most outlandish party venue? Or would it be a newly widowed older gentleman who had no idea how to plan a tasteful reception after the funeral of his beloved?

I never knew who would be on the other end of the phone, but I was always happy to meet with a potential client. Who knew four years ago that I would leave my secure career as a systems analyst to jump into this crazy, hectic world of event planning—and fall madly in love with it? But I did, and I really loved it.

After an apprenticeship with the prestigious Worldwide Event Planning in San Francisco, I took another chance and opened my own shop in Denver and was building my business slowly but surely.

"Yes, ma'am," I answered the caller with a twist of my lips. "We are the company that organized the birthday party for the mayor's dog."

My junior partner Juliet's head shot up from her desk. She waved her perfectly manicured hands wildly and gestured no, no, no!

I spun around in my chair to avoid her signals.

"Well, no, we don't exactly SPECIALIZE in pet parties. That was a very special event for the mayor."

I spun back around and stuck my tongue out at Juliet, who by this time was glaring toward my desk. I decided to tease her a bit.

"Tell me a bit more about your Crusher."

Juliet had a murderous look on her face, and she leapt up and struck a hands-on-hips pose. I decided to put her out of her misery.

"Of course. I'll be happy to get you the name of the pet bakery where we got the cake."

I looked up the name of Denver's premier pet bakery and gave her the phone number, but I decided to have a little more fun with Juliet—who by now was directly in front of me, tapping a neatly shod foot—before I hung up.

"But if you DO decide to have a full party for Crusher, do keep us in mind. Bye now." I smiled innocently as I neatened up my desk.

"One of these days ..." Juliet threatened as she strolled regally back to her own desk. Juliet was tall with a drop-dead physique and a striking head of natural curls, and she was often mistaken for the singer Beyoncé.

"Oh, come on," I cajoled. "You know you loved planning that event."

"Keira, you know full well that when you gave it to me, you didn't tell me it was for a DOG. You just said it was for the mayor."

"Ah, no. What I said was that it was for a member of the mayor's family. You know he's never seen without that ..." I struggled to finish the sentence.

"Mutt?" offered Juliet helpfully.

I shook my head.

"No," I said. "I was trying to think of the breed. Bernese? No."

"Does it matter?"

As a matter of fact it did. I have always prided myself in being accurate. My best friend, Alex, never missed an opportunity to point out that trait, and my mother often suggested that young men might find my tendency for accuracy a bit "off-putting."

"Swiss Mountain Dog!" There. I remembered.

"Great," said Juliet sarcastically. "Now I'll be able to sleep. But really, Keir. NO MORE PET PARTIES."

I grinned. "I can't promise that, Jules. Remember, that one with the mayor brought in big dollars and got us great visibility."

"Whatever." She waved my arguments aside. "Could we banish that one safely in the doghouse and look at what's really coming up?"

I whipped my blonde locks into a quick side braid, kicked off my high heels, and propped my feet up on my desk, and we got down to the daily business of reviewing upcoming events.

"Long term?"

Juliet began to rattle them off.

"We have the Donohue golden anniversary in six weeks at the Denver Botanic Gardens."

"Are the invitations ready to go?"

"Absolutely." Juliet held one up for me to view. "You know, I love the fact that they asked in lieu of gifts that people make a donation to any Denver museum of their choice."

I nodded. "If anyone truly knew the Donohues, they'd know they wouldn't have it any other way. Music?"

"That's the one with the grandson who is a member of the Colorado Symphony. We have a string quartet from there organized."

"Sounds good. How about food?"

"Hors d'oeuvres and champagne for the first hour, then the plated dinner. They're offering a filet or salmon, but people don't have to choose until that night."

We continued discussing the rest of the arrangements for that event, then moved on to the next one.

"We have the Sweet Sixteen for Caitlin Myers," said Juliet.

"That's the painting party right?"

Juliet nodded.

"At first the venue didn't want to close down for an entire evening for a nonalcoholic event. But when I told them who Caitlin's parents were, they were more than happy."

"I figured they would look ahead to future business." I grinned.

"To be honest with you, I wasn't sure why a teenage girl would want that particular type of party, but I get it now after meeting her."

"She is a quirky girl, definitely not the typical overprivileged teen who wants the over-the-top super bling party that you see on the reality shows."

"It's going to be fun," Juliet said.

We ran down the list of those arrangements and moved to the next event.

"Because it's off-season it wasn't that much of a problem reserving the entire stadium for the software launch next month."

"Did you order the specialized jerseys in the company colors?"

"Yes." She rolled her eyes.

"Jules, just remember the commission we're pulling in for that party," I said, smiling.

"I know, I know." She grinned. "I negotiated that deal, remember? I just shudder to think why some marketing person picked two very similar shades of green as corporate colors."

"Ours is not to question," I shrugged.

"I don't know how you stay so calm, Keira." Juliet looked back at her screen, tapped a few keys, then frowned. "Uh-oh. One small problem for the event this weekend."

"This weekend?"

"Witheroe," Juliet continued.

"I thought it had been running pretty smoothly."

"Oh, it has," she said, nodding. "The Tasteful Wedding Package. Church ceremony followed by catered dinner at the family's country club. Very very traditional. Bride's family is from money so old it has cobwebs on it."

"Well, the money does pay the bills, sweetie," I pointed out.

"No," she said, frustrated. "You know what I mean. They didn't want to explore anything creative. When we do those cookie-cutter events, I feel that people don't think we are the cutting-edge planners that I know we are."

I nodded. Despite a reputation for being very good event planners and having a steady stream of work, it was hard to get jazzed up over the bread and butter of our business: the tasteful, elegant weddings.

"I hear ya, Jules, but a majority of my first leads came from my mother's circle, and they weren't exactly nouveau riche."

My parents were both from generations of "old money" in Denver, and sometimes it was hard to escape the trappings that came with that. I had been presented at a debutantes' ball, for heaven's sake. One of the things I liked best about going away to college to Notre Dame was that for four years, I wasn't "the Graham girl." I was just Keira. But when I first arrived at the university, it took me awhile to break away from the thought that people might want to be my friend just because of my money.

My freshman roommate, Alexandria, was the first to put me at ease. We became fast friends and have been ever since. She's a ball of fire and wouldn't let me sit in the dorm; she dragged me to every event she signed up for. People called me Ice Princess because they thought I was so stuck up. Ha! Hopelessly well-bred was more like it. Little did they know how much work it was to undo all the years of having to be on my best behavior for Denver's high society. Luckily, with Alex's help, it didn't take too long. Ever since that freshman year, I've been able to be myself. I got my degree in systems administration—unheard of for girls in my "station"—and worked in high tech for several years until I took the leap to follow my dream and become an event planner.

After four years learning the event-planning business in San Francisco, here I was back in Denver, organizing some of the events that, once upon a time, I would have been on the guest list for. My business had come along so well that I was able to hire Juliet, who at this moment was snapping her fingers at me attempting to get my attention.

"Keira? KEIRA! What do you want me to order?"

"Hmm?"

"Were you even listening to me?" She pursed her lips. "I said that the Witheroes are not happy that the only choices there are for linens are eggshell and white. I can't exactly have the country club order brand-new linens, not on the budget we're stuck with. And don't get ME started on the fact that eggshell and white are, for all intents and purposes, the same."

"Ah. But Patrice Ellington Witheroe must have some reason for her stubbornness on this point. Let me make a call."

I picked up the phone and punched in a number I would never forget.

"Maeve Graham," answered the familiar voice.

"Mother, it's me." My mouth curled into a smile thinking of my mother probably just getting back from a charity breakfast, slipping off her impeccable heels to put on the comfy pink slippers I had knit for her when I was eight and going through my crafts phase.

"Keira, my sweet"—I heard the love in her voice—"I was just thinking about you. Can you come over for tea and let me show you the new mare we've gotten in?"

My mother lived on the 35-acre estate that my father had inherited in tony horse country right outside the city. It was where I grew up, and the word *home* to me always conjured up the sounds of horses in the background. The stables were not as full as they once were, but she still had a number of our own horses as well as some that she boarded.

"Sorry, Mother, but I am slammed with work."

"Oh." I heard the disappointment in her voice. Then she brightened. "That's okay, I'll see you at the Witheroe wedding this weekend, won't I?"

"Mother, you'll see me there but as the event planner, remember? Not as a guest." Although she had been the source of most of my first leads when I started my own event-planning service in Denver, my mother sometimes forgot that I was the hired help now.

"Of course, dear," she paused.

"Mother, is something wrong?"

"No, no. I just haven't had time to visit with you in awhile. I'd like to chat ... you know ... girl to girl."

What? Girl to girl? Had she been reading magazine articles on mother-daughter togetherness? We've always had a good relationship, but if she suddenly decided to follow some strange trend in family togetherness—eek!

"Keira? Darling, you called me. Was there something you wanted to talk about?"

"What? Oh!" I had forgotten the purpose of my call. Ever since my father died, I felt the need to take care of my mother. I had even moved back home from my own apartment until she found a good manager for the stables. Once she seemed to be back on her regular routine, I moved back to my own digs in the Washington Park neighborhood. At times like this, though, I tended to overanalyze her every word. Was she getting lonely on the estate? Hmm. No, I was sure everything was all right.

Back to the business of the call.

"Mother, let me ask you this. Is there a reason why Tish Witheroe is not happy with the country club's linens for her daughter's wedding reception?"

My mother laughed.

"Keira! Don't you remember? At Polly's Sweet Sixteen, the country club decorated with the eggshell cloths, and Tish thought she looked yellow in all the photographs. She completely neglected the fact that she had chosen a dress that perfectly matched the color of Big Bird's feathers."

I burst out laughing.

"Oh, that's right! Mother, thanks so much! Look," I continued not more than a little guiltily, "I can move some things around. If you promise some butterscotch brownies, I'll stop by after dinner tomorrow."

"Keira, you may think that making those brownies is work for me, but it's not. I'll see you tomorrow, dear. I love you."

"Love you!"

I hung up, tapped my fingers on my desk aimlessly for a minute, then swung my chair around to Juliet.

"I have it, Jules."

"Well, it better be something good."

"Tell Mrs. Witheroe that the linens are a shade called, oh, I don't know, panache. Then make sure that the lighting is a flattering shade of pink. Everything will turn out for the best."

"Genius!"

"Of course," I sniffed. As if there were any doubt.

CHAPTER TWO

I pulled my little car up the long, winding driveway that led to my childhood home, slowing only long enough to put the window down to breathe in the luxurious scent of the many flowering shrubs and bushes that lined the way. Although my mother still maintained a gardener on staff—who wouldn't with that much property?—she was very hands-on in the selection of the actual flowers and shrubs. She loved the colors and scents and wanted to make sure they were always just so.

I paused at my favorite place to take in the wisteria that lined the west wall of the house itself. Wisteria are tricky and don't necessarily bloom every year, and rarely bloom in Colorado at all. This wall was my mother's pride and joy and the envy of her garden club sisters.

I must have been parked a bit too long, because a trim figure with a neat ash-blond bob soon appeared on the porch.

"Keira?" called out my mother in her patrician school tones. "What are you doing, dear?"

"Just appreciating my wisteria, Mama, as if you didn't know." I had claimed the wisteria long ago, and my father told me the reason he planted them was just for me. I smiled when I remembered how as a tiny tot, I couldn't pronounce the name of the flower but still knew it was mine.

"Kee-wah's wist-ee-we-ah?"

"Exactly, Kee. Always your wisteria," my father affirmed.

I pulled the car the rest of the way into the rounded drive in front of the house, jumped out, and leaped up on the porch to embrace my mother. Mmm. Arpege. As sweet as the flowers were, the scent of my mother's classic perfume was always home to me.

"Well, sweetheart, they aren't doing as well as they should this year. William has been babying them, but I'm afraid he might have a bigger job on his hands than he thought."

"What? They're gorgeous!" I walked her over to lean across the rail to get a better view.

She shook her head.

"He's been working especially hard. I wish I had Marco D'Agostino here to advise him," she said, referring to my friend Alexandria's father, who ran a nursery back East. "These gardens are just an indulgence for me, I'm afraid, but I do so love them out here in front."

I nudged her.

"Trying to hide the ponies in the back?"

She smiled. "Now, you know I love everything about those horses! Sometimes, though, even with as great a manager as Martin, the stables seem so ... big and unwieldy."

What was this? My mother was sounding like a wistful heroine in a bad romance novel!

"Mother! What's up? You sound like Camille making her dying speech."

Wait ... she wanted to talk to me ... girl to girl ... oh no ... could she be ...

"Mama, you're not ..."

She saw the panic in my eyes and immediately hugged me.

"No, sweetie, I'm healthy as a horse."

I gave her a friendly punch on the arm. "Ha, ha. You'd think that joke would have worn out its welcome in this house!" Well, she had diffused the situation with one of my father's favorite corny sayings, but it only made my heart catch. What was up with me? Next thing you know, I'd be weeping uncontrollably, and THAT was just not my style!

"Keira, come in, because those brownies are not going to eat themselves."

We walked through the marble foyer past the elaborate living room down to the elegant kitchen, which had not changed much since I was a little girl.

"How's Rose?" I asked, referring to her live-in cook.

"She went to visit her oldest daughter. You remember Tessa? She graduated nursing school and is working in a hospital in Nebraska."

"Oh, right." I considered. "So it's just you tonight? What did you have for dinner?"

My mother laughed.

"You needn't worry, Keira. If I can operate the oven to make brownies, I can operate the rest of the equipment in the kitchen to make my own dinner." My mother's grand party days had slowly diminished over the years, and Rose had not had to prepare as many elaborate meals as she once did, so she was really less of a cook and more of a companion to my mother.

"So where are these brownies, lady?" I joked as I climbed onto one of the high stools surrounding the maple counters.

My mother unwrapped a tray of delicious-smelling treats and brought them over, along with a pitcher of fresh iced tea, and sat next to me. I grabbed a brownie and took a big bite.

"Mmm. Mother, these are sooooooo good!"

"Always your favorites." She picked up one, too, and took a bite that was considerably more dainty.

We sat in a companionable silence for a minute before I took a chance on opening this "girl to girl" talk she wanted to have.

"So," we both started at the same time and burst into nervous laughter.

"You go," I said.

"No, you," she said.

More silence.

"This is ridiculous, Mother." I felt like we were in a bad sitcom. "You said you wanted to talk to me 'girl-to-girl.' Now, unless you've taken your cue from endless episodes of some program on the Lifetime Channel, something is up. Spill!"

She dabbed at her mouth delicately with her napkin—private Catholic girls' school training had not been wasted on Maeve Graham—then cleared her throat and dropped a bomb on me.

"Keira, I've been dating a nice gentleman, and it's becoming serious."

I was dumbstruck.

"Keira? ... Keira! Say something!"

I paused. I wanted to make sure that just exactly the right mature, calm words would come out of my mouth. Then I spoke.

"ARE YOU KIDDING ME? HOW CAN YOU BECOME SERIOUS WITH SOMEONE? DADDY HASN'T BEEN DEAD ALL THAT LONG. I FORBID IT!"

Um. Perhaps not so mature.

"You forbid it?" To my mother's credit, she was very calm.

I mentally stepped back. After all, I had gone to private Catholic girls' school as well. I could be ladylike.

"NO, NO, NO, NO, NO!"

Oh. Yes. That was soooo much better.

My mother cleared her throat.

"Keira! Listen to yourself. You sound like you are five years old."

"I do not!"

Just kept getting worse! I jumped off the stool and ran to the window and looked out across the back grounds. That didn't help. All I saw were the stables. Daddy's stables. I whipped around.

"Mother," I started patiently. "Who? What? Why?" I trailed off.

She walked over to me, looped her arm through mine and walked me over to the small bay window seat where we spent many cozy winter mornings.

"Here. Sit." She sat down and patted the seat beside her.

I plopped down, staring straight ahead, my green eyes blazing.

"Keira, baby, do you really think your father would want me to spend the rest of my life alone? Was that the type of person he was? He and I had discussions about things like this long ago. We each decided that the best way to honor the love we had for one another if one of us died would be to find another companion in life."

I turned to her. "But—"

"No. Let me finish." Her tone became firmer, and her own green eyes bored into mine.

"I'm not a child, dear. I'm past sixty. I can make my own decisions. Your father has been dead nearly ten years. I've been through a mourning period. Russell has come along and is a fine man."

Hmph. Russell. What kind of name is that? Sounded more like a vacuum cleaner.

"Keira, I know you. I know exactly what's going on in your head. You're judging him by his name right now."

My head drooped down guiltily. If anyone could read me, it was my mother.

"But—"

"Keira." She shook her head. "You need to calm down. This is not about forgetting your father. This is about me making the best of the rest of my life. Can you at least see that and be happy for me?"

I pulled my legs up and hugged them close. I managed to calm down enough to be polite.

"I'm sorry, Mama, but you have to admit, you sprang this on me kinda fast!"

She threw her head back and laughed.

"Well, how would you have me do it? Send you a save-the-date to tell you I had some news, then run a PR campaign?"

I gave her a wry look. If there was any doubt as to where I got my sarcastic tendencies ...

"No. But you have to admit—"

"Yes, I admit this announcement was pretty quick. But now that the Band-Aid has been torn off, so to speak, do you have any questions? And I mean thoughtful questions," she amended when she saw the look in my eye.

I thought for a moment.

"Okay. Where did you meet this Russell?"

"Keira. Please don't call him 'this Russell' like he's a crook of some sort."

"Well, now that you mention it. How do you know he's not after you for your money? It's not exactly a secret that you're wealthy."

"Right, Keira. He found my name in 'Rich Widows Monthly.' We're all posted in there." My mother shook her head at me.

And my friends think I'M the snarky one!

"We met at church, if you must know."

Right. Like men out to troll for rich widows wouldn't haunt churches.

"He is the new director of family development programs at the archdiocese, and Father Anthony had him over for dinner at the rectory with those of us on the parish council."

Oh. Rats. Who could argue with that pedigree?

"How long have you been dating?"

"Six months."

I jumped up.

"SIX MONTHS! AND YOU'RE SERIOUS ABOUT HIM? Not to mention I'm just hearing about him!"

"Keira! Again, we're not children! We are intelligent enough to enter into a serious relationship. We've both been married before. He was widowed about the same time I was. And why would I need to bother you with all the gentleman callers I've had that weren't serious when you've been so busy?"

I guiltily ignored the last part of that statement and pulled myself together.

"Does he have children?" I asked patiently.

"Why, are you worried that I'll love them better than you?"

"Well, I WASN'T, but now that you mention it—"

"Calm down," my mother said, smiling. "He doesn't have children. And you know I couldn't love anyone better than you."

She pulled me to her, laying my head on her shoulder.

Hmm. Except this Russell character.

She said quietly, "I would love him differently is all."

Love him. How could she even dare to use that word for anyone but my father? We sat quietly for a moment, then I raised my head to look at her.

"Mother, you know I only want the best for you. This just hit me pretty hard! I'll really be happy, really. Just give me some time."

"I know, baby, I know."

At that moment, we heard the doorbell ring.

"That will be him."

"What?" My eyes were like saucers.

"I asked him to come over so you could meet."

"Mama!"

She got up, prettied herself in the mirror in the powder room off the kitchen, and with a girlish spring in her step started to walk through the house to answer the door. Well, no getting out of this meeting now. I stood up to make myself a bit more presentable, making sure my blouse was neatly tucked and pulling my ponytail a bit tighter.

I heard laughter approaching and imagined my mother's boyfriend? sweetheart? gentleman caller?—I couldn't even think of the correct term! I pictured a kindly widower with distinguished graying hair, the type of man you see on the golf course dressed nattily in a muted polo and tasteful khakis. I stood expectantly and watched my mother walk in, followed by the man who, let's face it, could one day be my stepfather!

"Keira, this is Russell Shaw. Russell, this is my Keira."

You have got to be kidding me.

This guy was—what?—10 years younger than my mother! I was expecting polo and khakis, and he was in designer jeans. Gray hair with a receding hairline? Oh no, he was years away from gray. His full head of light-brown locks were shorn in a super trendy cut. And those shoes? Definitely not Naturalizers!

I caught my mother's stern look in the corner of my eye and pulled my debutante self together.

"Sorry." I gave myself a mental shake of the head. "Pleased to meet you. Would you join us for brownies and tea?"

I ushered him to the counter.

"Thank you, Keira." He sat down, but I didn't need to worry about serving him. My mother fluttered around with a sparkle in her eye and a skip in her step.

"Russ, do you want to forego tea and have coffee in your usual cup?" she asked.

His usual cup? He'd been around long enough to have a USUAL CUP?

"Thanks, May-May."

Whoa! May-May? What was she, all of a sudden? A character in a Rodgers and Hammerstein musical?

I pulled my phone conspicuously from my pocket.

"Yikes! Would you look at that? I have a client meeting I forgot about!" I lied. "I gotta go."

I kissed my mother's cheek and stuck my hand out stiffly to Russell.

"Very pleased to meet you. I'm looking forward to getting to know you." I blurted out in what I hoped was a polite tone.

"Bye, Mother."

"Keira—" Her disappointed voice trailed after me as I dashed through the house, took the steps on the porch two at a time, jumped into my car, and tore down the driveway.

CHAPTER THREE

"Seriously?"

"Seriously."

"Coming over?"

"Nearly there."

Alex and I had reached the point in our phone conversation that would frustrate anyone attempting to listen in on it. We had known each other for so long that just by half-phrases and inflections, we could convey volumes. I had immediately punched in her number on the Bluetooth in my car as I skidded out of my mother's driveway, and began to fill her in on this disastrous meeting with my mother and her new beau. I had just reached this cryptic portion of the conversation. The only factoid I had left out was the age difference between the two of them. Somehow I couldn't bring myself to tell Alex that over the phone.

We hung up for the last portion of my drive, and I turned my radio up to full blast so that I wouldn't have to hear the voices in my head screaming, "Your mother is a cougar!"

I reached my best friend's restaurant in the trendy Highlands area of Denver, jumped out of the car, threw the keys toward the valet stand, and didn't even take my usual minute or two to bask in the flirtation of the cute parking attendant.

Pushing open the door, I flew past the hostess stand and through the busy establishment to plop in my favorite corner seat of the enormous solid-oak back bar.

"Wow! That's a record for even you, Speedy," said Alex as she pushed open the kitchen doors and walked through. She wiped her hands on a towel and pulled the chef's cap off her head. As she flopped onto the barstool beside mine, she signaled to the bartender to pour us each a glass of iced tea.

"No comments from the girl who made it from south Denver to Boulder in 20 minutes," I snapped, referring to an infamous drive she'd once made, cutting a normal drive time in half when we were in danger of being late for a concert.

"Ah, those were different times," she said importantly. "Now I'm a conservative, married businesswoman and mother."

"Pfft." I tossed my ponytail over my shoulder. "That was a month ago."

She kicked me.

"Hey! Don't let Cam hear you!" she reverted back to her sassy self, referring to her husband.

"As if that man didn't know exactly what you were like when he chased you and married you!"

A cat-eating-the-canary grin stretched across her impish face.

"I guess there were no secrets there, were there? I did get the better end of the deal when he caught me, though didn't I?"

At that moment, the object of our conversation appeared, shirtsleeves folded up and tie askew, with their young son perched on his shoulders.

"Ahem." He coughed. "Who exactly caught whom, Ally-Cat?"

Alex reached up and pushed an errant black curl from his forehead as I had seen her do so many times.

"Oh, that's an old story. I'll put it in my memoirs someday." She grinned. "Where are you boys going? Didn't you two just get back from the office, babe?"

Cam handed Marco to his mother for hugs and kisses and gave me a brotherly buss on the cheek.

"We're going for a quick walk by the lake, then off to bed," he said, referring to nearby Sloans Lake, which was one street over from their cozy brick bungalow. Cam was the vice president of engineering at a local software firm that had an excellent day care facility. On occasional days that Cam and Alex needed to take advantage of the day care because of their schedules, one or the other of them spent extra time with Marco in the evening.

"To what do we owe the honor of this visit, Keir?" he continued, leaning on the bar.

I shot Alex a look to let her know that I didn't want to talk with him about my mother just yet. Cam and Alex didn't have any secrets and he had always been like a brother to me, but I needed to process this latest news a bit more before I shared it with anyone other than my best friend.

"Oh, you know the Princess feels she needs to check up on the Queen occasionally," said Alex, using the abbreviated versions of our nicknames "Drama Queen" and "Ice Princess" that had stuck from our college days.

He looked from one to the other of us, and his emerald eyes didn't miss the fact that we needed a sisterly talk.

"Come on, Marco my man," he held his arms out to the child. "Mama and Auntie Keira want to talk about the sweaters on sale at Anthropologie."

"Nice," Alex said. "If I didn't know you weren't an evolved member of the male species, I would think that's all you really think we talk about."

"Well," he grinned. "I've sat at many a dinner with just the two of you, so—"

"Out!" Alex planted a kiss on his lips, then swatted him. "Take this child for his walk before he wears a hole in the floor jumping up and down."

"Seriously. Keira, can't you be a little less picky about these guys that chase you?" Cam teased. "Keep one around long enough so the four of us can learn to play canasta or something, and I'd have another guy around and half a chance against the two of you."

"OUT!" Alex wagged her chef's cap at him as he swooped Marco back on his shoulders and cantered toward to the door.

"Honestly. Canasta?" Alex smiled lovingly as she watched her two men go toward the door and heard Marco's gleeful laughter as Cam dipped him from side to side as they weaved through the regular clients, who laughed along with him.

I looked after him wistfully as well. I wanted to tell them both that it wasn't my fault I couldn't find as great a guy as Cam. Maybe they only make one in a generation. It's not like I was jealous of Alex. No one was closer to me than she was, and when she found her soul mate, I couldn't have been happier. It's just that I had not been able to find anyone to connect with. Shoot, even my mother had found someone now.

My thoughts screeched to a halt.

"What up, Keira? I know that look," said Alex as she swiveled her barstool back toward me.

"Drat, drat, drat, Ali." I pounded my head on the bar.

"Stop it, Keir," she said. "We can't afford to rebuild this bar just because you're having a bad day."

My head shot up.

"First of all, the bar is six-inch-thick oak, and my head could not possibly do damage because the physics of the situation—"

"There." She grinned. "I knew I could count on your penchant for correct information to pull you back."

My eyes slightly welled up.

"Hey, come on." She put her arms around me. "It can't be that bad that your mom found a nice man to get serious with. Your dad has been dead a long time, sweetie."

I took a gulp of my tea.

"It's not just that she has a serious boyfriend, Ali. It's who he is."

"Who? Is he an axe murderer? A drug trafficker? A frequent eater at the Olive Grotto?"

This last one was probably the worst insult as far as an Italian chef like my friend was concerned.

"No, he's a perfectly nice Catholic man. As a matter of fact, he works at the archdiocese."

"Ah, diocesan-approved," she nodded.

"Ali, I'm sure he would even pass Nonna's approval," I said, referring to her deceased grandmother and a woman of high standards. "It's just—"

"Oh, for crying in the mud, Keir, how bad could he be, unless he's a jillion years old or something."

"Oh. No. Not that direction," I said pointedly.

She paused, and her eyes widened as she got it.

"He's ... *younger*?"

"Yep."

She took less than a second, waved her hand, then said, "So what? Men marry younger women all the time. Society just has a weird hang-up about the age difference going the other way. What's the age difference, two or three years?"

I shook my head from side to side slowly.

"Five?"

"Um. I'm going to say a minimum of ..." and I held up ten fingers.

Her big blue eyes got even bigger.

"Come on, Keir, I think you're imagining things."

"Well, I don't think he would have appreciated it if I'd asked him to let me shoot a picture of his driver's license on my phone so I could prove it to you," I snapped.

"What makes you think there is such a vast difference?" she asked.

"Look, Alex. Either he's that much younger or he has the best plastic surgeon in town. Plus, not a smidge of gray hair."

"Oh. Right, I forgot that there wasn't a way for people to change their hair color." She gave me a whap on the back of the head.

"Ow. It's not just that. Clothes. Shoes."

She stared at me.

"What? Not wearing any? What ABOUT his clothes and shoes?"

I became impatient.

"You know. They were YOUNG."

"Holy Guacamole, Keir. People of all ages are welcome to shop in all stores. Well, maybe except for Arbor and Fletch. They tend not to even glance at you if you don't fit their demographic."

I shook my head.

"You just don't get it. He is YOUNG." I jumped up and started to pace.

Alex pulled me back on the stool.

"Shh. Don't drive away my business." She waved and smiled at a few of the diners who had begun to look at me quizzically.

"Look," she continued patiently. "Allegedly, he's—"

"Not allegedly. He IS—"

"Okay, okay. He IS a bit younger—"

"Not a BIT younger, a LOT younger—"

"Keira!" She was on the border of angry now. "You have no proof of age, and no, his clothing and hair color are not proof!"

"Fine," I allowed. "But, Ali, if he is at least 10 years younger—"

"So what?"

"SO WHAT?"

"Yes." She shrugged. "So what? Are they happy?"

I stopped kicking the bar.

"Um, I guess so."

"You guess so? Didn't your mother say she was happy?"

"Well, yeah," I allowed.

"I repeat, so what? If they're happy, then it doesn't matter."

I thought for a moment, then pointed up, aha fashion.

"Everyone will call her a cougar," I said triumphantly.

This earned me another whap on the back of the head.

"I cannot believe you just said that," Alex said, shaking her head.

"Well it's true."

You can say anything you want about the fact that it's no different than older man/younger woman, but the stigma of older woman/younger man is way different. It's an amazingly acceptable joke.

"Didja think that maybe, just MAYBE, if people would call her that, then, um, her DAUGHTER should be just that much more supportive?"

Oh.

Right.

I slurped my ice and pondered.

"You know, Ali, I hate it when you're right," I finally admitted.

"That's because you are usually the level-headed one, Princess." She punched my shoulder. "I've always been the Drama Queen, remember?"

I smiled halfheartedly.

Then I remembered another point.

"Well, how about this little melodrama, then, oh newly crowned wise one," I said. "It occurred to me earlier that part of my annoyance with this situation has nothing to do with my mother's new beau at all."

"Go on."

"It's just that, when Cam pointed out that I don't have a guy, it occurred to me that not only have I not found the right one yet, but even my MOTHER beat me to the punch. How's that for messed-up thinking?"

Alex blew her bangs out of her eyes and began patiently. "First of all, you know that Cam was not saying anything to hurt you, right?"

"Oh, I know, I know. He wasn't being mean in the least. But eventually you guys are going to get tired of having Auntie Keira around when all of her date prospects have vanished."

"Oh. Sure. You are always at the house in your saggy cardigan and sensible shoes with tissues stuck up your sleeves. That's you, all right," Alex laughed. "Keira, Cam and I can't keep track of all the guys who swarm around you. As a matter of fact, I made a bingo card and am crossing them off one by one: blond, blue-eyed doctor; brown-eyed sales manager. Just let me know when you date a redheaded musician, will ya? I need that one to fill my card."

"Ha-ha. That's the POINT, Alex. Lots of guys may be interested. Just not the right guy."

Her tone softened.

"He'll come along, Keir. When it's right, you'll know it. Remember all the frogs I had to kiss before I found my prince?"

I laughed. "And you're telling me that he's just a prince while you're the queen?"

"There's my snarky girl!" She hugged me. "And Keira, you can't compare your situation to your mother's. You're in different stages of life and looking for different things in a relationship."

"You're right," I nodded finally.

"Wow! Two rights for me in one conversation! Put it on the calendar, ladies and gents!" Alex hopped off her barstool and struck a pose.

I swatted her. "Don't get too comfortable in an uncommon position of being right, missy."

"I kind of like it here," she preened.

I hopped off my stool and hugged her tightly.

"I better scoot. You need to get back to the kitchen and let them know you're still the boss."

"Ha! As if they don't know! But you're right. My sous chef is more than capable, but I need to get back to help before the dinner rush really picks up," she agreed. "Are you going to be okay? Want to come over to the house and dig in to some leftover lasagna later?"

I laughed.

"Your Nonna would be proud. Solving the problems of the world, one lasagna at a time! No, I need to get back to my place and do some work." I paused. "I should call my mother."

"Maybe stop over on your way home?"

"Fine." I squinted. "I'll stop over, but not if my daddy-to-be is there. You have to give me that, Alex. I need to visit her alone to make things right."

Alex nodded.

"Sure, sweetie, but whatever you do, don't go to sleep without talking to her, okay?"

I hugged her again.

"Will do. And Alex, thanks for letting me freak out on you."

"Always, babe. It's what we do, right?" She smiled, placed her chef's cap on her head at a jaunty angle, and walked back to the kitchen.

CHAPTER FOUR

"Morning!" Juliet trilled from behind her computer as I entered the office the next day.

I removed my oversized designer shades from my eyes and perched them on top of my head.

"You are amazingly cheerful this morning," I said. "Did you talk the barista into an extra shot of espresso or something?"

"Oh, but even YOU will be cheery when you hear the news this morning, my maddeningly patient colleague. What is the one thing that we've been hoping for more than anything?"

"A winning lottery ticket?"

"No, and you do realize you have to actually purchase one to win, right?"

"Oh, is that how it works?" I asked innocently.

"Keira, focus. What would we both love to have?"

"A date with Chris Hemsworth?"

We both sighed.

"Unfortunately, no. He's married, remember?" She walked me to my chair and pushed me down by my shoulders and handed me a message slip.

I glanced at it.

"This? A note from"—I paused to read the name—"Alfred Sanford?"

Juliet nodded expectantly.

"Jules, I'm not a mind reader, dear. Who or what is an Alfred Sanford?"

She crossed her arms and pursed her lips.

"Think! What have we said would break us through from the Denver market to show how relevant and hip we are regionally and nationally?"

"Juliet! Seriously, now. I'm going to Java Junction and telling them you are absolutely banned. Alfred Sanford doesn't sound like someone hip, he sounds like someone who needs a new hip. People with those names are usually on the boards of—"

My eyes widened, and I jumped up. We both shouted together: "Food conglomerates!"

"OMG Jules, he's not related to SanFoods?"

Juliet nodded furiously and beat her fists on my desk.

"He IS SanFoods, Keir." She did an impromptu salsa. "The CEO of the largest international food conglomerate wants to hire us to coordinate an event—on a cruise ship, no less!"

"Whaaat? How did that happen? And just this morning before I arrived? Why didn't you call me?"

Juliet sat back on her own desk and began the story.

"What? And miss that look on your face?" She pointed at me. "Remember the Groveston wedding? Apparently, he was a guest of the groom. It turns out that SanFoods is sponsoring a specialty cruise for food lovers, and he was impressed with our "Around the World" theme at the Groveston reception and thought our company could handle their project."

I remembered that wedding. What an event. The couple were both seasoned world travelers and wanted practically every single cuisine that they had encountered around the world represented at the reception dinner—and they wanted the decor to seamlessly match. Not easy or cheap, but it was a fantastic challenge to tackle.

"Did you actually talk to Alfred Sanford?"

"Hey! Are you worried that I wouldn't represent?"

I threw a pen at her.

"No. If I didn't have faith in you, I wouldn't have hired you, silly." But I couldn't resist adding, "And it helped that you had references from here to forever. And, of course, if I didn't hire you, you would have set up your own shop and been my biggest competition."

She sniffed and tossed her long locks in true Beyoncé style.

"I resemble that remark."

"Jules, finish the story."

"Okay, it was the groom's grandfather who called to see if we were even interested. He gave me the briefest of details and said that if we were interested, we were to call Al—you see what I did there? Al and I, we're on a first-name basis."

I stared at the message. Taking on an event of any size for a major cruise line would be huge for us in terms of exposure. There was no doubt in my mind that I would return this call. And even less doubt that we would say yes to whatever this opportunity was.

"Thank you so much for the opportunity," I said to Alfred Sanford one week later following the presentation I gave as I sat across from him at his desk. "You won't be sorry."

After the initial phone call and an initial meeting where he described his concept for the event, Juliet and I had gone into overdrive. We devised an event that featured cooking classes by a mix of chefs and food bloggers, and then created a PowerPoint presentation to show off our ideas. Mr. Sanford was so pleased that he bumped the plan up from the original cruise ship to the *Ocean's Essence*, the largest ship sailing on the ocean.

"I'm sure we won't," he said, genially. He was a kindly man with receding graying hair and deep-set wrinkles around his eyes. Now THIS was the kind of guy I pictured with my mother, not ...

Stop.

I had promised myself that I wouldn't be judgmental (well, more judgmental) of my mother's blooming relationship. She was happy, and this Russell person seemed to be very nice to her. Besides, this was a moment to concentrate on my great new opportunity.

"I'll send you the full amended project plan this afternoon based on the discussion we had today," I said. He had made some minor tweaks and requests.

"That sounds perfect."

I looked through the paperwork once more to see if I had any further questions.

"Mr. Sanford, how do I make reservations for a stateroom for myself, my business partner, and the featured chef?"

He looked pleased.

"Keira, I see that you already sound like a seasoned cruiser, referring to a stateroom instead of a cabin! I can see we made the right choice. Those reservations are made through my assistant, Sharla. Just let her know what you need."

I smiled inwardly at his compliment of my knowledge. Apparently he didn't research me as much as I had researched him. I had left no stone unturned in my own fact-finding!

"Keira, as part of the package, I'd like to offer you the ability to invite your own family as well. Just let Sharla know how many other staterooms you'll need. Feel free to add four more rooms."

I was stunned.

"That is so kind of you! Thank you so much!"

"No problem, my dear. As executives, we reserve some promotional space on every cruise, and I am using my discretion to offer mine to you."

"Thank you so much!"

"Nonsense." He waved off my thanks. "I saw how hard you worked on that wedding for my godchild. My wife and I want to thank you for the happiness you brought the couple and the rest of the family."

Wow! Well, my mother always said to put your best effort into any job you do because you never know how it will affect you down the road. I doubt when she said it she thought it might eventually mean a free vacation for her.

We said our good-byes, and I exited his office. I maintained my businesslike composure as I walked to the elevator and punched in the number for the lobby of this downtown Denver high-rise. As soon as I reached the lobby, I calmly walked out of the building and down the street. The minute I turned the corner, I pulled out my phone, hit speed dial, waited for Alex to answer—and started to dance in glee!

"I got it, I got it, I got it!"

"Keir! That is so awesome! What is the actual deal? Did he tell you?"

"Duh. You know I didn't leave there without every *i* dotted and *t* crossed."

"Of course, what was I thinking?" I could picture her rolling her eyes. "So spill."

I recounted the plan to her amid shrieks.

"The deal was sealed when I told him that you were the keynote chef. At that point, he couldn't help but hire me!"

Alexandria's chain of restaurants had exploded in popularity, and she had written a cookbook based on her brand of Italian comfort food. Now she was occasionally featured on the Food Network as well as the *Today Show*. She had been contacted to compete on *Iron Chef* and was ecstatic when she got to match knives with one of her idols, Bobby Flay.

"Ahh. I'm just a little Italian girl who cooks," she said modestly. "Excuse me, can we get back to YOUR opportunity?"

"Oh, right. Me."

"Could you just reach around the back of your own head and give yourSELF a whap, please?" she said with impatience.

Alex was the only person beside my mother who could see through my cool Ice Princess facade and know how vulnerable I am sometimes and how reluctant I am to talk about myself.

I plopped down on a nearby bench and confirmed the details of the project, interrupted only by her occasional "ohhh" and "cool."

"So," she teased, "will there be room for me to sneak Cam along for a second honeymoon?"

"That's the best part," I said. "Mr. Sanford said I could take family and that I could get extra staterooms."

"WHAAAT!"

"I KNOW!"

"So, Cam and I can have a cabin? Wait ... You know I was totally joking, right? I wasn't angling for a free vacation for him."

"Stateroom, darling. Get the lingo right," I corrected. "But, of course, you goof. I would definitely want you to be able to invite Cam along."

"That's awesome, Keira! Your mother, too?"

"Of course my mother," I laughed. "I thought of something else, Alex. I don't have a lot of family, so I thought my D'Agostino family should share in my wealth."

"What? You mean Ma and Pop?"

"Do you think they could leave the plants and the nursery for a week?"

"Hmm. Well, they should. They never take a vacation."

"Is there anyone who can cover for them for a week?"

"I know Anthony could, of course. My brother could run a dozen companies without thinking." Alex's older brother was the only one to have gone into the family business and had even branched out into landscape design.

"I was hoping Anthony and Celia could come, too. And Damian," I said, referring to her other brother, the priest.

"Pop and Anthony out at the same time? I don't know, Keira, that's asking a lot."

We pondered silently.

"You know what?" Alex said finally. "Pop will just have to agree if we get Ma to see the importance of a family trip, right? Cousin Joey is his right-hand man and can keep things going for a week."

"Well, Alex, you know them better than I do. Just let me know how many staterooms I'll need, along with cots for the kids. Sweetie, I know this won't be much of a second honeymoon with the assorted offspring between you and Anthony along for the trip."

"The kids would be okay," she said, then stopped. "You know what? What do you think about this? Let's make this an over-twenty-one trip. Anthony, Celia, Cam, and I can do a kid trip to Disney or something another time. We can see if Celia's mother will take the little ones for this trip. They'd probably like that better anyway."

"Oh, like that is a burden for her!"

Alex's sister-in-law had a mother who not only didn't mind when grandchildren and grand-cousins came to visit, she insisted on it. Anthony's daughter had dubbed her warm and inviting home "Camp NannaPappa," and the rest of the assorted tykes had adopted the name as well.

"Your mother is going to love this!" Alex said.

"Oh rats!"

"What. Oh." Alex thought of the same thing I did.

"My mother will want her sweetheart Russell to come along, and I would not feel comfortable with them in the same stateroom, Ali."

"Hmm." Alex paused. "You know, Keira, you can't be sure that they don't stay together now."

"Please, Alex."

We both thought for a moment, then Alex had the best idea. "I know! He can share a room with Damian!"

That was the perfect solution. Except where would my mother stay? Before I could pose that problem, my resourceful friend rescued me again.

"That would make it easier for you. Your mother could share with Juliet, and you could have a stateroom to yourself that would be half sleeping quarters and half your office. You know you'd need that much room anyway."

"That would be the ideal solution, wouldn't it?" I said. "But do you think everyone will agree to the arrangements?"

"Keira, you're offering everyone a free Caribbean cruise for a week. Who argues with anything after that?"

I pondered for a moment. She was right.

"Sweetie, you call your people, and I'll talk to mine. In the meantime, I need to actually plan the business aspect of the cruise."

"Fantastic, Keir. Come over later so we can talk about booking the chefs." She paused. "Hon, is everything perfect now?"

Perfect. Everything solved. No problems.

"Mother, what is the problem? I'm offering you an all-expenses-paid cruise on the largest ship in the world!"

I was laying on the glider in the sunroom of our house with my hands wearily covering my eyes while my mother sat on a nearby lounge chair ostentatiously completing a crossword puzzle.

"No problem, dear. It's a lovely offer," she said.

It was as if she had taken out a big giant can of "tone" and lavishly painted the words she was saying with it.

"Then what is it?" I asked, picking up a small pillow and tossing it up and back.

She waited a moment, calmly laid her puzzle in her lap, took off her reading glasses, and began. My mother is nothing if not methodical.

"Well, Keira, look at it from my point of view. You offer me this trip, you tell me I can bring my friend, but then you direct me where he can sleep. Do I have it right?"

Uh-oh.

"Mother, are you telling me you are upset because of the sleeping arrangements?" Eek.

"No, Keira, I think they are perfect. I'm just upset because you came in and dictated it to me as if you think I don't have the morals to figure it out on my own."

Oh.

I stood up and went to the lounge chair where she sat, and scootched beside her. I hugged her and gave her a kiss.

"Mother, I'm sorry. I know you have your morals lined up. Who taught ME after all? I was just in organizational mode, I guess."

She smiled and patted my knee.

"Oh, if anyone is organized, it's you. And I guess it does my motherly heart good that you are keeping things proper. But the thought of you and Alexandria discussing my private life, well ... my goodness!"

I burst out laughing but composed myself when she gave me a look.

"Thank you so much for inviting Russ. He will probably be thrilled to share with Damian. They'll make excellent roommates. You know the good father IS my favorite priest."

"Oh, Mother, admit it. You know before he took Orders you would have loved to have snagged him as a son-in-law."

"Well," she picked up her crossword puzzle, "if I had to lose him to anyone, I guess I'm fine with losing him to that competition. Although, speaking of son-in-laws ..."

I pinched her cheek.

"All in due time, mama bear. How about you let me get through this tiny little cruise project before we have to worry about planning my wedding?"

"Mm-hmm," she said, propping her stylish reading glasses back on her nose, ready to get lost once again in her puzzle. "Who knows? Cruises are supposed to be extremely romantic, you know. Maybe Mr. Right will be on deck waiting for you."

CHAPTER FIVE

"Wow, this is the biggest boat I've ever seen!" Juliet tilted her head back and shaded her eyes from the sun as she attempted to take in the entire view of the behemoth before us.

"It's a *ship*, Jules," I corrected her. "A boat is the sleek little thing that we rent when we go up to Lake McConaughy for the day and waterski. And please move briskly. We have to sign in just like the other thousands of passengers, even if this is a working trip.

We had just been deposited from our cab at the dock at Ft. Lauderdale and marveled at the size of the *Ocean's Essence*, which would be our home for the next week. Shipside porters checked our larger luggage with brisk efficiency, and then we joined our 5,500 new best friends in the walk toward the ship to complete the check-in process. Our guest chefs and bloggers would be checking in at different times at their convenience, but I had booked a shipboard meeting room for us to all gather and cement plans later that evening after the ship set sail.

"I hope all the chefs make it," Juliet remarked, reading my mind.

"Did they all check in with you last night?"

"Yep. And the ones who didn't contact me got a phone call or text FROM me. I made sure to be in touch with each one of them personally."

The chefs and bloggers who had agreed to be the instructors for the seminars were paying their own way but had gotten a sizable discount. Many of them had never cruised before, so this was an exciting working vacation for them and one that offered them a lot of exposure. All of the pertinent information was in the packets we had distributed to them and was also posted on the login portion of our website. I was a big believer in backup plans.

"To be honest, I'm kinda more worried that the D'Agostinos won't show on time," I said. The clan had arrived in Ft. Lauderdale late the previous day, got in a bit of evening sightseeing, and attended a later Mass than we did this morning. Juliet had not yet witnessed "Hurricane D'Agostino."

As if on cue, a rented minivan pulled up, and I could hear peals of laughter spilling from the windows coming from my favorite family.

"There she is!"

"Keira! Keira!"

Juliet and I stopped and waited for the various members of the D'Agostino family to exit the van and then sort out and check their luggage with the porters.

Alex hurtled her petite body at mine, nearly knocking us both over.

"Girlfriend! We are cruising! On the ocean!"

"Ali!" I laughed. "Calm down. Anyone who saw you would never believe that we see each other practically every day back home!"

"Or that you are a renowned chef who shouldn't be acting as if she were fifteen years old," added her brother Anthony as he joined us, giving me a hug and kiss. He introduced himself to Juliet with a hug and tweaked Alex's ear. His attractive wife, Celia, joined us, arm in arm between Alex's parents. Another round of greetings, introductions, and kisses followed. When I first met the D'Agostinos I couldn't believe a family could be so huggy-kissy, but I got used to it and soon expected it. I quite enjoyed watching the calm, cool Juliet get caught up in the whirlwind.

"Where are Cam and Damian?" I asked, referring to the two least likely to be stragglers.

No sooner had I asked than they both appeared.

"Someone had to tip the porters," explained Cam with a shake of his head.

"Oh, as if Pop didn't take care of all that. You know that you two were just talking geek about the other ships around here!" said the sensible Celia with a wave of her hand.

"Caught us!" Damian had not lost his boyish charm even after his years in the priesthood.

Juliet had not said a word during any of these exchanges—quite a difference from her usual self.

"Come along, darling," I grabbed her arm. "Didn't I tell you last night that resistance is futile with the D'Ags? You WILL be assimilated."

The entire group laughed.

"Juliet, let's go!" I said. "We need to meet my mother on the Lido Deck. SHE had the good sense to check in early!"

Our group moved through the remainder of the check-in procedure as a unit. Because Alex and I were part of the "entertainment," we were able to bypass the normal line and go through the line that was reserved for first-class passengers.

"Are you sure we should be in this line?" Mr. D'Agostino asked with a tilt of his head, running his hand through his graying curls and blinking his blue eyes.

"Pop!" Alex's exasperation was evident in her tone. "Keira and I are getting a little bit of special treatment."

"Oh, does that make us your entourage, ma'am?" Anthony's own blue eyes twinkled as he and his brother, both looking so much like their father, prepared to tease their little sister.

"Cam!" Alex appealed to her husband.

"Huh? What?" Cam looked up from the document he was completing, but I could tell he had heard the entire exchange. "Did you say something, sweetheart?"

I sighed as I watched the exchange and once again prayed inwardly that I would find a nice man like Cam.

As if she'd read my mind, Mrs. D'Ag put her arms around me and said, "Your fella is out there, Keira."

"Oh, Mama D., I hope you're right!"

"I know I'm right," she asserted, fussing with the Peter Pan collar of my mint-green blouse as only a mother can. "You've been like a daughter to me since Alexandria brought you home from college, and I want the best for you as much as I do for my own little ball of fire and my boys."

We both looked over at Alex and the "boys" engaged in a heated discussion.

I laughed and pointed, "You know I've never been as outgoing as Alex."

She waved her hand and stopped me. "Stop that. You have a great personality. How else could you have run your business so well? Look at this event that you planned and the chefs you recruited."

I guess she was right. I always thought of myself as so introverted, but would an introvert be able to sell event planning? And run the events?

"I know I'm right," she said, reading my mind. "Oh, they're calling us forward. What do we do now?"

I snapped into action. This trip would never be successful if I couldn't manage herding these cats through check-in!

Forty-five minutes later, we had all deposited our carry-ons into our tiny staterooms, marveled at the efficiency of such small spaces, and assured Mr. D'Ag that our larger luggage would indeed be delivered. Finally, Juliet and I managed to leave to find the Lido Deck to search for my mother and Russ. The others took a more leisurely route and would eventually find us.

We wound our way on the deck through people sitting and listening to joyful island music blaring through the loudspeakers. I saw Russ sitting calmly in a deck chair but didn't see my mother. Russ was engaged in conversation with a sleek blonde. Wait. What tha—

Would my mother never stop amazing me? Instead of the suburban matronly bob that I was used to, she was now sporting a head-hugging pixie haircut. And were those highlights a lighter shade of blonde?

Before I had an opportunity to comment, Juliet whapped me on the back of the head.

"Hey!" I rubbed my noggin. "Where did you learn that?"

"I guess I've been hanging around your East Coast family for a while," she shrugged. "In any case, cool it. I know what you are thinking. But your mother looks awesome in the new haircut, and the new style of dress is pretty cool, too!"

What? I didn't even look at what she was wearing. Hmm Instead of her conservative capris and button-down pastel top, she had on a bright, floral mid-calf sleeveless dress, a "statement" necklace and jeweled wedgie sandals! All unquestionably tasteful, but still ...

"Mother?"

She turned to look at me, and her face was one of pure joy. If I didn't know better, I would've thought she'd had some sort of face-lift. She spoke, and only when her cultured tones came forth did I know this was my mother.

"Darling! Russ and I checked into our staterooms and had time to wander around the ship a bit! It is so lovely. Why did I put off going on a cruise for so long?"

Because your crowd was more the firmly-on-the-ground type? Or used to be! Who knew with her these days?

"Keira, are we all in staterooms that overlook The Commons?" asked Russ. He was referring to the deck of the ship that was designed to resemble a large city park and was ringed by small shops and restaurants.

I guess I still wasn't comfortable with the idea of my mother having a suitor, much less the fact that he had inspired an extreme makeover. I hesitated. Luckily, Juliet jumped in.

"All of our staterooms are in a row, so yes, we all basically have the same view, Mr. Shaw."

"Call me Russ. So that means all our balconies are connected?" he asked. "If we have room service breakfast, we'll see each other bright and early."

"You bet," said Juliet, brightly, obviously trying to fill the emptiness in the conversation. "So make sure you have your robe on if you step out there after your shower!"

I shot her a look. Was she not even listening to what she was saying?

"Well, Juliet," my mother inserted with her usual delicacy, "I'm sure we'll take that into consideration. And since you and I share a room, you can remind me."

Really, Juliet.

"So ..." I attempted to rescue the situation. "The rest of our gang seems to be arriving."

Alex and her family arrived, and I paid particular attention to how they greeted Russ and how they assessed my mother's makeover. Of course, they are the nicest people ever so they didn't show any shock or amazement.

"Look, they're doing the Electric Slide!" Alex grabbed Cam and pulled him to join the group of dancers lined up in front of the small stage on the deck. Juliet lost no time kicking off her sandals and scampering right after them. The three jumped immediately to the front of the group and fell right into step, laughing and making new friends. The music stopped, and the smiling crew member leading the dance began to teach the steps to the next dance. After the new song started, she came over to recruit more of us. Her jet-black hair fell down her back in a thick braid, and her name tag improbably identified her as Neil.

"Let's go, Celia," said Anthony, with his hands on her hips. "We can't let little sister have all the fun!"

"And you?" the crew member asked me in a Down Under accent. "You look like you'd like to dance, mate."

"Just sitting this one out ... Neil?"

"It's Cornelia, actually, but I grew up mostly around boys, so I wouldn't have lasted long with a girly name."

"Was that in Australia?"

"Bite your tongue! I'm a Kiwi from New Zealand through and through, and don't forget that," she laughed and went to the next group of people to recruit more dancers.

Damian moved to the railing where I was leaning and scooted himself beside me.

"Keir, I sense something is troubling you," he said.

"Oh, not really," I stared ahead.

"I've known you a long time, little sis, so please share with me," he said.

"Well," I paused, then turned toward him and couldn't help spilling it all out.

"Don't you guys see that my mother is dating someone practically young enough to be her son? And look at how she's dressing! What? What are you smiling at?"

"Keira," he began patiently. "I do know that Russ is younger than your mother, only because Alexandria told us. But honestly if there's more than about six years there, I'd be shocked. Besides, what are you worried about?"

"What?" I began and noticed heads turning at my volume, so I took it down a notch. "I mean 'what?' I don't want people to think my mother is a cougar."

"Keira, please don't use that term. It's not very kind." He drew me closer to him. "NO one who knows your mother would think that. As for her wardrobe, she's an amazingly classy lady, no matter what she wears. What could be wrong with that?"

"Well. Um." I really didn't have an answer. I looked at my mother, trying to see her through a stranger's eyes. And I actually saw an attractive older woman with an age-appropriate hairstyle and an age-appropriate outfit. The more I thought about it, I wondered why I hadn't helped her modernize her look myself.

"And stop right there," Damian said. "I know you're feeling guilty that YOU didn't help your mother with a makeover."

"Actually, yes, why didn't I? Do you realize how many shopping expeditions your sister and I have had since my father died?"

Damian shook his head. "She just wasn't ready for a change until now, for whatever reason. Instead of beating yourself up over it, why don't you embrace the change and help her now?"

Hmm. I didn't think about it that way. As a matter of fact, her haircut was cute, but I think the colorist and stylist that Alex and I frequented would probably be a step up.

"Damian," I finally said. "You're the best."

"Oh, I don't know about that," he said with true modesty. "But listen, I'll be sharing a room with Russ this week, remember? If I discover anything that is worth worrying about, I'll let you know."

"What do you mean?" My senses were back on alert. "What could you discover?"

"Oh, that he sleeps with a childhood teddy bear. Or that he is attempting to contact aliens in his spare time," Damian teased.

"You!" I punched his shoulder. "How can you be so wise one minute and so exasperating the next?"

"It's a gift, sister, it's a gift. Now listen, there's the whistle to call us all to our mustering station to show us what to do in case of emergency. We'd better get there early, because with all of this gang going to the same mustering station, at least one of us needs to be standing close to the front and paying attention."

"Too true."

We had barely taken two steps when a tall man dressed in typical cruise attire for the crew—navy blazer with crisp khakis—stopped us.

"Are you Keira Graham?" he asked seriously.

I was not sure I liked his tone.

"Who is asking?" my natural defenses responded.

He stepped backward, obviously not accustomed to people questioning him. After a beat, his face broke into what can only be described as a practiced dazzling smile that reached all the way to his sapphire eyes.

"Sorry. Let me start again. I'm looking for Keira Graham." Was his tone a bit too polished? "Might you be her?"

"Again," I started. "Who's asking?"

"Keir ..." Damian shook his head from behind the stranger, who whipped around.

"Maybe I'll have more luck with you. I'm looking for Keira Graham. Who should be able to direct me to someone traveling in her group?" He glanced at the paper in his hand. "Father Damian D'Agostino."

Damian's eyes widened.

"What? Why are you looking for me?"

CHAPTER SIX

I crossed my arms and tilted my head in a smirk. Ha! Not so funny when a stranger is looking for you, is it Damian? I only regretted that the others had already moved on.

"Are you Father Damian?" Damian was not in his clerical collar, so it was understandable that this man was confused.

The stranger was as tall as Damian with a slightly more athletic build, and his stylishly tousled brown locks with just a hint of blond made an interesting contrast to Damian's own dark curls.

"Well, yes, but—"

"Fantastic." The man grinned. "The purser said that you identified yourself as a Catholic priest. Because the cruise line doesn't assure that priests are on board every cruise, when we discover one who has identified himself, we ask if he would be willing to say daily Mass. We generally have many passengers on each cruise who would like that."

"Certainly," said Damian, without hesitation. "Just tell me where. How will we arrange for the necessities? How—"

"Show up at the purser's office after mustering and ask for me." He handed Damian a card. "We'll get this sorted out. As I said, we are prepared to do this if we find a priest and are thrilled when we do find one," said the man as he prepared to move on to his next task.

"Wait a minute," I jumped in, grabbing the card from Damian. "Just who are you? And how did you know I was me?"

"Oh, simple," grinned the man over his shoulder. "You and I need to meet anyway later this evening. I was told to look for the regal, ice-cool, stunning, green-eyed blonde who looks like she'll snap your head off."

"What? Why would we need to meet?" And who gave that description?

"I have to go. We'll speak later about the event you're managing. I'm your boss this week. I'm Brennan McAllister, the cruise director."

I managed to make it through the entire mustering process, learning how to manipulate a life vest and how to arrive at the correct lifeboat in case of an emergency, all without making one comment about the weird encounter. But the words of Brennan McAllister kept ringing in my head: "regal, ice-cool, stunning green-eyed blonde."

How was it that these words could strike such a nerve? Admittedly, being called stunning was a tremendous compliment, but other than Alex, who called me Princess, no one had made a joke about me being regal in a long time—since college, in fact. Who was this Brennan McAllister anyway?

"What is up with you?" whispered Juliet, standing next to me during the mustering process. I shook off her inquiry, knowing that if I attempted to explain that bizarre encounter, it would engender many more whispers from the entire gang.

When the horn blew to break us up, I made a mad dash for the room assigned for meeting with the chefs, secure in the knowledge that the rest of the family would spread out to random activities until meeting up for dinner at our large appointed table. I was not prepared to share the details of that odd meeting until I had time to process it.

In the room, I had intended to take comfort in the routine of work by busying myself with a review of the week's agenda before the meeting started, but Juliet caught up with me almost as soon as I'd sat down.

"Give it, Keir. Why did you arrive at muster looking like you had just been to the principal's office?"

"I'm sure I don't know what you mean." I kept my eyes down and focused on my iPad.

"Hey! Don't forget that I share a tiny, tiny office with you on a weekly basis!" She crossed her arms. "Don't make me go get your mother!"

My head shot up.

"All right." I glanced at my watch. "But we only have a few minutes, so just the details."

I shared the bizarre conversation and tried to describe the person who had identified himself as our new boss.

"Weird," she said. "I mean, I get him looking for Father Damian, but what a bizarre way to go about it."

"I know, right?"

"Although I guess the way he identified you was pretty spot-on—"

"What!" I glared at her and pulled myself to my full height. "Exactly what gave that away to him, if one might ask?"

"That!" Juliet pointed at me. "That's the whole regal thing you have going on."

I opened my mouth to protest, but it was true. There was my nickname coming back to haunt me again. But somehow it sounded different coming from him!

"Oh, I wouldn't worry about it, Princess," began Juliet. I wadded up a piece of paper and threw it at her. "I'd be more worried about what the definition of boss is. Does that mean he is suddenly in charge of our project?"

At that moment, our food bloggers and chefs started to stream into the room, claiming seats and chatting with one another. Some of the chefs were professionals who had been on the scene for a long time and either had their own restaurants or were well-known for working in popular eateries all over the country. Some were new to the restaurant world. We had everyone from chefs trained at Le Cordon Bleu to homegrown foodies who had a lot to write about. Most of them had cookbooks that had already been published or were being released in the very near future. We tried to recruit a variety of styles and cuisines to give the attendees the maximum experience.

Alex arrived with her usual bouncy energy and managed to greet every single one of them in the space of moments.

I began the meeting and explained the week's agenda. The demos would run every day, whether the ship was in port or at sea. Since those attending the conference were all dedicated foodies, they clamored for this type of activity and would gladly fit it in with their fun in the sun.

"Each of you is assigned to one of two rooms fully equipped with the items you requested for your assigned time and class. The ship's crew will manage the switchover between classes. I suggest that you show up early to make sure you have everything you need and are prepped."

"How many students are signed up for each class?" asked Arless Schneider, who specialized in gluten-free recipes.

"Don't worry, we'll bring in ringers if no one wants to see your presentation," yelled Roland Branshon good-naturedly from the back of the room. The crowd laughed. Arless and Roland had competed in a cook-off on a local morning show in their home city recently, and Roland had come out the winner.

"No one has to worry," I laughed. "Every class will be filled to capacity. Almost as soon as we posted this cruise on the website, it sold out."

"How will we know if someone is registered for our specific demonstration?" asked one of the bloggers.

"When they made reservations with us for the seminar and paid, they were each sent a packet containing, among other things, a name badge along with their personalized schedule so that they wouldn't have to register again when they got here," I said. "Each of you has your class roster in your packet, and you just need to match the name badges to the roster as the attendees arrive. They've already given us permission to share their contact information with you. We'll distribute that after the event, so you don't need to collect any of that information. We recommend that you have whoever is stationed at your book sales table do the checking in right at that table. All of this is written on your Important Facts Sheet." I pulled out that sheet and pointed to it.

We continued with other practical questions and answers, and then someone asked, "I see that Alexandria isn't in one of the two rooms, but is booked in a theater for her demo. How'd she get that?"

There it was. I had been hoping that no one felt I'd played favorites with Ali and was prepared for a discussion about that perception, but I didn't need to worry. Roland immediately jumped back in:

"Hey, you get booked on Iron Chef with Bobby Flay, and you get to play the big room next time," he interjected.

The room cheered and applauded, and Alex stood up and struck the iconic Iron Chef pose.

"Okay. This will be our last meeting as a full group," I said. "Just remember if you need me for anything, my stateroom office is listed on your Important Facts Sheet. Even though most of you have given up your cell phones for the voyage, Juliet and I have not, and you can have either of us paged anytime at the numbers on your sheet. Anything you need, you let me know. I'll be bouncing from demo to demo during the day, so I should be easy to find."

"And if you can't find her, please look for me," came a vaguely familiar voice from the back of the room. Heads swiveled.

Brennan McAllister jumped from his perch on a table on the back of the room and made his way to the front, shaking hands along the way like a politician stumping for votes.

I could see the women eyeing him appreciatively as he moved through the group. He had changed from his formal Cruise Director togs into a stylish pair of jeans and a polo jersey with the ship's logo over the breast. Did he only take the job with this cruise line because their signature blue color matched his eyes?

"Hi. I'm Brennan McAllister, your cruise director," he said when he reached the front of the room. "Now, I know you might think I'd be too busy to attend to you, but let me assure you that this project is extremely important to the *Ocean's Essence*, and we're more than happy to have you folks on board to entertain our guests."

Hey, did he just take over my meeting?

"I'm personally thrilled to have added Keira and Juliet to my staff, if only for a week." He winked my way. "I know I can count on them."

HE could count on US? Why, this entire event was planned by us! I'll wager he didn't even hear about it until today!

"Mr. McAllister," began Arless.

"Brennan," he smiled.

"Brennan. Should we check in with you after our classes?"

Whoa, whoa, whoa.

"Folks, all you need to do is follow the check-in/check-out procedure listed in your packets," I jumped in, feeling a bit more flustered than I cared to. I looked out into the group to find Alex grinning at me. I felt thrown back to college days when we would go to fraternity parties and she would whip an unsuspecting jock my way and say "Haaaaave you met Keira?" and then walk away, leaving me on my own.

I pulled myself together.

"Mr. McAllister," I began.

"Brennan," he reminded me with an even bigger smile and a boyish tilt of his head.

"Brennan," I shot through my teeth. "Thank you for joining us. We don't want to keep you from your other duties. Ladies and gentlemen, let's give our cruise director a round of applause as he leaves us." I grabbed his elbow and pointed to the door.

He gave a quick salute and strolled to the door. While his newest adoring fans followed his every move, I pulled myself together and prepared to conclude the meeting.

"Now, folks, are there any last questions before I turn you loose?"

"Where's the best bar?" came a voice.

The crowd laughed.

"There are quite a few of them on several decks of the ship. Take your pick," I said. "Just be responsible, even if you don't have to drive!"

CHAPTER SEVEN

"Um, Keir? Who's the dish? He wasn't on the menu." Alex laughed at her own pun.

Juliet answered for me while I ostentatiously collected leftover extra papers in the meeting room.

"THAT is the cruise director," said Juliet.

"I get THAT, Jules," Alex patiently answered. "But WHO is he to our girl, here?"

They both plopped down in chairs in the front row, crossed their legs and arms, and blinked up at me.

"He's no one," I answered, not catching either of their eyes, hoping to sound calm.

Alex looked to Juliet for more information, but Juliet just shrugged and rolled her eyes innocently.

"Keir?" Alex continued impatiently.

I knew if I didn't answer her, she'd continue grilling me and never let us get to dinner. So I sighed and began:

"He came looking for Damian. Somehow he knew he was part of this group, and since this group is under my name, he looked for me to point him toward Damian. That's all."

"That's all?" Alex said in a tone that I recognized from many years of our friendship.

"That's ALL, Ali. You heard him. He's my 'boss,' apparently." I flicked my hair back over my shoulders. *We'll see about that.*

Alex turned to Juliet as if to cut me out of the discussion. "Have you ever noticed that when the Princess flicks her blonde locks back like that, she's planning to go in for the kill on someone?"

"I know!" Juliet bobbed her head. "She's definitely plotting something here."

I rolled my eyes.

Silence from the peanut gallery. I could stand it no more and jumped in: "What? WHAT?"

Alex calmly flicked a piece of nonexistent lint from her shoulder.

"Keira, Keira, Keira," she affected the tone of a much more mature individual than we both knew she was. "Don't try to kid us. Mr. Blue-Eyes back there doesn't know who he's dealing with, does he?"

I jumped up to sit on the table.

"It's just that, this event could be my big break, you know?" I leaned back on both elbows. "I can't stand the thought of all my work"—I caught Juliet's eye—

"*our* work getting credited to some pretty boy just because he swoops in and claims it."

"Hey, that won't happen," Juliet said, not unkindly. "This has been a Keira Graham Events production from the beginning. I don't think anyone would be confused."

"Keir," Alex added, "don't you think he came here because he has to make sure that it gets the stamp of approval of the cruise line for legal purposes? Didn't you sign some sort of paper to that effect?"

I pondered.

"Well, yes. But for him to come in and say he's my BOSS."

"Ah. That's really it more than anything, isn't it?" Alex said wisely. "It isn't necessarily that you have to coordinate your movements with the cruise line. You can't stand the idea of reporting to anyone specific."

She had a point. Ever since I started my own business, I was proud of the fact that I answered to no one but myself.

"Come on, Keira, couldn't you see he was just trying to get at you because he was frosted by your icy-green stare?"

I leaned forward and pointed at her. "That's the other thing. How did he glom on to calling me regal? I thought that was just something that we— What?"

Alex and Juliet were laughing and snorting.

"Keir, did you think that the Ice Princess nickname fell out of the sky way back in college?" Alex asked finally. "We love you, but anyone who knows you for half a second reads that don't-mess-with-me 'tude."

"Well." I jumped from the table and tucked in my blouse. "I shall take my 'tude into the dining room to enjoy supper with the rest of the family, thank you very much. You two are of course welcome to join, if you wish."

With that I strode away purposefully, aware that my exit only proved them right.

"Where are Alexandria and Juliet?" asked my mother as I reached the large table in the formal dining room and took the empty seat next to hers.

"Oh, I'm sure they will be here from the day care center shortly," I quipped.

"What? Day care?" Russ asked from the seat on the other side of my mother as he motioned the waiter to bring me bread. He hadn't been around us and was not used to the snarky shorthand we engaged in.

"Keira," interjected Mrs. D'Ag from across the table, "how elegant this all is! I feel so underdressed."

"It's okay, Mama," said Celia. "You can see that most of the guests are casual tonight because all of the luggage hasn't been delivered to their staterooms. When you read the daily *Lodestone* newsletter that gets delivered to your stateroom, you'll know what the dress code is for dinner each night and come in the right clothes."

Anthony kissed his wife on the cheek. "That's what I love about this woman! Never been on a cruise before and knows the dress code for dinner on the first night!"

"Oh, Tonio," Celia grinned, "I just looked it up on the Regal Cruise Line website before we came. We have two formal nights, three 'smart' nights, and one casual night."

"What's a smart night?" asked Mr. D'Ag, scanning the menu.

"Nothing Damian or Anthony is able to take part in!" Alex said as she sat down next to her husband.

"You kids settle," began Mr. D'Ag.

"Or what, Pop?" said Damian. "You'll turn this ship around?"

We all laughed, and Mr. D'Ag shook his finger at Damian.

"Look, Padre, you're still my son."

"And he's our priest," interjected Mrs. D'Ag. "Damian, please lead us in the blessing."

Afterward, Mrs. D'Ag continued, "Damian, what's this about you being the priest for the whole ship as well?"

"Leave it to Ma to promote Damian practically to bishop," whispered Alex across the table to me. I winked back. No matter what had happened in the meeting room, we were back to being comrades in minutes.

Damian explained the circumstances to the table.

"That's marvelous!" said my mother. "I know I'll be happy to attend Mass every day."

"One of the best things is that the crew will have the opportunity as well," said Damian. "If there isn't a priest on board, they can go for several weeks without the opportunity."

"Too bad Nonna isn't here," Cam said, referring to the late matriarch of the D'Agostino family and the namesake of the restaurant chain that he and Alex owned. "She'd love the fact that you're able to do that."

"Oh great, that's all we would need," drawled Anthony. "One more reason for Nonna to prove that Damian is the favorite."

Heads at tables around us turned as we burst into shrieks of laughter and then into loving imitations of the late Nonna. I couldn't help but notice that Russ was enjoying himself. I guess if he could hold up to a dinner with my adopted family, he couldn't be that bad after all.

Our table was nearly the last one to finish all of the courses, including double desserts for some of the guys. We conferred about plans for the next day, knowing that the next time we'd all be together would be at dinner that night.

Juliet and I would be tied up with business the next day, but we listened and advised as the others discussed their plans for a day in Nassau.

"Well, you kids can go snorkeling with dolphins or whales and such, but your mother and I are going to have a leisurely stroll around the city," said Mr. D'Ag.

"Pop! There aren't any whales there and you know it!" Alex kissed the top of her father's head.

"Well, dolphins, whales, sharks, or guppies," said my mother, "I'm with Marco. Russ, shall we join them and be leisurely tomorrow?"

"Absolutely, Maeve."

"Pshaw," said Anthony. "You oldsters take it slow, the rest of us are going for excitement. Ow! Celia!"

He realized what he said after Celia kicked him in the shin, then said, "Sorry, Russ!"

Now that was something we hadn't counted on. If my mother continued seeing Russ, would he forever be too young to be with the "old crowd" and too old to be with the "young crowd"? I tried to peek at him from the corner of my eye.

"No offense taken, Anthony," he said with a grin. "I'm just not a dolphin man."

"Aaaanyway," began Cam, always one to smooth out awkward situations. "It's getting late, and if anyone is going to go a-wandering for any reason tomorrow, we need to get some rest."

We all headed in different directions, some going directly to their staterooms, some going for a late-night stroll on deck, and some stopping to listen to music in one of the theme bars.

My plan was to head directly to my stateroom, but I was waylaid by two elderly women.

"Excuse me," said one, tugging at my sleeve, "they told us that you are the girl in charge of the cooking seminar."

"Yes, ma'am, that's me, Keira Graham." I smiled inwardly at the term *girl*. Well, I did probably seem like a teeny-bopper to these women who must have been in their late eighties. Both had neatly shorn white hair and were dressed in expensive resort wear. They reminded me of many of the doyennes at my mother's country club.

"Good," nodded the one who had tugged my arm. She hooked her cane over her arm in a practiced move, opened her large tote bag, and pulled out a folder. "Well, Keira, my name is Elizabeth Grant and this is my sister, Rose. We registered for our classes, but Rose has a situation."

"Lizzie," said Rose, "get to the point and don't waste her time."

"I am getting to the point, Rosie. She needs to know the details."

This reminded me of so many conversations I'd had with Alex.

Elizabeth turned back to me.

"Rose has been put on a new diet and can't eat a lot of sugar. Now, is it at all possible to change from these classes that are making desserts?" She looked doubtful.

"Ms. Grant," I began.

"Oh, you can call us Elizabeth and Rose, dear." Her smile was wreathed in the type of lines that a person only gets from a lifetime of smiles.

"Elizabeth," I continued, "we can certainly switch you around. Let me see here."

I found the appropriate folder on my iPad and scanned the demonstrations. I quickly deleted their names from the lists for the dessert classes and added them to two other classes that I knew would not be so sugar intensive. Then I wrote two notes for them with the new classes and my signature indicating that I had approved the change.

"Take these notes with you to the new classes. Before you get there, I'll let the instructors know that you'll be added."

"Just like that!" Rose exclaimed.

"I knew it could be done," nodded Elizabeth. "Thank you so much, my dear."

"It's my pleasure, ma'am." I made a note to myself on the tablet to contact the new instructors.

"You are as efficient as you are lovely." She turned to her sister. "Rosie, doesn't she remind you of that actress? Kim Novak?"

"I was thinking Tippi Hedren."

I wondered when these ladies had last been to the movies.

"No! I have it!" Elizabeth snapped her fingers. "Grace Kelly. Doesn't she just LOOK like a princess."

Oops. Definitely my cue to leave.

"Ladies, I appreciate the compliment, but I need to let you get back to your evening. Please let me know if there is anything else I can do for you."

I shook each of their hands and continued on my way.

Princess Grace. I was just glad the family hadn't been around to hear that because I would NEVER have heard the end of it!

I left the sisters and headed to my stateroom to unpack my personal belongings and organize the other half of the room into a proper office area. If one of the bloggers or chefs came calling early in the morning, I wanted to represent myself professionally. When I arrived at the stateroom, I was pleased to see that my luggage had arrived, and I noticed a small envelope tucked behind the identifying number on the door. Thinking it was one of the daily notices from the cruise ship, I waited until I had organized my room before walking outside on my tiny balcony to sit and read it.

Luckily our level was well above The Commons Deck so other guests couldn't hear me exclaim, "You have got to be kidding me!"

"Keir?"

I heard my name but didn't know where it was coming from.

"Keir, look to your right." It was Juliet, leaning over her own balcony in her pajamas and slippers. "What's wrong?"

Since she shared a room with my mother, and since I didn't know who else from our entourage was sitting on their balconies, I motioned to her to come to my stateroom.

"Look at THIS!"

I shoved the small paper into her hand when she walked through my door. She sat back on my bed and scanned it while I paced the length of the tiny stateroom.

"Well?" My expectant voice was on the brink of impatience.

"Well what, Keir?"

I grabbed the paper from her hand.

"Juliet, do I need to read this out loud to you?"

"No, Keira," she shook her head. "I am capable of reading it. I just don't get why you are so upset about it."

I took a breath and began.

"Our BOSS expects me to meet with him every day and give him a status report on how the event is progressing!"

"Keira, I get it." Juliet gingerly pulled the paper from my hand. "But, look, it's not out of line when you think about it. He just doesn't want to be blindsided by any guests who might come to the ship's office with comments. At the end of the day, they are the ones who have a reputation to uphold."

I plopped down on the bed and crossed my arms. She had a point. I didn't know every single one of our cruise director's duties, but I did know that no matter what happened, everyone looked to him to make sure that all the entertainment ran smoothly. That was everything from the nightly shows to the daily trivia games to bingo and any poolside activities. It was a version of my own event planner job in a microcosm on the ship.

As far as this cruise was concerned, we were a major attraction. If any one of the cooking classes didn't go according to plan, the students wouldn't blame the instructor or Keira Graham Events; they'd blame the cruise line.

"Fine, Juliet," I concluded. "That makes sense. But why do I have to meet in person with him every night? Can't I just fill out some kind of form?"

"I don't know, Keira. Maybe he's just a type-A control freak. Know any of those?" she asked the question pointedly.

"Hey, was that aimed at me?"

Juliet grinned, stood up and flicked her hair back over her shoulders. In polished tones, she began imitating my voice: "Jules, did you color-coordinate the notes for the Bremerton wedding? Jules, don't forget to have the Reception Hall measure to see that the knives are exactly as far from the spoons as they are from the plates. Jules—"

I stopped her.

"Is that really me?"

"Uh, yeah."

I rolled my eyes.

"Keira," she sat back down and put her arms around me. "I may have exaggerated just a skosh, but you are a tad controlling sometimes, don't you think?"

"You say controlling, I say well-organized," I sniffed. "Where would the world be without order?"

Juliet said nothing and smiled at me.

Oh. It hit me.

Brennan wasn't out to get me, this was just his own particular way of keeping order. Why on earth did I take it so personally?

"Don't take it so personally," said Juliet, reading my mind. "Just do the little report, have this little status meeting, nod and smile, and go back every morning and do things your way. You know that nothing he says is going to change your own meticulous plans, don't you?"

I smiled a smug smile and pulled my ponytail tighter.

"You're right. I always run my show. All I have to do is have these bothersome meetings with him to check a silly little detail off my list every day."

I hugged her.

"You'd better get back to your stateroom or my mother will wonder what you're up to," I said.

"She wasn't there when I left," Juliet shook her head. "Not sure when she'll be back."

"Nice try," I pursed my lips. "I know my mother would not go out carousing all night. Besides where would she and Russ go? To his room with his roommate the priest?"

Juliet grinned. "Ha! I just wanted to see if I could get you riled up again. Your mom was tucked into her bed doing a crossword when I ducked out. She knew by the fact that I was in my pajamas that I wasn't going too far and figured I was headed here, so she asked me to tell you good night again."

Yep. I knew my mother. Well, except for her new hair and wardrobe.

"Juliet, what do you think of her new look?"

"Keira, she looks awesome. Stop worrying." She started out the door and then stopped. "Take this as a compliment: If that's what you'll look like at her age, you'll still be pretty stylin'."

Maybe. But she had already been aging gracefully side by side with my father, and now had apparently found love again. Geesh. She was on love number two, and I hadn't even found bachelor number one.

CHAPTER EIGHT

"Keira, do you want to join us for breakfast?"

My mother's polished tones followed her ladylike knock on the door of my stateroom the next morning, the first full day of our cruise. I took the few short steps from where I was sitting at my desk to open the door.

"Good morning, Mother. Who's 'us'?" I peered around her, expecting Russell because I knew that Juliet was hitting it hard at the ship's gym.

"Russell and I are forgoing the buffet upstairs and going to the little cafe in The Commons. It looks like fun." Her upbeat tone matched her teal sundress and coordinating sandals.

I thought for a moment.

"Now Keira," she began.

"Oh, no," I said hurriedly in case she got the wrong idea. "I was just thinking of my time. The first cooking class starts in little over an hour, and I wondered if I could sneak in some more work before I went down there."

I gestured toward the second bed in my stateroom, which I had converted into an office space last night.

"Keira, I realize this is a working trip, but you have to eat. What kind of mother would I be if I didn't insist on that?"

I smiled and hugged her.

"Are you kidding? Between you and Mama D., I'm sure I'll have plenty of reminders to eat. Plus I'll be around food all day every day with the cooking classes. I'll be sure not to miss the tastings."

She waved that last comment off.

"Oh, those bits and bites don't count, and you know it. I don't want you to be the first person to come on a cruise and lose weight!"

We both laughed.

"I promise I'll maintain an official cruiser's eating plan, okay? It's just that today is the first day of the event, and I want to make sure that everything goes well." I stood up and looked into the mirror to straighten the collar of my blouse.

"I have no doubt that it will, darling," her voice trailed off. I caught her eye in the mirror and spun around.

"Mother, that's a funny tone."

"No tone, sweetheart, I just forget what a successful businesswoman you are sometimes, that's all."

"Well, I never was cut out for the debutante-ladies-who-lunch world, was I?"

"No, you were not. While the other little girls played tea party, you had your Barbie dolls imitating career girls who answered to a demanding CEO."

I turned back to the mirror. I didn't want to remind my mother that the other little girls never included me in their games and thought I was too stuck up to play tea party; in reality, I was just really shy.

I started to put my hair into a crisp, professional French braid.

"Come sit here and let me do that. I haven't braided your hair in ages."

We sat on my bed, and I turned my head, offering my hair to her. The feel of her delicate hands gently pulling my hair brought back fond memories. She must have been feeling the same way.

"Keira," she sighed. "You know, your father always said your hair was spun gold."

I chuckled. "He should have taken out an insurance policy on it before I decided to get that awful perm in high school. Remember?"

"Oh, all teenagers go through phases, I suppose." She finished the braid with an expert twist. "If the perm was the worst experiment you tried, I guess we were lucky."

"It really made it difficult to get my hair up under my riding helmet though."

Mother feigned a shudder. "Oh, sweetheart, you know I love you, but the photographs from that era are, shall we say, a little awkward."

We both laughed, then turned to the door when we heard a soft rap.

"That's probably Russ." Mother looked at me expectantly. I decided my bit of work could wait.

I took her hand in mine and kissed her cheek. "Let's go with him to the cafe. I'd better get my first of many breakfasts of the day in, to stay on that cruiser's diet."

"This is so charming!" my mother exclaimed as we sat at a small table outside the cafe. The three of us had gone through the self-serve line, selecting yogurt, fresh fruit, and bagels. Russ had returned inside to retrieve tea and coffee for us.

I nodded. "I know that the large buffet on the Lido Deck by the pool is ample, but this is nice and quiet, isn't it?"

Small marble tables suitable for two or three were clustered near the entrance of the cafe, but toward the center of the deck were groupings of chairs and couches with low tables to accommodate plates or glasses. Lush live greenery covered half of the deck, making it feel as if we were in the middle of a charming city park.

Russ joined us with our beverages.

"Here you go."

As he sat down, his hand brushed my mother's shoulder and she reached up to pat it lovingly. They already had a shorthand of sorts with these casual touches and smiles.

"Yoo-hoo!"

We looked up to see Angela and Marco D'Agostino walking toward us.

"Mama and Papa D.!" I smiled and gestured for them to join us. "Are you having breakfast?"

"Oh my, Keira!" Mr. D'Ag waved that thought off. "We ate with the kids earlier up at that buffet. Goodness! That was more than enough."

They pulled up two chairs from another table to join us.

"Maybe a coffee though," said Mrs. D'Ag, motioning toward the cafe. "Marco, I'll have a cup, and see if they have a cookie to go with that to keep these folks company."

I suppressed a smile. I had been around my best friend's family long enough to know that food was an integral part of life and companionship and that no matter how recently one had eaten, there was always room for just a little more.

"Isn't this deck beautiful?" my mother asked.

"Marco could spend his whole time right here, I'm sure," Mrs. D'Ag agreed.

"I'd love to know more about these plants," Mr. D'Ag said as he returned with the coffees. He sat next to his wife and tilted his ball cap, which was emblazoned with his own nursery logo, back on his head.

"Well, you can, sir," came a voice that I was now beginning to recognize as one that could pop up behind me at any moment.

I closed my eyes, counted to ten, and spun around.

"Mr. McAllister, what brings you here at this moment?" I asked as politely as I could.

"It's Brennan," he reminded me, smiling, flashing those infuriating dimples. "The cafe is my favorite breakfast spot when I don't have an obligation in the morning."

"Keira?" My mother's inquisitive tone reminded me of my girls' school training, which had somehow deserted me.

"Mr. McAllister," I began, then corrected myself "Brennan ... this is my mother, Maeve Graham, our friends Russell Shaw and Marco and Angela D'Agostino. Folks, this is Brennan McAllister."

"The cruise director," finished Russell. My head swiveled.

"He was the one who made the announcements last night, Keira," added my mother. "He's also listed in the *Lodestone* newsletter that we get every day."

"Of course, Keira," finished Mrs. D'Ag. "He's the one who Damian worked with to be able to celebrate the Mass."

Does everyone know this guy already? I get that the cruise director of a ship is supposed to be visible, but I'd sure like to forget this one.

"Mrs. Graham, I see where Keira gets her stunning looks. Mr. Shaw, it's a pleasure to meet you. Mr. and Mrs. D'Agostino, it's delightful to meet the parents of our priest-in-residence. And of course, you also must be the parents of our featured chef, Alexandria?"

What tha—?

Smiles all around at his encyclopedic knowledge. Charm by the bucket, this guy had.

"Oh, and Mr. D'Agostino, check your *Lodestone* for the final day at sea. We have a guided tour of these plants by our head nurseryman. You won't want to miss that. Now if you fine folks will excuse me, I'll get to my breakfast and let you get back to yours. Have a regal day!"

His azure eyes sparkled, and he worked in a wink as he walked away.

"Well, Keira, he seemed awfully nice," said Mrs. D'Ag, expectantly.

"Very sharp young man," agreed Mr. D'Ag.

"Is he the one you'll be ... working with?" This was my mother asking tentatively.

I looked from one to another.

"Well, Russ," I said, "you might as well jump in."

I could tell he was trying not to saying anything that might jeopardize our already tentative relationship, but then even he had to comment.

"Well, all I can do is give you this," he handed me a table knife with a smile, "you know, to cut the romantic tension?"

Very funny.

"Ha-ha" I retorted and punched him in the shoulder. He gave me a friendly wink as the others laughed. Maybe this Russell guy would fit in after all. I was just glad my back was to the interior of the cafe and I wouldn't need to worry about catching the twinkly eye of the Charming Cruise Director.

By the time Juliet was able to join us, it was nearly time for the others to leave for their stroll in Nassau and time for the two of us to attend the first cooking demonstration of the day.

"Keira!"

Juliet's stunning looks and unique fashion sense make her hard to miss in any crowd. Even with the emerald camp shirt and khaki shorts that we had adopted as our uniform for the week, she carried her own look with her edgy hairdo and flair for accessories. She bounced over to our table.

"Hello family!" She grinned and circled the table to distribute hugs. Even though it took her a moment last night to get used to the hugs and kisses of the D'Agostinos, she had fallen right into their ways.

The group at the table smiled right back.

"Juliet, my dear," my mother spoke for the entire gang. "We're thrilled to see you, but we need to leave so that we're able to get onto the island in enough time for a nice stroll and get back for some pool time before dinner and tonight's show."

"Sounds fine," said Juliet. "You know that Keira is chomping at the bit to go over the first demo again, even though it has been planned and replanned. Is there a musical this evening?"

"I believe the show tonight is *Grease*," said Mrs. D'Ag. "I hear it is great. Will you girls be joining us?"

"You bet." Juliet affected a dance move made famous in the stage play.

"Come on, prima donna," I laughed and hooked my arm through hers. "We need to get to the demo room. We actually do sing and dance for our supper, remember?"

Kisses all around, then we all left to attend to our various activities.

"Let's go back to the office," I said as we entered the elevator. "I need to get my iPad."

"You do know that it isn't actually an office, right? This is a temporary situation," said Juliet. "Or has my worst nightmare come true, and you've decided that you like sleeping in the office and you'll be giving up your apartment when we get back to Denver?"

I nudged her with my hip.

"No, silly," I rolled my eyes. "Can you imagine me giving up my tasteful apartment to live in our office, even if the office itself is tasteful?"

"I don't know, Keir." She shook her curls. "Lately you've spent a lot of time there."

"Well, to get ready for this trip, yes, but don't worry. And don't worry about that slip of tongue of mine, calling my stateroom the office. I just have to keep the two halves of the room straight in my head, you know?"

"Yep," she said. "That's you. Precise. To the nth degree." She slouched to lean on the railing that circled the small space.

The elevator door opened, and two particularly attractive men entered, garbed for a day's excursion off the ship, and pressed the button for Deck 15. Juliet's posture improved immediately.

"You guys going to the island?" she asked prettily. "Shouldn't you be going on a 'down' elevator?"

I suppressed a smile. She could teach a class in Flirtation 101.

The taller of the two turned toward us and flashed a brilliant smile.

"We're actually headed to grab a bite on the Lido Deck first. Have you two ladies had breakfast yet?" His dark chocolate eyes moved from one to the other of us.

"Actually, we had our breakfast at the cafe in The Commons," she said.

We?

Hunk Number Two, with matching dark flashing eyes, joined in the conversation. "Is it good there?"

"Delicious," Juliet's curls bobbed. "You should try it one morning."

"Or maybe for a quick coffee this afternoon?" Hunk Number Two turned fully to address both of us.

I jumped in at this point, seeing where the conversation was going. Not that I had a problem with either of these two guys, but seriously, we were here to work!

"Jules, our schedule is booked this afternoon, remember?"

"Jules. What a great name. And you are ...?" Hunk Number One addressed me.

"She's Keira, and we'd both be delighted to meet you but unfortunately we're running an event that will keep us pretty busy during the day."

By this time, the elevator had reached our stateroom floor and the doors opened. The guys held the doors open and one of them asked, "What event? Is it something we can attend?"

"It's the 'Cooking at Sea' event, and it is fully booked unfortunately," Juliet pulled two flyers from her tote and handed them to the guys. "I'm sorry, we didn't catch your names."

"I'm Langston," said the taller of the two, "and this is my brother, Owen."

"Too bad about your schedule," said Owen, looking over the flyer.

"Oh, but I'm sure we could meet for a cocktail after the last demonstration to tell you more about it, couldn't we, Keira?" Juliet tilted her head, and her smiling eyes caught mine.

I knew that if I said anything about "paperwork" or "catching up on the day," her look would turn in an instant.

"Sure," I laughed. "How about in the Sports Bar at about 5:30?" I picked the bar that was in the most common area of the well-traveled Promenade Deck. Sure, these guys seemed nice, but still they were unknown to us, right?

I continued, "You fellows need to let these doors close. I can only imagine how many people are fuming right now."

Langston took his hand off the open door button and leaned back into the car. "They'll be fine. It's vacation time, remember? No worries, no hurries." The door closed on his flashing grin.

"What?" Juliet said innocently, looking at my smirking face.

"You know what," I bumped her hip.

"C'mon, Keir, I know this is a working trip, but why

can't we 'work in' a little bit of fun?" She grinned at her own wordplay.

I just shook my head and started walking toward my stateroom. She grabbed my arm.

"You aren't angry, are you?" she asked with a tilt of her head.

"Of course not, Flirty Gerty," I laughed. "I just wonder why it took you even this long to get us dates for drinks."

"Hey, you knew my outgoing personality when you hired me," she flounced.

"Yep. The only girl I know who can go from zero to having guys drool over themselves in sixty seconds."

"I shall take that as a compliment." She ruffled her curls even more buoyantly.

"Oh, it is, sister, it is."

"Besides," she added, "you know that I know the difference between harmless flirtation and advertising something I'm not selling."

We reached my stateroom. I hugged her.

"Jules, you know it and I know it. Just make sure the guys know it."

"Hmmph," she sniffed. "I know I didn't go to Catholic girls' school like you did, but my aunties could have given some lessons in propriety to the nuns!"

We laughed, then I went into the stateroom and retrieved my tote containing my iPad and other materials I'd need for the day. I gave myself one last look in the mirror, patted my immaculate French braid, and rejoined Juliet. We returned to the elevator to descend to Deck 3 for the first demo of the day.

"Here we go," I said. "Day One."

CHAPTER NINE

We reached the conference room, which had been divided into two demo rooms, and walked into the first room—and felt as if New Orleans had been transported lock, stock, and barrel onto the ship. Exuberant Mardi Gras music blasted from speakers, and tables were decorated in the trademark purple, green, and gold colors. I couldn't resist smiling as the guest chef, Louisiana Annie, yoo-hoo'd toward us from the front of the room.

Annie was well known in regional circles and had quite a following on her website and blog. She was a petite ball of energy, with a slim figure and a smile that stretched across her entire face.

"Keira, come on down to the front, *cher*!" she said, motioning.

Juliet and I couldn't help but bounce to the zydeco beat as we moved toward her.

"Annie, I feel like I'm at Mardi Gras!"

She gave each of us a giant hug, then handed us equally giant hurricane glasses.

I took a sip of the rum and fruit juice drink. It was the same one that had been made famous by Pat O'Brien's restaurant in the French Quarter but was now being served in nearly every establishment in New Orleans. Wow! Potent.

"Annie," I cautioned.

"Oh, *cher*," she waved me off. "Don't you think these folks can handle a little rum?"

My face must have shown my disbelief.

"Now, doll, these folks are on a cruise!" She winked. "This is the only otha' place where booze is running twenty-four hours a day besides Mardi Gras!"

Her husband and partner of many years, Bobby Ray, stepped in.

"Keira, my pet," began the jovial bearded giant, "she's just a-funnin' you. She made that one for you triple strength to pull yo leg a little! We're not gonna have anyone walkin' outta here and straight to the medic!"

Juliet snickered as Annie whipped the towel from over her shoulder and, with a practiced move, snapped me on the behind.

"C'mon, now, girlie, you know Annie. I'll keep it under the legal limit," she said with her trademark impish grin. "Of course now, if someone asks for a stronger recipe, I'm gonna have to provide it." Her ice-green eyes sparkled as she turned her face innocently to the ceiling.

I handed her back my glass and pulled Juliet's from her grip as well.

"Annie, you are a pistol," I shook my head. "But seriously, are you all set? Do you need anything that I can help you with?"

"*Cher*, you go help one of those amateurs," she said with a grin. "Bobby Ray and me got this covered!"

I looked at my list. She was teaching the class that included how to make her signature bread pudding and, of course, the wicked Hurricanes. I was positive that not only would people have a great time in her session, but she would sell a good number of cookbooks and videos. We had debated on whether to place Annie on the first day, worried that people might be let down afterward with chefs that were not as buoyant, but in the end we knew we had to come out of the gate strong or we would lose word of mouth and risk some students dropping out of some of the rest of the sessions.

I observed Annie heaping Juliet a huge portion of bread pudding and knew we had chosen correctly.

"Jules, let's go check on the other demo room," I said, smiling.

"Keira! Neither of you leaves this room without finishing your bread puddin', now!" Annie barked. "*Laissez le bon temps rouler,* child!"

Juliet and I managed to finally leave Annie's demo room and turned to walk toward the other room that would hold the next demonstration. We would come back in time to watch Annie's actual presentation.

"That Annie is something else, isn't she?" Juliet remarked. "How is it that she hasn't gone national?"

"Oh, I'm sure that's coming soon," I said. "She actually has recently kind of exploded on the scene. She has just been asked to open a restaurant, you know."

"Really? Do you think she'll do it?"

"Could you imagine containing that little ball of fire in one place?" I shook my head. "It was hard enough getting her to sit still long enough to finish the cookbook, as I understand it."

"How did it happen, then?"

I smiled. "Her husband is actually the one who does the blogging and keeps the website up-to-date. He put the book together with her recipes and barely managed to get her to stop and do photo shoots and other things."

"Does he cook?"

"Nope. Not a lick."

Juliet shook her head. "They're two halves of a whole, aren't they? To look at them, you'd never know it, though. He's the big Papa Bear, and she's the little Tinkerbell. Opposites really bring out the best in one another, I guess."

I stopped in my tracks.

"What?" Juliet stared at me.

Silence.

"Please don't tell me you left your favorite pen in the stateroom or something," she said.

I started walking again. I didn't necessarily want to share my epiphany with her.

"Ah, you caught me," I lied. "But here it is in my tote."

"Seriously, Keira, sometimes ..." and she was off teasing me, but I didn't hear her.

Her offhand comment, that "opposites really bring out the best in one another," just kept turning over and over in my head.

Fine. I get it. Russ and my mother. Opposites bring out the best in one another. I didn't need a two-by-four to hit me over the head.

"Keir? KEIR!"

Juliet's voice shook me out of my thoughts.

"Juliet, I'm right here. What?"

Her curls bobbed up and down as she inclined her head down the passageway.

"Ook-lay oo-hay is oming-kay," she whispered conspiratorially.

Why was she suddenly resorting to pig Latin?

"What do you mean 'look who is coming'?" I was mildly exasperated. I turned toward her, but she had managed to slip into the next demo room. At that moment, Brennan McAllister strode into view, having exited Annie's demo room. His tanned face was a perfect setting for those impossibly blue eyes and gleaming cover boy smile.

"Well, here's our event princess!"

"Hello, Mr. McAllister." I caught his look. "I mean Brennan. To what do we owe this visit?"

"I just thought I'd stop by to see how our chefs were doing."

Aargh. There it was again. OUR chefs. He just met these people last night. How dare he be so territorial! At that moment, I heard Louisiana Annie's distinctive "yoo-hoo!"

"Brennan, doll, you forgot your takeaway!"

She bounced down the hallway with a wrapped tray.

"Annie, you angel! You didn't need to do that!" He sparkled.

She just giggled girlishly.

"That's right, Annie," I added. "Brennan could have waited until after your class to get leftover bread pudding."

"Now, Keira, *cher*, I wouldn't have him leaving with any leftover puddin'," Annie said. "I whipped him up a shrimp po'boy!"

What! Annie wasn't making po'boy sandwiches in class today!

"We got to talkin' and our Brennan here said he loves po'boys, so I just ran on into the kitchens and found the ingredients to make one," Annie said answering my unspoken question as to where she acquired the fixings.

"Now, Annie, you really didn't need to do that!" I'm sure my tone was more admonishing than it needed to be.

"Pshaw, girl. Man like this needs to keep up him up some strength for his work!"

I glanced at Brennan, who just ran his fingers through his artfully disheveled locks and stood looking wordlessly innocent.

"Yeah. He's a worker all right," I said. "In any case, thank you, Annie, and I'll see you in class." I spun toward Brennan. "I'm sure you have something to do, like a cruise to direct?"

"You bet," he smiled. "Annie, you're a doll. Ladies, I shall see you later."

With a tilt of his head, he ambled down the passageway, whistling.

"Mmmm, mmmm," Annie observed. "If Bobby Ray wasn't in the picture, I'd be chasin' that."

"Annie!"

"What, *cher*?" she burst into laughter. "Oh, he isn't for an ole bayou gal like me. He's more for a young city gal like you. What do you say, Keira? We're all stuck on this floating city for next few days. You want me to whip up a love potion for ya that my granny taught me?"

I could only repeat, "Annie!"

She laughed even harder. Juliet returned at that moment.

"What's going on here?" she asked.

"Oh, I offered to whip up a love potion for Keira to help her catch that blue-eyed Brennan McAllister and you'd think I offered to whip up voodoo. You know I was just offerin' to make you another Hurricane!"

Annie's Hurricanes were like magic, but really, me and that overbearing Brennan McAllister? I hardly think so! I drew myself up regally.

"I believe you have a class to attend to, Annie. And Juliet, I don't know why you conveniently slipped away, but shall we continue the rest of our day?"

I proceeded to walk away with as much dignity as possible while they whistled and catcalled.

Juliet joined me in the next demo room, empty except for the setup and audience chairs. Since the chef for this demo wouldn't be going on until after Annie, he wouldn't be checking in for at least another hour. I walked to the front of the room to review the demonstration materials.

"I get it now," Juliet said.

I opened my iPad to review the notes for Joe Laughlin who would be doing a variety of dips. His cookbook was called *Dip, Dip, Hooray!* and was a collection of the best dips and spreads from around the country.

"I said, I get it now," Juliet repeated, raising her voice and cupping her hands around her mouth.

Again, I didn't give Juliet the satisfaction of a reply.

"You know, you think can ignore me, but I won't let you out of this room until I get a response."

I rolled my eyes.

"Fine, Jules. What is it?"

She dashed over to join me.

"I get why you weren't interested in the handsome brothers in the elevator. Your heart is otherwise engaged by that cobalt-eyed Adonis."

"Uh, no, Juliet. We're not living in a romantic comedy," I said wearily. "I'm not frustrated by my secret love Brennan, and we're not destined to 'end up together'."

"Are ya surrre?"

Really. Juliet could be so patronizing sometimes.

"Yes, I'm SURRRE."

She narrowed her eyes, unconvinced.

"Right, Keira. If that's the case, then what's with the attitude with him back there?"

Crossing my arms, I began patiently, "Jules, I'm just a bit peeved that he took Annie off course, okay? And as for the brothers act, I agreed to meet up with them, didn't I?"

"But not with much enthusiasm."

"Geesh, Juliet, how enthusiastic can I be about two guys—good-looking, I'll admit—that we met for about three minutes?" I laughed. "Can we at least have drinks with them before we order the wedding gowns?"

"Funny," she allowed. "When will Joe get here?"

I reviewed his demo table. Since he would not actually be cooking anything, his setup was not as elaborate as Annie's, but I still expected him to arrive and check and double-check things. Joe was as meticulous as he was cheerful.

"Early, I'm sure. He has a lot of chopping and blending to do."

At that moment, the topic of our conversation entered the room.

"Hey! Don't you two vixens sabotage my demo!" Joe wheeled himself toward us in a wheelchair that was so personalized it positively screamed JOE LAUGHLIN wherever he went.

Joe had been injured in an IED explosion in the war in Iraq and lost both his legs. He returned home and, after hospitalization, entered and graduated from a prestigious cooking school in Denver. Defying those who questioned what he could do with cooking training—how could a "cripple" run a kitchen, after all?—he opened his own cooking school for the physically impaired. His larger-than-life personality was legend, and the cooking blog he maintained was hysterical. Today's class on appetizers was one of the first to fill up, because of Joe's combination of cooking knowledge and comedic delivery.

"Joe! You're early!" I leaned in to kiss him on the cheek after he wheeled up the ramp that was built to accommodate his display area.

"Well, you know how difficult it is for a sad wheelchair victim to get around," he mugged with his large puppylike eyes.

"Ha! Pull that bit on someone else," I swatted him. "I saw you zip around this ship last night."

"Caught me," he grinned. "Actually, I wanted to pop in for a bit of Annie's demo and see if I could scam a Hurricane."

"Oh, I'm sure you wouldn't have to scam one," Juliet allowed. "Can we get anything for you while we're here?"

Joe's practiced eyes scanned the tables, set up in a U-shape for his convenience.

"Looks like I'm all set. I'm teaching this crowd how to make Nan's Veggie Dip, Olive Crostade Dip, and Tex-Mex Corn Salsa-Dip. We might make a cocktail as well if we have time. Can't let Annie have all the fun." He winked.

"Sounds perfect. Give me a buzz if you need anything," I said.

"Anything?" he leered toward both of us.

"You know what I mean!" I shook my head, and Juliet and I walked out of the room.

There. First two demos set. Maybe we'd even get a little pool time in the afternoon. Then drinks with Juliet's new friends, dinner, and the show. A perfect day.

CHAPTER TEN

"You would not believe how annoying that meeting was with that Brennan McAllister." My beach cover up whipped behind me and my sandals flipped noisily on the Lido Deck as I raced over to where Alex and Cam sat companionably side by side in lounge chairs, catching the last of the afternoon rays.

"What happened?" Alex swung her legs to one side and patted her chair for me to sit with her.

"First, he pointed to his ridiculously overpriced watch and said I was late."

"What does the cost of his watch have to do with anything?" asked Alex.

I glared at her. "NOT the POINT."

"Sorry, sweetie," Alex patted my knee. "Go on. How late were you?"

"I wasn't late! I was early."

"Apparently he does not have an accurate timepiece," said Cam.

I turned my icy-green stare toward him.

"Just sayin'," he shrugged.

"Keira, please tell me you didn't go down the rabbit hole of arguing about the TIME rather than getting on with the meeting?" Alex gestured for the roving waiter and ordered me an iced tea.

Unfortunately, I had done exactly that. I had actually spent a bit more time discussing clock management with him than I should have, but I didn't feel like sharing that little tidbit with Alex and Cam. My non-reply to her statement was a dead giveaway.

"Aha! That's exactly what she did," Alex turned to Cam, then turned back to me. "You know, Keir, sometimes you could let accuracy go for the sake of moving a conversation along."

"What! I don't do that!"

"You've always done that! You will go to the ends of the earth to prove a point," Alex said. "You absolutely know that you were thrilled when smartphones became available and you could look up a fact to prove a point at the drop of a hat."

"I seem to recall you dragging me into conversations so that I could prove points for YOU on more than one occasion," I began. "For example, in junior year at the Theta Nu Christmas Ball—"

Cam reached over and poked me. "You two know that I love your Lucy-and-Ethel comedy show more than anyone, but, Keir, back to the topic at hand. What was so awful about your meeting?"

"Oh." I stopped to take a sip from the frosty glass that the server had slipped into my hand, and took the opportunity to gather my thoughts again.

"Well, after he incorrectly accused me of being late"—I looked at each of them, challenging them to disagree with my assessment of the time discussion—"he began an incessant list of questions. 'How many attendees?' 'What kind of questions were asked?' 'What types of questions did each attendee ask?' It was endless."

"Are you telling me you didn't have actually the information?" asked Alex.

"Well, of course I had the information. Do you think this is the first such event I've planned?"

"Did he disagree with any of your findings?" Cam asked.

"No." I thought for a moment. "That was part of what was odd. He would just nod as I gave him the answer and barely look at me. He didn't even take notes."

Cam and Alex looked at one another, then back to me.

"What?" I asked.

"What?" Alex mimicked then turned to her husband. "Cam, you're a guy."

"Last I checked," he drawled as he lay back on his lounge chair.

Alex continued, unfazed. "Don't you think that a reason a guy would not take notes in a meeting and avoid eye contact could be that he was not necessarily interested in the topic but the person?"

"Ally-Cat," Cam said, his eyes closed and his hands crossed comfortably above his head, "I think you are speculating. As a GUY, I suspect he just got the information he needed and didn't need to take notes."

"Maybe," she answered slowly, "but I agree it sounds strange."

Cam shrugged again. "Strange or not, it's what happened. Keir, how did you leave it with him?"

"Well, he got a call and had to leave, so the meeting just sort of ended abruptly." I sipped thoughtfully, then nodded my head. "You know what, Cam is right."

"Hey!" Alex sounded insulted.

I patted her knee. "Sorry, sweetie, but I think Cam has it here. I can't judge the whole meeting because there WASN'T a whole meeting. I'll just have to see how it turns out at tomorrow's meeting."

There. All settled. With any luck, I wouldn't see my "boss" and his frosty blue eyes until our meeting the next day. Whew. Time to relax. The lounge chair next to Alex became free so I moved over to it, prepared to stretch out. I took off my cover-up, kicked my sandals under the chair, then undid the perfect French braid my mother had concocted for me early in the morning and fluffed out my hair into the crimped, natural waves that fell out.

"Seriously, Keir, do you have to pull your Sports-Illustrated-cover-model-oh-so-casual-cascading-hair routine? Give some of the other girls around the pool half a chance, will ya?" Alex mocked.

I playfully struck a cover model pose in my throwback black-and-white, Marilyn Monroe polka-dot bikini, leaning my elbow on my knee and resting my chin prettily on my fist. "Here she is, boys." I affected a voice even lower than my usual throaty one.

"Well, I don't know about what the rest of the boys think, but 'she' walked out on my meeting." I heard the distinctive tones of Brennan McAllister.

I shot a look at Alex that I knew she understood to mean "Why didn't you warn me?" but she had ducked her head into the cooking magazine she was perusing.

I hopped up to face him. Well, after I hopped up I had to also look up since he stood a good foot over me. Darn it, why was I barefoot? I could have commanded a bit more respect in heels.

"Brennan, I thought our meeting was over since you took that call and left the room."

"Is that how you conduct your business?" His usual grin was absent.

"What! How long did you expect me to wait when you were nowhere to be found?"

He looked down to the sheaf of papers he carried and handed them to me. "That is neither here nor there. I expect this report to be completed. Please leave it at the purser's desk, and I'll pick it up. If I don't see you, I'll see you at the same meeting time tomorrow, and please be on time."

I opened my mouth to comment but didn't get the chance. He turned to Alex, his dimples back and face split once more into that infuriating smile.

"Alexandria, so good to see you again. I'm looking forward to your demo on Thursday. Are the two of you attending the show this evening?" he asked, indicating both Alex and Cam.

"The whole family is coming, aren't we, Keir?" Alex answered, her own blue eyes sparkling.

I was nothing if not properly raised. "We're all looking forward to it," I choked out.

"Terrific," he clapped his hands together and straightened his cruise-director blazer and slacks and moved on, greeting cruisers along his way across the deck.

I sat back down on the edge of my lounge chair and began shuffling through the pile of documents he had handed me.

"You have got to be kidding me," I murmured.

Alex stood up and peeked over my shoulder. "What, what, what ..."

I shrugged her away but answered, "All the questions he asked me are right here! He could have just given me this document to fill out this morning, or he could have taken notes. The worst thing is, I can't even make a copy and have it ready for tomorrow's meeting because everything is specific to this day."

Alex sat back on her own chair and could not keep from laughing. "I knew your chickens would come home to roost one day!"

I rolled up the document and began to beat her with it.

"Stop, stop, stop!" she laughed. "You don't want to get in trouble for turning in sloppy work, too, do you?"

I reluctantly stopped and smoothed out the sheets.

"What chickens?" asked Cam.

"Oh, Princess Keira here was the only undergraduate ever selected to run the computer lab back at college."

"So?" Cam seemed confused.

"So," continued Alex, "she was the strictest, most orderly person to run that lab EVER."

I glared at her. "Um, if they hadn't given me the shifts when the marketing majors were assigned, I think I wouldn't have had to be as strict." I looked at her pointedly. "The math and computer majors were more respectful."

"Wait," said Cam. "You can't mean to tell me that our little Ali and her marketing crew didn't follow the rules?"

"Hush," said Alex. "We followed the RULES, just not to Keira's specifications. She had us fill out million-page documents just to reserve space—"

"Really? A million?" I couldn't contain my sarcasm.

"Well, not a million, but a lot more information than you would think!"

"You know who you can blame for that? The frat boys who would want to use the systems 'just for a minute'." I turned to Cam to plead my case. "You're a tech guy, Cam."

He sat up and pushed his shades up on his head. "Hey! How did I get dragged into this? I wasn't even there."

"You wanted to hear the story!" Alex and I said in unison, then looked at each other and burst out laughing.

"In any case," I continued, "not everyone had their own computers or access to the Internet at that time, so they needed to use the lab for more than if they were taking computer classes. Some of those guys would want to log on and, well, do some pretty sketchy 'research' and—"

"I get it," Cam said, nodding. "And you would be responsible for what was found on the server. Ally-Cat, I hate to say it, but Keira probably had a point, running the lab the way she did."

Alex waved her arms at him. "Oh, you would take up for her, you uber-geek. In any case, I really believe that this system that Captain Blue Eyes—"

"He's not the captain," I interrupted and corrected.

"Okay, Cruise Director Blue Eyes has set up is perfect for our own uber-organized gal."

"Pfft. Whatever." I patted the papers. "Does he think I can't get through these? I'll be done quicker than anyone ever has."

"I really don't think it's a contest, Keira."

"Uh-huh. Sure. Right." But in my mind it was a contest. And I was going to WIN!

Alex and Cam convinced me to put my "assignment" aside and fill them in on the first day's activities. By the time I caught them up on Louisiana Annie's enthusiastic class and Joe's uproarious session, Damian joined us.

"Padre! We haven't seen you today," Cam said and pulled over a nearby lounge chair for Damian, who deposited his lanky frame in it.

"After I celebrated Mass, I joined the folks for their walking tour of Nassau," he said. "What a beautiful little town. Did you guys get a chance to visit?"

Cam shook his head.

"You know your sister and brother. Celia and I spent most of our day playing referee between them in their various competitions while we all snorkeled and kayaked."

"Ha! You were right in the thick of it!"

"I think that the others might see it differently," Cam laughed. "Maybe we should pause this discussion until we're together at dinner and Celia can back me up."

Alex swatted Cam lovingly with her rolled-up magazine, then turned her attention back to Damian.

"Did Ma and Pop seem to have a good time?"

"Oh, you bet," Damian said. "You know Pop stopped at every example of flora and fauna along the way, and Ma shopped for tons of souvenirs for the grandkids."

"I hope she brought an extra empty suitcase for that," said Alex, smiling. "We have a few more days on the journey."

"Don't worry, she bought a bag on the island."

"How about my mother?" I asked cautiously. "Was she with you?"

"She and Russ were with us and had a great time as well," said Damian.

"Good."

"Keira, are you still worried about—" Alex began.

"No, no, no." I rushed to correct her. "I've accepted them as a couple. At least I think I have."

My face must have looked doubtful.

"You don't sound so sure," Alex said.

I shrugged.

"Okay. Let's just say, I'm working on it. Can we not make it the main topic of conversation? We have dinner and the show to think about tonight."

"Just dinner and the show?" asked Damian pointedly.

"Why? What else is going on?" Alex sat up eager for information. Really, sometimes it was as if we were still eighteen years old.

"I don't know," Damian grinned. "Ask Keira. All I know is that I ran into Jules in the passageway outside our staterooms, and she said that if I saw you to remind you not to be late for your meeting at the Sports Bar. Is there some activity we need to know about not listed on the *Lodestone*?"

"Whaaaat!" Alex swatted me. "You've been sitting here all this time and haven't bothered to bring up THAT little tidbit of information?"

"Calm down, Alexandria!" I scooted away. "My gosh, always with the drama."

Her eyes could not squint smaller, and she opened her mouth to remind me that her nickname was, after all, "Drama Queen," but I cut her off with a look.

She crossed her arms, expectantly. I looked to Cam and Damian for support but found none. Traitors.

"Fine," I allowed, knowing that Juliet and I were not going to be able to have quiet drinks with the handsome dark-haired strangers now without at least one member of my extended family cruising nearby to observe.

I recounted the meeting with Langston and Owen and the invitation for cocktails.

"That sounds promising!" Alex's eyes glowed. "What will you wear? How are you doing your hair? You always look good when you let it flow like that—what?"

She stopped when Cam reached over to embrace her and give her a loud kiss on the cheek.

"My endlessly hopeless romantic," he said.

"So?" she grinned. "I'm not saying she has to MARRY the older brother, I'm just saying he would be nice to chat or dance with or have a midnight stroll on the deck—"

"Whoa," I interrupted. "First, how did we get from one cocktail in the Sports Bar to a midnight stroll? And second, how did you assign me the older brother? Why not the younger?"

Alex shook her head from side to side.

"It's obvious. He sounds more like your type."

"By whose definition? You've never met either one!"

"I can tell by the way you described him," she said illogically.

"Augh." I laid back on my lounge chair as Cam and Damian laughed heartily.

I sat back up.

"Okay, Ali, here's the deal. I'm leaving here to complete this ridiculous report for my 'boss,' then to shower and change to join Juliet and the two nice gentlemen in the Sports Bar for one cocktail. Please, please promise me that you will not follow me to give me wardrobe or hair advice. Most importantly, promise me that I will not see your elfin face anywhere near the bar preparing to render judgment on a man who at this moment has no idea is already being fitted for a tuxedo!"

I finished with a flourish as I gathered my things and stood to leave.

"I promise you. I ... will not," she said.

"Good. I will see you at dinner." I turned to Cam and Damian. "And I thank the two of you for providing me no protection."

"Anytime." "Love you, sis," they chorused as I walked away.

It did not hit me until I reached the elevator that Alex paused just a little too long on the word "I" when she made that promise.

CHAPTER ELEVEN

Juliet's door opened the moment I arrived at my stateroom. "I know what time it is, Juliet," I said as I unlocked my door. Geesh, was she standing with her eye glued to the peephole?

"More importantly, do you know what time we're supposed to be downstairs?" she followed me into my stateroom.

"Please, come in," I said drily.

"No time for niceties, sister, we have a date."

I looked at my watch. It was early even by my early-bird standards.

"Juliet, if we get ready now, we'll be absolutely wilted by the time we get there!"

Clad in her brightly patterned kimono, with no makeup on yet, she wasn't ready, but she obviously was in preparation mode.

"Keira, I know you. If you think about this for too long, you might come up with a reason to not even go. I'm here as sort of a—"

"Cheerleader?" I suggested as I flopped down on the bed and kicked off my sandals. "Are you going to have a pep rally for me?"

"Ha," she said as she sat next to me. "But you know that when you are in business mode, sometimes you can come up with excuses to ignore your social obligations."

"My 'social obligations'? You sound like my mother."

"You know what I mean," she nudged me. "Lately, at home you've been passing up more and more nights out to spend time with your best friend the computer."

"What exactly do you think I'm doing when I'm logged on? Playing video games? Might I remind you that I've been making sure every *t* is crossed and every *i* is dotted for this project? Which, if you recall, can break open our business if it turns out to be a successful event."

"Keira, you know we had this project buttoned down weeks ago. You actually had a spare minute here and there and could've taken a night out for dinner or something."

"I have gone out to dinner!" I defended.

"Going over to Cam and Alex's doesn't count, and you know it."

I pondered. Juliet was not a slacker and was definitely dedicated to the business, but still always managed to find time to have a healthy social life. Come to think of it, I thought I usually did, too. Besides, having a healthy social life also contributes to networking that is so important to keeping the business alive.

"You know we have to network to keep the business going," Juliet echoed my thoughts.

"Oh, I know," I agreed. "I guess I've just let planning this project take over a lot of my time."

"Well, we're here now, and there's no more planning to be done. You know as well as I do that, barring a catastrophe, it will run smoothly. Relax!"

"I'd love to relax, Jules, but Brennan McAllister is being a real thorn in my side."

"What! Didn't you have your little check-in meeting with him? What could possibly have happened there?"

"Well ..." I shared the story of my earlier meeting with him and ended by showing her the multipage report that I had to complete.

She grabbed the document from my hands and scanned it.

"Are you flippin' kiddin' me?" she asked.

"I wish I was."

"Keira, this is so silly," she began, then sat back. "But we agreed that we have to put up with this minor annoyance so that we can make sure we get a positive review from the cruise line, didn't we?"

She suddenly stood up and headed toward the door.

"Hey," I said, "if this is a 'we' situation, where are you going?"

"He asked you to fill out the report, not me," she smiled.

"So?"

"Do you need my help?"

"Well, no."

"Will my being here get this done faster?"

"No, but—"

"Then I'm getting out of here, because I know you. Until you get that blasted paper finished, you won't get ready for our drinks date, and I'm not doing anything that will stand in the way of THAT."

"Seriously?"

She paused and turned in the doorway.

"If you need help with an answer from me, buzz me. Otherwise, get it done, get showered and dressed, and be ready to go in precisely ninety minutes."

"Am I taking orders from you now?"

"In this instance, you are. There are two dashing strangers waiting to admire us, and I need to get ready to be admired."

"You are ALWAYS ready to be admired!"

"Yes, but I want to strut into the bar and pick my best pose at just the right moment, so that they are stunned as they look up and view us walking toward them." She struck her best Beyoncé stance.

"Get out!" I laughed and threw a small pillow at the door as she closed it.

Precisely ninety minutes later, I heard a knock on the door.

"How's this?" I whipped open the door and struck my own pose.

"I don't know, dear, what are you going for exactly?" asked my mother, trying but not succeeding to hide her smile.

"Mother!" I grinned. "I thought you were Juliet. Come in."

"No need to, Keira. I just wanted to check in with you since I hadn't seen you all day. Russ will be here in a moment. We're headed down to take a stroll around the ship before dinner, and I wanted to wish you good luck on your date."

How did she—? Oh, right, she was Juliet's roommate.

"It's not a date, Mother, more of a casual meet for drinks. I ... we—"

"You don't have to explain anything to me, dear. Do I know every date you have back home?"

"Well, no, but—"

She patted my cheek. "You deserve to have fun with a nice young man."

Why did I suddenly feel like I was back at St. Mary's going to a school dance with one of the boys from Regis Jesuit Academy? Russ walked up and joined us.

"Keira, you look stunning," he said. "Your date is a lucky young man."

How did HE know? Oh, right. Damian's roommate. I wondered at that moment why I thought it was a good idea to travel with my entire family, real and extended.

"Russ, I was just telling Mother it's not a date—"

"I know," he smiled. "But any young man who is lucky enough to even sit for a moment and buy you a cocktail is very lucky indeed."

I looked at him. He was sincere.

"Well. Anyway," I said. I felt I needed to close the conversation. "You two scoot along. I need to see why Jules is late!"

Mother gave me a kiss on the cheek, and Russ squeezed my hand. They turned to walk to the elevator hand in hand. I sighed. Even from behind, you could tell they were truly happy.

I went back into my stateroom to retrieve my small handbag, and at that moment Juliet popped in.

"Keira! For crying out loud, let's go! What are you waiting for?"

"Well it's Keira!" The charming Elizabeth Grant smiled at us as the elevator door opened, and we joined them on the trip down.

"You look lovely, dear, and so does your friend," added Rose.

"Thank you. Juliet, this is Elizabeth and Rose Grant, two of our seminar attendees. Ladies, this is my colleague Juliet Fernandes."

"Good to meet you," Juliet said. "Are you enjoying the seminar so far?"

"Oh yes." Rose's head bobbed. "We are learning quite a bit. And thanks to your friend, we were able to switch our classes to accommodate my new diet."

"She's the best," Juliet smiled.

"We can tell that." Elizabeth's smile matched Juliet's. She continued, "So where are you gals off to before dinner, dressed so beautifully?"

"Oh, meeting a few friends."

"Lizzie," Rose began in an exasperated tone, "look at them. They're off to meet a couple of young men, can't you see?"

I choked back a laugh. Just because these ladies were older certainly didn't mean they weren't wise to the ways of the world.

"Of course, of course," Elizabeth said, nodding, as the door opened to their chosen floor. "Well, have a nice evening and make sure they don't stick you girls with the bar tab."

"We won't!" we called after them before the door closed, then looked at each other and giggled.

I would be lying if I said that admiring heads did not swivel as we approached the Sports Bar.

Juliet was striking in her stylish ensemble that combined a flirty short skirt in a delicious shade of yellow and a coordinating sleeveless top with a lace yoke. Her trademark springy curls were pulled back with a silk scarf bandeau and cascaded down her shoulders.

Although we hadn't planned it, I had coordinated colors with her with my simple ice-blue sheath with a V neck and cap sleeves.

"I'm glad you let your hair down, Keira," said Juliet.

"Is that some sort of metaphor, Jules?"

"Uh, no," she grinned "but I'm glad in that way, too. What I meant is that I always see you with a ponytail or with your hair in a bun or braid. When you let it down like that, it's magnificent."

I reached up and flicked it back.

"Shh. It's my secret weapon!"

We laughed as we arrived at the Sports Bar and scanned the area. Our dates were sitting together and hopped up when they saw us approach.

"Ah, the lovely event virtuosos arrive!" said Langston. Or was it Owen? Darn! I forgot who was who. Not a good start to the evening.

"Hello, Langston," I said, careful to face both without focusing on one in particular until Langston acknowledged my greeting, then "Hello, Owen" to the other. Having grown up attending many formal functions, I had learned the fine art of avoiding an embarrassing mix-up.

"Gentlemen," Juliet slipped into ladylike character and held out her hand delicately to be kissed. Really, Jules? Was there a camera filming some modern episode of *Downton Abbey*? I chuckled inside.

"We were waiting for you here," indicating the bar that faced the Promenade Deck, "but we can go inside and get a table if you wish."

"Oh, no," I said. "I like sitting here and being able to people watch."

Somehow it just felt better being a bit more out in the open.

Juliet and I took the chairs that the brothers had been occupying, and they stood next to us. We ordered a bottle of wine to share and began the "getting to know you" routine.

"So." I seemed to have drawn the short straw for asking the first question. "Where are you two from?"

"We grew up in Toronto, but I moved to Vancouver. Owen still lives in Toronto."

"So you're Canadian?"

"Is that a problem?"

"No, just an observation. What do you do?"

"I'm a lawyer," said Owen, "and Langston is a doctor."

I sighed inwardly. Why did this seem like the beginning of every date I'd been on for the last several years? The only difference was that Juliet was along to take over some of the compulsory questions. Maybe things would get better after the compulsory round and we got into the free skate. What? Why was I thinking about ice skating? Focus, Keira, focus!

"What?" I knew a question had been addressed to me, but I hadn't heard it. "I'm sorry, the music is a little loud."

The others just looked at me, since the tune at that moment was a light jazz piece.

"He SAID," repeated Juliet with some annoyance, "what made you decide to go into event planning?"

"Oh." Right. First Date Question Number Twenty-Five. I could spit out the answer to that one while juggling fire batons.

Honestly. These two were handsome, professional men, and since we were only together for a week, there was an expiration date to any potential flirtation. Why was I so off my game? Just no spark. Oh well, this was only supposed to be a meet and greet anyway, so no harm. But I did owe them my full attention while I was there. Besides, I should always be networking. That was how we got some of our best events. Network, network, network. But was connecting from Toronto or Vancouver to Denver a reach at this point?

"What?" Darn it! The only reach I needed was one to pull myself back to the conversation.

"Sorry."

"We know. Loud music." Juliet surreptitiously pinched my arm.

I took a sip of my wine.

"What made you decide to take this trip?" I asked, thinking it would be better to have them answer questions for a while. But by the way the three of them stared at me, I could tell that they had already discussed that topic. I decided to be honest. Well, sort of.

"I really have to apologize. My mind wandered off. I was thinking about the results of the event today and doing a bit of thinking for tomorrow."

"We understand," said Langston politely, helping me cover my poor manners. "What chefs are featured tomorrow?"

Did they really want to discuss the event?

"Oh let's let Keira clear her head," said Juliet. She changed the topic skillfully. "What did you two for the rest of the day after we saw you earlier?"

Langston answered, "We went on a snorkeling excursion, then came back to the ship for the afternoon."

"How was the snorkeling?" Juliet asked.

"Well, we had a great time like we always do when we snorkel, and this time we went kayaking as well. But I have to tell you we had the best time with the people sharing our excursion. That made the trip worth it."

"Really? How so?"

"Well, they were two couples who were brother and sister with their spouses. First of all, they were animated and personable, but what made it fun was that they—"

"Made everything a competition!" I finished for him with a laugh.

"How did you know?" asked Owen.

"Let me see if I can describe them for you: the brother and sister had matching bright blue eyes, and even though it seemed that they were fighting, you could tell it was all in fun? And the sister's husband secretly egged on the competition, and the brother's wife patiently shook her head throughout it all?"

"Hey! Exactly!"

"You were in a group with my best friend and her family!"

"What are the odds!" exclaimed Juliet.

"Well, pretty good, if you look at how many people actually signed up for excursions," I began, but caught Juliet's eye. I knew that a discussion of mathematical probability and statistics would not go over well at the moment.

"We were worried that the excursion was going to be boring, but they really livened it up," said Langston.

"Oh, they're lively, all right," I said, nodding my head.

"Well, you'll appreciate this, the ringleader—"

"Alex," I said.

"Yes. Alex said that she had girlfriends along on the cruise that she wanted to introduce us to."

Juliet and I looked at one another.

"Us!"

"Of course we had to politely decline, because we told them we were meeting two ladies."

"Ah, but that wasn't the real reason, was it? You thought her girlfriends were going to be less than attractive, didn't you?" I wondered if maybe I needed to rethink these two.

"No, no, no!" Langston looked at Owen.

Juliet jumped in. "Well, what was it, then?"

"Well, to be honest, we didn't believe anyone could actually be as fabulous as she described."

I laughed.

"Alex is my BEST friend. Of course she's a bit biased."

Langston put his hands on each of our shoulders.

"Oh, but she did not exaggerate."

What kind of players were these guys? I wouldn't have considered me fabulous based on my less-than-tuned-in conversation to this point.

"Oh, Alex is pretty good at selling. She used to be in marketing."

I swiveled my chair around to survey the Promenade Deck. More people were making their way to the splendid dining halls for dinner. Large family groups with young children, bright red from a day in the sun and squeaky clean from a fresh shower, mingled with young couples strolling slowly arm in arm, oblivious to the hustle and bustle around them. Here and there were groups of young men or young women traveling separately in laughing groups, perhaps destined to meet later in one of the ship's bars. Everyone had an air of expectancy. Why was I being such a downer?

I swung back to face the brothers, prepared to thank them for the drink and to say my good-byes, when the announcement system came on and a familiar voice emerged.

"Good evening, ladies and gentlemen! This is your cruise director Brennan. I hope you had a great day in Nassau today. Just a reminder of tonight's activities ..."

He continued with his announcements, and his voice just reminded me of his infuriating personality. I needed distraction.

"Langston," I began on a different note, "this was lovely. What do you say we all meet up again later, after the show? Maybe in the Piano Bar?"

His eyes widened, as did his grin.

"That sounds great! Owen? Juliet?"

"You bet!" said Owen.

"Well, I sure wouldn't disagree," said Juliet, and I could tell from her tone that she thought I was the last person who would have suggested another meeting that evening

CHAPTER TWELVE

Was it my imagination or did everyone at our dinner table become unusually interested in their menus as Juliet and I approached?

We stopped a few feet from the table and paused.

"Ahem," I said. Nothing. I repeated loudly, "AHEM!"

"Oh, Keira, there you girls are," said Alex.

Why no, Alex, you weren't waiting on pins and needles. Hmmh. Two could play at that that game. I winked at Juliet.

"Hi guys. What looks good tonight?" We sat and took our menus and studied them as closely as if winning lottery ticket numbers were hidden on them somewhere. Their curiosity was conspicuous in the absence of a bombardment of questions.

"The seafood special looks good," said Juliet, playing along, "but I think I'm in the mood for prime rib tonight."

"Sounds good," I nodded. "But, you know, you can order two items."

"Really? I didn't know that! I think I may order two desserts," said Juliet. "I heard that the chef is preparing a chocolate—"

"All right!" interrupted Alex finally. "While we are all fascinated by your menu selections, I think you know we really want to know about the two mystery strangers! How did it go? What did you talk about? Who hit it off with the one in the linen blazer?"

She clapped her hand over her mouth.

"Aha!" I pointed to her. "I knew you would manage to show up and try to monitor the situation!"

Juliet jumped in, "Where were you? I didn't see you!"

"I wasn't there. I promised I wouldn't be there, remember?"

I thought back to the people walking past us in the Promenade Deck.

"Alex, you little sneak! You managed to get Gerard Marten to spy for you, didn't you?" I recalled seeing one of our featured bloggers sitting across the way at the coffee bar while we were talking with Langston and Owen. But I didn't think anything of it, since one was bound to see familiar faces over the course of a cruise. And Gerard wasn't even looking our way, so I assumed he hadn't seen us.

Everyone laughed.

"Don't you know that once Ally-Cat sets her mind to something, she achieves it?" asked Anthony.

"So," said Mrs. D'Ag, "now that you brought up the subject, how were these boys? And why didn't they walk you over to meet us?"

Cam did a perfect spit take.

"What?" Mrs. D'Ag's innocence was delicious. From the fact that she called them "boys" to the thought that we would subject them to the family after a casual drinks date. There was only so much room on a ship for them to run away from the inevitable interrogation.

"Mama," Cam patted her hand, "do you remember the gauntlet I had to run through the first time I was introduced? Alex and I had been dating for ages by the time I met the family."

"Oh pfft," Mrs. D'Ag said, with a wave of her hand. "We just like to know that our girls are with nice boys, right Maeve?"

My mother laughed, "You're right, Angela. Cam forgets that he is just lucky he passed the test."

"Hey!" Cam stopped buttering his roll and pointed it at Damian. "I got the priestly seal of approval first! That should count for something."

"Besides," I added, "these two today were approved before Jules and I even sat down with them."

"How is that possible?" asked Mrs. D'Ag.

"Well ... Alex and Anthony wanted to fix us up after meeting them THIS MORNING."

"What? No!" said Anthony. "Are they the snorkelers?"

"Snorkelers? I'm confused," said my mother.

Celia explained the events of the morning to the table.

"Hmm," said Russ in his calm way. "It looks like they've already met some of the family, girls. I'm afraid I have to agree. When do the rest of us get to meet them?"

You too, Russ?

The others joined in.

"Yes, bring them around!" "We need to meet them!"

I sat back and crossed my arms.

"Vultures ... all of you ..."

Mr. D'Ag was the one who finally saved us.

"Now come on, leave these girls alone. I'm sure they don't need their dinner upset in this way."

Thank you so much, Papa D., my eyes shot to him.

He smiled and continued, "After they finish their desserts, we can see what plans they have and maybe join them."

I dropped my chin to my chest in the midst of the good-natured laughter.

The rest of the dinner passed enjoyably, with everyone sharing stories about the events of that day.

The snorkeling entourage had several close calls, and Anthony and Alex made sure to work in comments about Langston and Owen whenever possible. Juliet and I managed to deflect any questions neatly.

The group that went for a walk on the island had ended up grabbing a cab and going to the enormous Atlantis Hotel and Casino.

"Wow, mother, how was that?" My mother was not someone who frequented casinos.

"Your mother is quite the gambler," said Russ.

"Oh, Russ, stop." She turned to me. "I think I spent a grand total of five dollars in the nickel slot machines."

"You were able to find a nickel slot machine in that luxurious place?" I asked.

"Oh yes. I wasn't about to drop a hundred dollars a hand at blackjack."

My mother was nothing if not fiscally responsible.

"Pop and Russ spent a little at the tables, though," said Damian.

Normally a quiet man who only opened up in a discussion of plants, Mr. D'Ag laughed. "Russ and I kept our betting to a minimum, thank you very much. But I don't know if I can really trust a man who is a New York Giants fan."

Uh-oh. The D'Agostinos were die-hard Pittsburgh Steelers fans, so the discussion of pro football was off and running. Russ held his own, but I could see that Juliet was lost.

"Sorry, Juliet, football discussion is a rite of passage with this family!" I checked my watch as we all were finishing our desserts and coffee, then I reminded the group that the musical show would be starting soon. I had to admit one of the advantages of a cruise vacation was the ability to get up from a delicious meal and walk directly to a first-class show. Tonight we were going to see *Grease*, and everyone was looking forward to it.

"Let's go, kids!" Mrs. D'Ag marshaled us out of the dining room and toward the theater.

After the final applause at the show, Mrs. D'Ag was once again in charge as we stood in our row and stretched.

"All right, now, let's get to bed," she said. "Tomorrow is a long workday for Keira and Juliet, and according to the *Lodestone* there's a lot of activities the rest of us can participate in for the day at sea."

"Bed?" exclaimed Alex. "Ma! We're on vacation."

"Well, that's your choice, but if you're tired tomorrow, don't blame me," answered the practiced mother and grandmother.

We all laughed, but it was Cam who had the best comment.

"You're absolutely right, Mama. I'm going straight to bed. C'mon Ali," he ushered Alex by the elbow, then stopped. "But, you know, I'm just going to stop in that Promenade Cafe and see if they have any of those little pizzas or sandwiches."

Mrs. D'Ag stopped and turned.

"Pizzas? Well, I guess it won't hurt to stop for a coffee."

The rest of us burst into laughter.

"What?" asked Mrs. D'Ag.

"Oh," said Russ, hooking her arm, "I think your son-in-law believes he's clever, but we know better, don't we?"

She smiled at him. "Oh, these kids!"

My mother hooked Mr. D'Ag's arm to join them, and the others started to follow, chattering about the show. She turned to me.

"Keira? Are you joining us, or are you and Juliet going up early?"

I didn't want to tell her that Juliet and I were meeting Langston and Owen and start another round of questions.

"Something like that. See you for breakfast?"

"Sounds good, dear," she kissed my cheek. "I'll see you in The Commons Cafe."

Juliet and I watched them leave, then we left to find the Piano Bar for First Date Part Two.

The Piano Bar was located on Deck 6, so we didn't have a long trip. Juliet took advantage of the journey to assess our dates on the way.

"They're nice guys, aren't they, Keir?"

"Sure, from what we could learn in that brief time, I guess."

Juliet stopped in her tracks.

"No, no, you're not going to go into that hyper judge-y mode, are you?" she asked. "How did they fall short of the measure?"

I laughed. "No, nothing like that. I mean that we really didn't have time to get to know them, that's all."

"Uh-huh," she pursed her lips. "I'm not buying it. I know you too well. What could possibly be wrong with them that you already figured out?"

"Seriously ... nothing! You saw me. I was just distracted, and I don't feel that I got to know them, that's all."

Juliet resumed walking, then whipped back toward me.

"Well, you seemed like you were going to call it quits after the Sports Bar. What made you think you wanted to give them a second chance?"

"I TOLD you. I was distracted and felt that I owed them another opportunity."

She searched my face, then started walking again.

"Okay, I'll buy it. Remember, we're not marrying these guys just because we enjoy a tune in the Piano Bar with them. The music in this bar can't be that magical."

When we reached the door to the bar, we could hear the strains of Train's "Marry Me" filtering through.

Doubled over in laughter, we entered the intimate venue and searched for Langston and Owen. They hadn't arrived, so we took two stools at the bar encircling the piano. The piano player launched into the next request, with the crowd joining in.

"This is fun, isn't it?" Juliet said over the merrymakers.

I nodded, looking toward the door to see if our dates were anywhere nearby.

Juliet swatted my shoulder.

"Stop! We said we'd be here after the show, we didn't give a precise time. They can't be late for a time that wasn't set."

"I know, I know," I said, but my mind had wandered back to Brennan McAllister and his accusations of MY tardiness. Well, I'd show him the next day.

"Keira, what are you thinking? Your face is positively murderous!"

"What?" I came back to the present and shook off those thoughts. "Nothing. Must just be the lighting. Come on, let's think of a request."

I flipped my hair back over my shoulders and grabbed the sheet of songs that the piano player had on the bar. We were studying the list when I heard a voice over my shoulder.

"Ah, the lovely Keira and Juliet."

We turned, smiling, to find Langston without his brother.

"Langston! But where is Owen?"

"I'm afraid when my brother and I made the plans with you two, he had forgotten he had promised to Skype with our favorite aunt," Langston said smoothly. "Surely you two are not disappointed with only having the lesser of the two?"

Hmm. Who would pay the exorbitant online costs at sea, and what favorite aunt would not have encouraged her single nephew to cancel a brief electronic visit and instead court a lovely young woman? Not any aunt of a young man of marriageable age that I had ever met. Of course, we couldn't exhibit disappointment.

"No, we totally understand!" Juliet said. "We're glad to have you to ourselves to chat with this evening."

I concurred. "It will be our honor."

Langston's black eyes flashed and his giant smile showed off blinding white teeth.

"Great! So, have you lovely ladies chosen a song request?"

He leaned forward and put his arm around Juliet.

Ah. I got it. I knew exactly which lovely lady he had his eye on. And if I had any doubt, it was sealed when he scooted between us and faced Juliet directly.

I smiled to myself and spun around on my stool to give him more room. I'd give it a moment or two, then excuse myself. Juliet didn't need a chaperone; woe be unto Langston if he had any wild ideas. I suppose I should have been hurt in some way, but I wasn't. I realized that if Owen had been there, I probably would have become bored at some point anyway. He was nice enough but kind of bland. Better that he kept his "date" with his aunt.

After a suitable amount of time, I hopped off the stool and managed to catch the attention of the flirtatious couple.

"Hey guys, I'm sorry to bug out on you, but I really want to get back to my stateroom and get things ready for tomorrow."

"Do you need me to help?" came Juliet's cursory offer. I debated on teasing her a bit by telling her that I would love her to help, but I was straightforward.

"No, Jules, I got this."

"Oh, but Keira, we want you to stay," said Langston. I almost believed him, he was that good.

"Oh, Langston, I think you have more than you can handle with Jules, there," I patted his shoulder. "You kids have fun."

I left the Piano Bar, suddenly relieved that I wasn't going to have to make small talk for the next hour or so.

CHAPTER THIRTEEN

My eyes sprang open when my travel alarm buzzed the next morning. After a quick shower—I still marveled at how tiny the shower stall was—I dressed in the Keira Graham Events uniform, applied my makeup, and pulled my hair back into one of my trademark ponytails. Glancing in the mirror, I saw myself as I wanted others to see me: confident, knowledgeable, and prepared.

I gathered the materials I'd need for the events of the day as well as the day's *Lodestone* and made for the door when I took a peek at my watch.

Forty-five minutes early.

Well, I could sit in the stateroom. No. It was lovely but a bit cramped with my personal traveling materials fighting for space with the event materials. The balcony was always an option, but I felt like going a bit farther afield.

Early to the cafe? A possibility, but I was feeling even more adventuresome.

I strolled down the passageway to the interactive map by the elevator and scanned it.

Aha! I entered the elevator and made my way to a tiny part of the forward deck that looked quiet and secluded and might capture the morning sun. Alone on the small deck, I made myself comfortable in a lounge chair and pulled out the day's itinerary. I would spend about a half hour preparing for my day in this charming spot, then I would descend to meet my mother for breakfast.

Lost in my paperwork, I was nearly startled when a voice interrupted me.

"So how did you manage to find my secret thinking space?"

"What brings you here, Brennan?" I shaded my eyes to view my intruder.

"Oh, I like to start my days up here," he said as he pulled a lounge chair beside mine. "It's one of the only spaces on the deck of the ship where I get fresh air and a minute to breathe."

"What? I would think that you'd want all your adoring fans swarming around you at all times."

"Oh, I do, I do." He leaned back, with a cocky grin on his face. "But I have to build up an air of longing and desire, you know."

Whatever.

Oh well, I didn't have to talk to him just because he was there.

I should, though.

No, said my inner petulant voice. After his smart-aleck attitude toward me in front of Alex and Cam, I didn't owe him anything. I focused on my papers.

I couldn't help but sneak a sidewise glance, though. He was comfortably settled back with his hands clasped above his head and ankles crossed. Rather than his usual Cruise Director duds, he had on shorts and a random T-shirt. He could easily have been mistaken for any passenger. Tanned and healthy, his brown hair had natural blonde streaks that glinted. I presumed his blue eyes were closed behind his shades.

"What, Keira?"

Darn it. He caught me looking at him!

"What do you mean 'what?'" Great. I was suddenly twelve years old again.

His dimples flashed.

"You looked over here. Do you have a question?"

I decided that the best defense was an offense.

"If you must know, I was looking at the *Lodestone* and was going to ask you what the deal was with this '70s night."

Smooth. Like anyone couldn't have figured that out based on the name of it.

"That." He sat up. "That is one of my favorite activities! The whole crew dresses in throwback, and we encourage the passengers to do so as well. We have a parade in the Promenade, then it breaks into fun music, lots of dancing. Hey, you know what?"

Suddenly I did not want to know what.

"You and Juliet are part of the crew. You should participate in the parade with the crew!"

"What! We don't have any '70s costumes with us!"

He shook his head. "That won't be a problem at all. Check with Neil—she's the crew member who led the line dancing on deck the first night."

"From New Zealand?"

"I see you DO know Neil. She's my second in command and will be able to hook you up."

"Seriously?"

He became more animated.

"Absolutely," he affirmed, then looked at his watch. "Look, I have to get to a meeting. I'll have Neil find you and get you set up, and then I'll see you at the beginning of the parade."

"What about our daily meeting? Won't you see me there first?" I stopped short of saying "And I'll be on time, AGAIN."

"You're right." He snapped his fingers, then pointed at me as he walked backward away from the area. "The report you handed in last night was top-notch. What do you say you just generate a report like that one and drop it at the purser's desk, and we'll see if that works for today."

He disappeared around the corner.

Huh? After all the clatter yesterday about that report and today's meeting?

I looked at my watch and realized that I needed to hop if I was going to meet my mother for breakfast.

My logical mind could not process what had just happened. Oh, well, I shrugged. I just needed to remember to stay in Brennan McAllister's good graces if I wanted to get good feedback from the cruise line, no matter how oddly he acted.

"Over here, dear!" Mrs. D'Ag waved me toward the small grouping of couches and short tables outside The Commons Cafe where she and my mother had settled, rather than sitting at the regular tables.

"This is nice." I kissed them both. "Where are the others?"

"It's just us. The rest have gone somewhere to eat mass quantities of giant pancakes or waffles or something," my mother said. "Go in and get your breakfast and join us."

I grinned. I was sure that if the guys were engaging in a pancake-eating competition, Alex would be right in the thick of it. I couldn't imagine her dad and Russ participating in it though.

When I returned with tea, fruit, and a bagel, Celia had arrived.

"Were you involved in the pancake-palooza, Celia?" I asked.

"What? Oh, no. I went for a walk around the jogging track on Deck 5 before coming here. Is that what those guys are doing?"

"I think your father-in-law and Russ are even involved, and Alex."

"Well, of course, Alex." We laughed. Growing up with two brothers, Alex had always felt a keen sense of competitiveness.

"Do you know how many competitive activities she dragged me into at college?" I asked.

"Please don't tell me you girls competed in anything unladylike!" my mother said.

"The Graham name remained intact," I assured her. I decided to tease her a bit. "Wet T-shirt contests don't count, do they?"

"Keira!"

"What?" My face was pure innocence.

"Relax, Mrs. G." Celia patted her knee. "You know these two girls must have been the poster girls for proper behavior."

"Well ... mostly proper," I continued to egg her on.

My mother shook her fist jokingly and laughed.

"So what are you folks doing to pass the day at sea?" I asked.

Celia pulled out the *Lodestone*.

"Well, speaking of competitiveness, I see that Anthony has highlighted every contest on the schedule today, so I assume he wants to participate in each of those. General trivia, '80s trivia, progressive trivia—"

"I sense a theme," I said.

"You know this family and trivia contests. Other than that, I think we're going to try out the zip line."

"The zip line?" asked Mrs. D'Ag.

"You can see it on the tippy top deck. It's the one above the boardwalk on the other side of the deck we're on now," I said.

"Oh, the side with the carousel," she nodded.

"Right."

She turned to Celia and grabbed her hand. "You mean that rope that goes all the way across the ship? You're going to slide across that?"

"Mama D., it's safe as anything. Little kids do it!"

Mrs. D'Ag shook her head. "I guess so, but it just looks so high!"

I reassured her. "They lock you in with a close-fitting, tight harness, and it really doesn't go all the way across the ship, just across that part of the deck." Although, come to think of it, that part of the deck was as long as the decks of most smaller cruise ships! "It'll be fine. Come on, you have to come and take pictures."

Mrs. D'Ag shuddered. "I could come watch. I suppose it will be nice for the babies to have one last picture of their parents."

"Mama D.!" Celia and I cried in unison.

She turned to my mother "Are you going to witness this craziness?"

"Well, Angela, who am I to miss that? Russ and I are going to attend the art lecture a little later, then play some bingo, but we'll catch up with the group there if they tell us when they are going to dangle for their lives."

At that moment, the pancake crew joined us, laughing and joking.

"Kiss me, my love," said Anthony to Celia, "I am the champion."

"The winner by a flapjack," said Russ.

"I think I might place a formal challenge to the commissioner. Oof! I gained a ton!" joked Alex as she sat on the arm of her mother's chair and rubbed her nonexistent belly.

"Are you still claiming that your last pancake was thicker than Tonio's?" Cam sat companionably next to me with his arm draped around my shoulders.

"Uh, yes," Alex said.

Celia broke in with her usual calm. "Okay. Enough of this flap." Groans all around at her poor pun. "We were just comparing plans for the day," she continued, unperturbed.

Moments passed as plans were discussed and confirmed, and people left to begin the day's activities. Soon Alex, Russ, my mother, and I were the only ones left in the cozy chairs.

"When will we see you again, Keira?" asked Alex.

"Well," I looked at my schedule. "I think I'll be tied up all day with the event, but I'll be ready for dinner. What shall we do tonight?"

"I see there's a '70s parade on the Promenade Deck afterward," said my mother. "I wonder what that is?"

"Oh! I almost forgot! It's supposed to be fun, I guess."

"You guess?"

"Well, the crew dresses in throwback '70s costumes and parades through the Promenade Deck. Then afterward they play '70s music for everyone to dance to. Passengers are encouraged to look as '70s as possible, too!"

"Awesome!" Alex said. "I bet we have enough stuff between us that we could look '70s. Juliet could definitely pull off a Foxy Brown look."

"Well ..."

"Oh, come on, Keira, you have to come out with us."

"No, it's not that." I dreaded the response to what I would say next. "It's that Juliet and I were asked to sort of ... be ... in the parade."

A chorus of disbelieving reaction followed.

"And when were you going to tell us this?" asked my mother.

"I'm telling you now."

"Uh-uh. You have to tell us exactly how this happened." Drat. I knew Alex wouldn't just let it go simply. I blew a stray wisp of hair out of my eyes and began.

"I ran into Brennan McAllister this morning—"

"What! Your nemesis? Where?"

"You realize this is why I hate telling you people anything?"

"Ah, but you are such a good storyteller."

"Okay. I was up on a tiny little piece of the forward deck earlier, where it's basically secluded and private, and who should appear but everyone's favorite cruise director. He told me about the parade and said that since Juliet and I were part of the crew—"

"Oh, I bet you loved hearing that." Alex's sarcasm was not well hidden.

"SINCE Juliet and I were part of the crew, we should participate. He said we could come down and get costumes and get ready with the rest of them."

"I think it sounds like fun," said Russ.

I pondered. "It does, actually. We're supposed to find Neil—remember the crew member who led the line dancing?"

"The Australian?"

"New Zealander. Anyway, Neil is supposed to get us some costumes."

"What does Juliet think about this?"

"What does Juliet think about what?" The object of the question walked up at that moment, fresh from her daily gym workout, ready for work, her normal curls tamed into a more sedate bun, but with wrists full of jangling bracelets that accented her uniform.

"Keira signed you up to be in the '70s parade this evening," said my mother.

"Sounds like a kick!" said Juliet, never one to be caught off guard. "How did that happen?"

I recounted the story for her.

"I guess you girls need something more exciting to do than last night, right?" asked my perceptive mother.

Juliet looked at me quickly, then looked away.

"Waiiit. They're not telling us something," said Alex. "Did you girls not go straight to your staterooms after the show?"

"We may have taken a detour." I tried to deflect the tale of meeting Langston in the Piano Bar.

"And?"

"It's no use, Keira. We have to tell them," said Juliet. She took a deep breath. "We went to the ship's casino and gambled our money away at poker all night."

"Ha." Alex squinted.

"Come along," Russ took her by the arm. "We will hear this story, if indeed there is a story, when these two want to share it. But I think they need to get to the event room, if I'm not mistaken, to earn their pay. And you need to join your husband in the Outrigger Bar for the first round of many trivia competitions that you will dominate."

"This isn't over," Alex said over her shoulder.

No, I knew it wasn't.

I turned to Juliet expectantly.

"Well, missy, you got off the hook with them, but you better start talking to me!"

Her eyes were earnest when she blurted, "He's the most wonderful guy I've ever met!"

I searched her face to see if she was kidding but could see no signs of joking. How could this be? She just met this guy yesterday! In an elevator! On a cruise ship!

"You just met this guy yesterday! In an elevator! On a cruise ship!"

"I know, I know, I know," she said, nodding. "If I heard me say what I just said, I wouldn't believe it either. But seriously, Keira, he's more than just someone to share a dance and a few laughs with."

I pulled myself back from saying all the things I wanted to say and kept it to an edited version.

"Look, Juliet. Do you think you might be swept up in the romance of being on this ship? You can't honestly tell me you're buying into that playboy image?"

Oops. Not a terribly supportive statement. Yes. I could tell by her flashing eyes that she didn't appreciate my "concern."

"What? Just because he's dashing and well-dressed with a killer smile, it means he's a playboy?"

"No. It's not that." It kinda was that.

"Or is it because he preferred me over you?"

"Hey! Wait a minute! What makes you think that?"

She stopped and turned to me. "I could tell last night that you expected Langston to be for you and Owen to be for me and got upset when Langston paid more attention to me after his brother didn't show up."

Where was that coming from?

"Juliet, can you hear the words that are coming out of your mouth? I didn't expect either of them to be 'for' either of us. If you remember, we were just going to have a nice evening of drinks. Geesh. When only one of them showed up, I didn't realize we were going to have to play a game of rock-paper-scissors to see who 'got' him."

"Then why were you so weird, Keira?"

"What do you mean 'weird'?"

"It just seemed to me that after he made his choice obvious—"

"Again, I wasn't aware that you and I were like items on a menu."

"You know what I mean. After he started paying more attention to me, you seemed distant."

"Juliet," I began, unsure of how to proceed. "I was actually relieved."

"What? Are you saying you really DON'T think he's good boyfriend material."

"How did we circle back to that?"

"Well?"

"I was RELIEVED that I didn't have to make small talk with EITHER of them," I hastened to finish. "They seemed like perfectly nice guys, but I just was not up to small talk with anyone last night, okay?"

"Really?"

"Really."

She was mollified, and we continued walking.

"But, Keira, do you really think he's just a playboy?"

Hmm. I knew Juliet well enough to know that she had good judgment in these matters and could spot a fake. I decided that I really needed to step back.

"You know what it is, Jules? I just never see you all giggly and squeally. This is new for me, and I overreacted."

"Believe me, Keira, I know what you mean. The whole time we were talking, I just kept thinking that there is no way this can be for real. But the more we talked, the realer it got."

"Realer?"

"More real. You know what I mean. It wasn't about the grammar, Keira."

"I know." Wow. She was serious if she couldn't take a bit of ribbing.

"Sooo, what else happened?"

"Well, we left the Piano Bar after a while and went out for a stroll on the deck. Eventually, we just sat on deck chairs and talked for what seemed like hours."

"It must really have been a lot of hours if my mother noticed how late you came in."

"It was pretty late, but he was a real gentleman and walked me to the door."

"No wild moonlight kisses on deck?" I joked.

"Well, there might have been some smooching in the moonlight," she said with a cheeky grin, "but a chaste good-night kiss at the door."

"It all sounds normal. What now?"

"I don't know." She turned from cheeky to pensive. "I'm kinda falling for him."

Seriously? After a couple of glasses of wine and romance in the moonlight?

"I know what you're thinking, Keira. You're thinking this is really fast."

"Aren't you thinking that, too?"

"Well, yes, but ... I don't ... It's just ..."

Was this my calm, poised Juliet? Juliet who could chew through dates and leave them wondering what happened.

"That's ... great?" I couldn't help sounding skeptical.

"Here's the thing. I know that on the surface, he is tall, dark, and handsome."

"Why yes. All qualities that we run from."

"Hush. You know what I mean. He *looks* like he's just surface. But when you talk with him for a while, you get to the real man. You remember he's a doctor?"

"Right." I guess I remembered that's what he said was his profession.

"Well, he's a heart surgeon specializing in pediatrics at a Children's Hospital, and he spent time with Doctors Without Borders—what?"

By that time, it was supremely difficult to hide my skepticism.

"Nothing, Juliet. Well ... can't anyone say that?"

"Yes. But can anyone have pictures on their phone?"

"I guess not."

I burst into laughter.

"What now, Keira?"

"Oh, honey. I'm picturing you demanding photo evidence to back up every statement he made."

"Ha ha. It wasn't like that. Well, sort of not like that."

"No, no. I'm proud of your detective skills. Remind me again why you are an event planner and not working for the CIA?" She took several steps away from me, stopped, turned, and waited for me with her hand on her hip. "Oh, come on, don't flounce away from me, Beyoncé."

I caught up to her and hugged her.

"Come on. I'm sorry. Tell me more."

"Well, he wants to take me to dinner at the Steakhouse or Giorgio's—you know, one of the specialty restaurants."

I nodded.

"I definitely want to go."

"Well, why not? Although, you realize that for all intents and purposes, you're part of my extended family while on board, and you'll have to introduce him to them, right?"

"I know. I thought of that. But it will be good practice for him meeting my big Portuguese clan."

What! She was already talking about taking him home to her family. She really must be falling for him.

"And I'll have to meet his family, too."

What? At that rate, Father Damian might have to perform a wedding as soon as we return to port.

We reached the event space.

"I'm happy, Jules. Seriously. We'll have to chat more about him, but I see that our first chef is here for the day. And from the look on his face, I sense that we may have a few nonromantic questions coming our way."

Corey Webb bore down on us with a look of sheer determination. A proud, self-proclaimed amateur-for-life chef, he had combined the cooking tips he learned from his melting pot of a family and wrote a highly popular blog featuring Asian, Italian, and Eastern European recipes. His shipboard session was entitled "Rice, Rice, Baby."

"Corey, how's it going?" I was afraid of the answer.

"Keira, do you see the steam coming out of my ears?"

He could be a bit dramatic for such a big bruiser of a guy.

"I take it that it's a metaphor for some problem you're having?"

"Well, that's the only steam we have. My rice cookers aren't working properly."

"I'm on it," said Juliet, who dashed away.

"Other than that, Corey, how are things?" I hoped that the rice cooker situation was the only problem. I knew Juliet would come up with a solution.

Corey ran his hand through his erratically chopped dyed-scarlet hair and shook his head.

"I guess we're fine. Are all these chairs going to be full?"

"Packed house, Corey. You are very popular."

He took several deep breaths.

"I'm not sure I can play to a packed house."

Corey was notorious for his stage jitters. I knew that once he began his presentation, he would engage with the crowd and be fine.

"Look, let's run through your menu. All rice today?"

"Why, should I have done some pasta?" His eyes looked forlorn. I looked around to see if his wife, Anitra—usually the only person who could calm him down—was anywhere nearby, but I did not see her.

"It was just a question, Corey."

"Oh. Right, right." He pulled a tiny sheet of paper from the pocket of his immaculate chef's apron and read from it.

"We're doing Mama's Stuffed Peppers, Tessie's Cabbage Rolls, and What's Shakin' Bacon Fried Rice.

"Sounds delicious! Rice, rice, baby."

Juliet returned, a determined look on her own face.

"Well?" Corey wrung his hands.

She began, "Here's the deal. I can't find anyone to repair the cookers. BUT"—Corey's eyes widened, so she hastened to point to the cell phone in her hand—"I have them on standby to cook as much as you need. Just tell me, and I'll call them."

Corey paused, then breathed a sigh of relief. Even as a jittery cook, he knew that sometimes a backup plan was the only solution.

"Let me call them. Thank you so much, Juliet."

He dialed the number and began the discussion. Anitra walked up to join us, and as we helped her unload the boxes of materials she had wheeled into the room, we filled her in on the situation.

"Thanks, guys," she said, pulling a bandanna around her own hair that perfectly matched Corey's in scarlet hue. "I guess I should have come down to this room with him before I went to the storage area."

"No problem, Anitra. That's what we're here for," said Juliet.

"Juliet once again has proven to me that I made the right decision to hire her."

"As if there was a doubt," my colleague grinned.

Corey finished his call, handed the phone back to Juliet, and welcomed his wife with a kiss. He had regained his composure and was less dramatic.

"Thank you both. Are you sticking around for the demo?"

"For your stuffed peppers? You bet!" Juliet said.

"Awesome!" His face split into a grin. "Well, let's get back to prep."

The couple hustled back to the front of the room.

"Crisis averted. Do you think it will be the only one today?" Juliet asked.

"Are you new to this?" I joked. "We'll be lucky if it's the only one this *morning*!"

CHAPTER FOURTEEN

Fortunately, the demos for the day at sea were relatively crisis free. Janet Walsh, the lively host of "Let's Do Brunch," was also an award-winning quilter and had brought samples of her designs to display. She actually managed to give a mini-lesson in quilting between whipping up her famous Darby's Chicken Salad and other brunch favorites.

"I don't know how she does it," Juliet said as she attempted but failed to complete a neat row of stitches on the tiny square she was working on.

"Years of practice, I guess." My stitches were better than Juliet's but still not as precise as Janet's. "You're just lucky you haven't ended up stitching your square onto your lap."

"Funny," Juliet said.

Eventually we reached late afternoon, and in the middle of our final demo, Juliet and I relaxed in the back of the room. Gabriel Francis was completing the last offering in his session, "Saintly Sinners Desserts." The crowd was oohing and aahing over his Aunt Lydia's Cheesecake and waiting for the tasting. After a day indoors, and after his earlier Deluxe Lemon Bars, I felt the need to get some fresh air and a walk.

"Jules, do you care if I go for a walk?"

"This is the last demo. I can handle it. Why don't you just call it a day."

"Really?"

"Sure."

"Well," I looked at my phone, "Alex just texted me that they were getting ready to go on the zip line. I might get up there in time to catch them going across."

"Won't you do it, too?"

I shook my head.

"Probably not today. They book specific times for it, and I doubt I can get in line at this point. I would like to try to get pictures of the others, though."

"Get going, then. Oh and Keira?"

I sensed that she was going to drop some information on me.

"You won't mind if I don't come and do the parade with you, will you? If Langston and I go to dinner, well ... you know ... I don't want to have to leave early."

"I get it. Sure, no problem."

"You'll still do the parade, though, right?"

"Oh, I don't know. I'll see."

"Come on, Keir! You're not going to bug out!"

"Oh, no, not like you are?" That was unfair.

"That's unfair."

I didn't want to hurt her feelings.

"Don't worry about it. Look, I need to get up on the top deck, then I need to finish that little report for our 'boss,' then get ready for dinner. I've got a lot to do before parade time."

She still looked unconvinced.

"Okay. Just make sure you don't give up on it," she said. "It sounds like fun."

I tapped my watch.

"Gotta go. Catch up with you later."

It felt good to walk out of the elevator and into the bright sunshine and breeziness of the Sports Deck. I saw Anthony and Celia at the far end of the deck where the zip liners concluded their wild ride. I waved and walked over to join them.

"Have you guys had your rides?"

"Omigosh! It was so much fun!" Celia had the same glee in her voice that I'd heard so often in her daughter Elisabetta.

"You need to do this, Keir," agreed Anthony.

I leaned on the railing.

"Is one of our crowd coming next? I didn't miss everyone, did I?" I was sure that Alex would whoop and holler all the way across.

The next rider pushed off. It was definitely a female and she kicked with obvious glee as she careened toward us. No, not Alex. That wasn't her bathing suit.

Wait. I knew that bathing suit.

Mother!!

My mouth must have been agape as my mother slid into the pile of cushions beside us.

"Did you get that, Russ?"

I realized that Russ had come behind us to capture a video of the spectacle of my mother—dignified Maeve Graham—zip-lining across the deck of a cruise ship as if she were a teenager!

"May-may, you were fantastic!" he embraced her and kissed her.

"Keira!" She turned and saw me there. "Did you see me?"

"I saw you, Mother."

"Wasn't that something?"

Oh, it was something all right.

"Mother. How? What?"

At that moment, Cam slammed into the cushions.

"Mama G., you were amazing!" He said after he was unhooked from his harness.

"I know!" Her eyes were still sparkling.

Damian was the next zip-liner to arrive.

"Mama G., you are my hero!"

Et tu, Damian?

"Well, you boys wore me down with your persuasion. And that little daredevil Alex, of course."

Of course.

The daredevil herself screamed and screeched upon her arrival. After embracing my mother, she saw me.

"Keira! Did you see your mother?"

"How could I not?" I deadpanned.

"What? Are you mad that she did that?"

My silence spoke for me.

"Keira! You can't tell me that you're upset that we encouraged your mother to take a chance!"

"Why no, Alex. And where are your parents?" I peered across the way. "Are they next?"

"No. But what does that have to do with it?"

"So it's okay for MY mother to act foolish then?" My voice must have been a little too loud because the others stopped laughing and comparing rides, and turned toward us.

"So you think what I did was foolish, Keira?" my mother asked in her normal patrician tones.

"No, Mother, I didn't really mean that. That was an unfortunate choice of words."

"Because, I might remind you—AGAIN—that I'm old enough to make my own decisions. I don't need my adult daughter watching after me."

"Mother!" I called after her as she walked away, and stopped before making a scene. A normally quiet Russ looked as if he was going to speak up, but just shook his head and strode off to follow her.

"Keira! That wasn't nice at all!" Alex began.

"Really, Alex?" I just wasn't in the mood. "Remind me, just where are your parents, again?"

"They're playing bingo. Besides, what difference does it make if they did this or not? Or is it that you're jealous that your mother is more daring than you are, Ice Princess?"

I looked around to see others outside our group were starting to stare again and thought it was better not cause a scene.

"I'm just not in the mood for this right now. I'll see all of you ... DAREDEVILS ... at dinner. Right now I have to do a boring report for my boring job."

I stomped off. Luckily when I reached the elevator, it was already there, and the doors opened with a passenger inside.

"Hello, mate! Brennan told me to look for you, and your co-worker said you might be up here. Are you ready to suit up for the parade tonight?" Neil greeted me with a smile.

"You know what, Neil, I am sooo ready!"

I'd show them who's a daredevil!

I managed to make polite chit-chat with Neil as the elevator descended to the crew deck, one of the lowest decks on the ship. The doors opened to a scene a bit different than the passageway outside my stateroom.

Crew members dashed back and forth preparing to arrive at their next assignment. The "kids"—the crew that worked for the cruise director and who seemed to be everywhere on the ship at once—were all dressed in their polo-and-khaki combination and comparing notes:

"Who's manning the board?"

"Isn't that you, Gianni?"

"No, no, I'm early ticket one."

"It's Olga's turn. She's on bingo. Syd will get there when ice melts."

A combination of accents all mixed together speaking in the kind of shorthand that only comes from working closely in a group that has many responsibilities and little time.

Neil could sense my amused confusion.

"It's all shorthand around here. Can you even guess what's going on?"

"Let me see. Gianni will be taking tickets for the early show, Olga is calling bingo and will run the shuffleboard tournament. Syd will help her after the ice show?"

"Good on ya! You managed to crack the code! We have some crew members who still haven't managed to decipher our crazy shorthand." She stared pointedly at the tall red-headed young man with the name tag "Bryce."

He swooped her up and gave her a laughing embrace.

"Aye, Neil, me love, tell me again why ye won't make me the happiest Irishman and run away with me to raise a family in County Derry."

"Because you have been too long at the Blarney Stone and don't mean a word of it, me lad," Neil said, echoing his accent, and pushed him toward the elevator. "Now get to the Lido Deck and use that charm on the teenyboppers who'll be waiting for you to teach them cowboy line dancing."

"How about you, me flaxen-haired green-eyed filly?" he turned to me and waggled his eyebrows.

"She's here on real business, not monkey business. Now scoot!" She pushed him once again.

"They seem like a fun crew," I said.

"Oh, it's nothing but high jinks around here sometimes. I have a devil of a time keeping them on task, especially the head prankster."

"Bryce?"

"No. I mean the head imp himself. Brennan."

"Brennan? Surely not. He's the director."

"Oh, he's the director, and a great one at that, but when it comes to pulling pranks, he's the worst ... or, should I say, the best."

I thought of smooth, cool-eyed Brennan with that ear-to-ear grin. Surely, he must run his crew with the same tough-as-nails attitude he showed me the other evening in our meeting.

"But what does he do if you don't complete your reports correctly?" I asked.

"Reports? What reports?"

"You mean you don't have daily meetings and reports?"

"What gave you that idea?"

"He did. He said we had to meet after my event every day for a debrief."

"Keira, we don't have daily reports! We barely have time to get the work done during the day!"

Suddenly I felt quite the fool. I had to endure that meeting with him yesterday AND I completed that report last night AND I was prepared to complete one tonight and every night.

"Neil," I asked as we entered a storage area filled with props and costumes. "What else can you tell me about Brennan McAllister?"

She began pulling costumes and holding them against me. "Not a lot, really. He hasn't had this ship for long. He moved up from being cruise director on one of the smaller ships. This is actually my first cruise with him."

Hmm.

"I do know one thing. The girls all love him."

Big shock there.

"I mean they LOVE him. Apparently his transfer followed some sort of incident with a passenger."

Another big shock, I thought drily.

"What about you? Aren't you under his spell?"

"Me?" she laughed. "I'm taken, mate. My husband is on this ship as well."

"Is he on the cruise director's crew?"

"Not exactly. He plays piano. Here, see if these boots fit."

"Is he in the band?" The white go-go boots zipped up perfectly.

"He's in all the bands. When you're a musician on a ship, you go where you're needed. Wig or no wig?"

"I'd prefer no wig if possible. So you all are multitaskers then." I did recall seeing some of the same faces of the musicians in different venues.

"That's the key to working on a cruise ship. Lots of tasks."

"I noticed so many different accents. Is that normal?"

"Definitely. People apply for jobs from all over the world and speaking different languages is a plus because we might be assigned to ships that sail with cruisers from all over the world. We're a real mixed bag on the cruise director's crew. If you do no wig, can you pull off a Farrah Fawcett look?"

"Oh, definitely. What about a dress?"

She snapped her fingers.

"Give me back those boots."

"Hey! I like these."

"What you wear on your own time is up to you, love. No, I have a better idea for you, blondie. If you're going Farrah, you're going glam."

She pulled out a form-fitting kelly green silken dress with spaghetti straps and a handkerchief hemline.

"Wow! That is stunning!" I ran the material through my fingers. "Is this vintage '70s? It has to be."

"You bet it is. And here ... and here ..." She handed me a white fur stole and a pair of high-heeled silver sandals so wispy they seemed to be made of mercury itself.

"Do you think I can pull this off?"

"I can't think of anyone else who could. Look, come down here early and let Magda do your makeup. She'll send you back a couple of decades for sure.

I looked at the ensemble.

Why not? It was daring. And wasn't *daring* the key word of the day?

"Did you do a bit of shopping?"

I met Mr. and Mrs. D'Ag in the passageway as I was walking toward my own stateroom.

"What? Oh, this." I held the exquisite green '70s disco outfit against myself. "It's for the parade tonight. What do you think?"

Mrs. D'Ag said, "I think it's perfect! You'll look like you stepped right out of *Saturday Night Fever*!"

"That's the look I'm going for."

"Where are you headed now?" she asked. "Why don't you join us by the pool for a while. I'm sure you must be tired of being inside all day."

After the temper tantrum I had pulled on the Sports Deck, I felt like I needed time to cool down before I saw my mother and the others and apologized.

"I need to do some paperwork and clean up before dinner."

"Are you sure?"

"Angela, let her do her job. Remember she's here to work, not to fritter away her days by the pool," said Mr. D'Ag. "Keira, doll, you do what you need to do, then we'll see you when we see you. Here."

He handed me a stick of gum from his front pocket. I had seen him do this wordless fatherly gesture to Alex many times, and it was one that he began sharing with me when the family "adopted" me as their second daughter, back in college.

My fancy dress crushed against him as we hugged. "Papa D., thank you so much."

He waved me off awkwardly.

"It's just gum, not diamond earrings, sweetie." But his smile stretched across his face. "Come Angela, we'll miss getting a good chair."

Despite my inclination to not complete Brennan's report, or to fill it out with joke answers, I did the correct thing and filled it out properly. What could it hurt? I reasoned that it was valuable to my own record-keeping in any case. I did, however, refuse to jump through any hoops to get it to the purser's office before dinner.

Once the detestable paperwork was done, I took a leisurely shower and prepared my hair for later in the evening by drying it so that it cascaded in a long golden column. When it was parade time, I would employ a curling iron to give the sides the classic '70s Farrah "wings." That night was a smart casual night, so I slipped into my off-the-shoulder swing mini in a bold geometric print. I looked into the mirror and felt as if I was already in '70s mode.

At the precise moment I finished my preparations, there was a mad rapping on my door.

"Let's go, Keira, this is just dinner, not the prom!" came the teasing voice of my best friend. Could she possibly have forgotten my rudeness of earlier?

I whipped the door open, and Alex nearly fell in.

"Calm down, Alexandria! You don't need to alarm the entire ship." I peered out to see Cam, Damian, Anthony, and Celia, appropriately smartly dressed. The men wore linen slacks and summer sport coats, while the women wore dressy halter numbers—pastel floral for Celia and bold color-blocking in primary colors for Alex.

"Yikes! I didn't realize I needed this much of an escort."

"Ma was afraid you were going to order room service, so she sent us to strong-arm you," said Anthony.

"I knew better," I laughed as we started toward the elevator. "Where are your parents, anyway? And my mother and Russ?"

"Oh the grown-ups are having dinner in the Steakhouse specialty restaurant. So it's just us kids tonight."

I stopped short of the elevator.

"No! I think Juliet is having dinner there with her beau!"

"What? She'll be ambushed. Not by your mother, certainly, but definitely by Ma," Anthony said and turned around. "How would she not have discussed this with your mother?"

"I don't know. I suspect she got ready and left the room before Mother came back to get ready."

"Ooh," Alex said with a hint of diabolical glee. "I think we should go there ourselves and watch that happen."

"No!" we chorused.

"That's a nice steakhouse," Cam said. "It's not dinner theater."

Celia herded all of us into the opening doors of the elevator. "We will go to our table in the dining room, as planned, and have dinner as planned," she said sensibly, but ended with, "Of course, if we end up taking a stroll in The Commons near the steakhouse afterward, well, it is a nice area, after all, and open to everyone who wants to walk there."

"Ceil, we thought Elisabetta got her devilish streak from Tonio, but you contribute pretty heavily, too, don't you?" Cam gave her a hip bump.

"I don't know what you're talking about!" she sniffed, then winked.

Despite the missing diners at our table, the decibel level of conversation did not seem to have gotten any lower. For a day at sea, the family managed to fill time with myriad activities in addition to the infamous zip line.

"The bowling was pretty cool," said Cam.

"Especially when the guy who kept bragging about what a good bowler he was got crushed by the lady who just learned the game today," agreed Celia.

"They have a bowling alley?" I asked.

"No," Cam shook his head. "It was on the Wii gaming system hooked up to a big screen in the Sports Bar. You have to play it pretty carefully."

This led to a demonstration of video game bowling that resulted in almost catapulting a nearby wine bucket to the floor, along with a few stares from neighboring tables.

"So, we KILLED at every trivia competition," said Anthony, neatly changing subjects.

"I am not shocked," I said. "And did other people eventually learn who you were and begin to groan when they saw you approaching?"

"As a matter of fact, yes they did," said Cam. "They thought they finally had a chance when they saw Damian, because some of them had been at daily Mass and figured that surely a priest would not be competitive."

"They don't know Damian."

"I was just being honest about the answers that I knew," said the man in question. "Can I help it that the topic for the one competition was rock and roll?"

"Well, when they let you pick the category, I don't think they knew you nearly had a successful rock and roll career before you became a priest, Padre!" said Cam.

"Ouch. Nearly?"

"You kids stop fighting," said Alex, in a perfect imitation of their father, and we all laughed. "Anyway," she continued turning toward me, "you need to carve out some time to join us tomorrow in the shuffleboard tournament."

"What are we, senior citizens?" I asked.

"No," she shook her head. "It's fun. All ages participate. As a matter of fact, most ages participate in everything."

I remembered my meltdown over my mother and the zip line.

"You guys, I'm really sorry," I began.

"Stop," said Damian. "We know it wasn't your best moment, Keir. It's okay."

"But it's not okay. I was mean to my mother. You guys should hate me."

"We know you need to make it right with your mother. But we love you, okay?"

I looked around the table. Their faces were sincere.

"Okay. So what about this shuffleboard?"

"Oh, it's so cool, not what you'd think at all." And Alex was off and running.

CHAPTER FIFTEEN

The dinner table was clear of everything except our coffee and teacups when Alex remembered. "Oh! We need to get down to The Commons if we're going to get a peek at Juliet's young man, don't we?"

"Are we really going to do that?" I asked. "Isn't that kind of a *Brady Bunch* thing to do? Spy on Marcia and her date?"

"Yes. So?"

I looked around the table but didn't see any disagreement. The one person who might have been the voice of reason, Damian, had excused himself earlier to attend to a contingent of the staff who had scheduled pastoral meetings with him.

"What's the harm?" said Anthony, taking me by the arm. "We're just going to sit in the Tidal Wave Bar in the park."

"The one that moves up and down from The Commons to the next deck on hydraulics?"

"Right. It only sits in front of the Steakhouse for fifteen minutes before it moves up, so if we catch a glimpse of them, well, then so be it."

"Yes. That sounds oh-so-nice and innocent, doesn't it?" I went along, but I had a nagging feeling that something wasn't quite right.

"What else do you have to do before the '70s parade, Keir?" asked Alex. "It's not like you're the grand marshal of it or anything, right?"

Hmm. She hadn't seen my disco togs, so maybe I would keep that a secret.

"You're right. I just have to get down to the meeting space in time to march in with the crew. Neil did say something about doing my makeup, so I might go a little early."

"Do you have a groovy outfit to wear?"

"Something like that. You'll be able to pick me out."

We negotiated our way through the ship to the relative calm of The Commons Deck, marveling again at how many different "neighborhoods" were contained on the floating city.

"After this, before the parade, we should go over to the Boardwalk and get a hot dog," said Cam.

"Seriously? Did that short stroll give you an appetite?" asked Alex.

"I don't know, there's just something about being on a ship that makes me hungry all the time," he shrugged. "Besides, you should talk. Have you walked past the Promenade Cafe ONCE without having a chocolate brownie?"

"That's different. I'm doing research," she said. "We might want to carry them at the restaurant, and I want to figure out the recipe."

"Oh, you'll be carrying them into the restaurant—on your hips!" cracked Anthony.

We reached the small bar that was "parked" on The Commons Deck outside the Steakhouse, which would afford us a prime view of entrances and exits.

"Here. It was meant to be. Perfect." Alex settled front and center on a stool facing the Steakhouse. The rest of us took our places around her.

Although the restaurant didn't have large windows, it did have walls that could be opened to imitate the open-air concept of restaurants on land. All in all, it was a charming venue.

"I see your mother and Russ, but I don't see Jules and the doc," Alex declared. "I'm pretty sure they can't see us out here."

"'Jules and the doc'? What are they, a Vegas act?"

"You know what I mean."

"You took exactly one second to look! Besides, you don't know what he looks like."

"Uh, I went snorkeling with him, remember?"

"I forgot! Hey, I thought you said he'd be perfect for me," I teased.

"Tomato, tomahto," she waved me off. "He would fit into the group one way or another."

"Thanks, pal. Nice to know you're looking after my interests."

"Hush. I'm concentrating."

Alex did indeed concentrate on scanning the diners, while the rest of us lost interest and instead turned to one another and began a new conversation.

"Keira."

Alex's voice was different.

"Please prepare to look, but don't turn your head quickly."

Why do people always do that? They know the first inclination is to whip your head immediately to where they are looking. I managed to keep myself from performing a cartoon turn, however.

"What will I be looking at?" I whispered out of the side of my mouth.

By this time, I noticed that the others had fixed their gaze at the point where Alex was focused, and I turned quickly just as the theme bar began its descent.

Just in time to see Russell Shaw reach into his pocket as if ready to present my mother with the universal romantic gesture—no doubt a black velvet box that contained an engagement ring.

In retrospect, I guess it shouldn't have been a surprise, but even when you sort of expect something to happen, you're still shocked when you see it with your own eyes.

"Keir?"

Alex's voice was tentative as the bar reached its final destination on the next deck.

"Keir? Say something."

"What? Oh. Well. I guess that's that."

The others gathered around me, waiting patiently for a more elaborate reaction.

"What do you mean 'That's that'?" Patience was never Alex's strong suit.

"What do you want me to say, that I'm upset? I guess I can't be. She gave a pretty clear indication of how she would factor in my feelings earlier in the day, didn't she?"

"Well, you have a right to your feelings, Keir," said Cam sensibly.

"What?" I was still somewhat in shock. "Sure, sure. I guess I just ... just ..."

"You just wanted to know about it?" offered Anthony.

I thought about that for a minute.

"No. Not really. It wouldn't have been much of a surprise for her if I knew first, right?"

"Well, I guess," said Celia. "I suspect, however, that you might have wanted him to run it by you? You are her only family."

"What, like ask for her hand?"

"Not really," Anthony shook his head. "This is a big step. You two are close and maybe not ask for her hand, exactly, but maybe make sure you were there?"

That was it. I guess I just wanted to be part of it. I blew it with my temper tantrum earlier though, didn't I?

"But your parents were there for it."

"No. They were at a table for two. I don't know where Ma and Pop were," Alex said.

The Tidal Wave Bar was ready to ascend back to The Commons Deck.

"Are we riding back up?" asked Celia.

"We might as well." I was not ready to walk anywhere yet.

When the bar reached its destination, our eyes immediately went to the table where my mother and Russ had been sitting. They were still there, sitting quietly enjoying what looked like dessert. From their faces, they didn't look like a couple who had just gotten engaged. Mr. and Mrs. D'Ag were with them.

I whipped my head toward Alex.

"I thought you said they were at a table for two."

"They were alone! I don't know where my parents were. Can I help it if those tables are tiny. Come to think of it, I'm not sure that's really optimal for serving."

"Hey! I don't need you to be a restaurant critic right now!"

My mother's head happened to turn and look out into The Commons. She saw us, so she motioned for us to come over.

I took a deep breath. Well, now is as good a time as any to learn the good news. But, even for my calm mother, she was being amazingly quiet.

"Here are the kids," said Mrs. D'Ag. "How was your dinner? You have to try this dessert. It is delicious!"

"I love how we're still kids even though we have kids of our own, Ma," said Anthony as we crowded around their table.

She patted his hand.

"You'll always be our children, right Maeve?" she addressed my mother.

My mother reached up and pulled me down for a kiss.

"Absolutely. And we'll always love you, no matter what." She pushed a wisp of hair away from my face and winked at me.

"Mother ... I ..."

"Hush," she whispered, "I know what you're going to say, and I already forgive you."

"What's this?" Mr. D'Ag. "No sad faces! Pull up chairs and order some of this dessert."

He motioned to the waiter. Luckily the restaurant was mostly cleared out and we could push another table and chairs toward theirs.

While I was happy that all was well, I was still confused. Who gets engaged, then goes on as if nothing happened?

"Is this how blue bloods get engaged?" whispered Alex.

"Just because we don't jump around like your hot-blooded—"

"What's with the whispering?" asked Mrs. D'Ag.

"Nothing, Ma." Alex became inspired. "Mama G., I heard you had a great new manicure. Let me see your hands."

"I don't have a new manicure," my mother said.

"Smooth." I shot daggers at my best friend, while Cam kicked her, not so subtly, under the table.

"What's going on with you two?" asked Mr. D'Ag. "And don't say nothing, because I've known this one"—he pointed to Alex—"since birth, and this one"—pointing to me—"since she was a teenager."

We looked guiltily at one another, suddenly feeling as if we actually were teenagers.

"All right," began Alex. "We saw Russ pull an engagement ring out of his pocket. So what happened?"

Collective groans from Anthony, Celia, and Cam and a whap on the back of Alex's head from me followed, then all eyes turned to Russ.

"Keira," my mother assumed her breeding, "I don't know what you amateur sleuths think you saw, but earlier Russ pulled his handkerchief out of his pocket. Could your eyes have deceived you? Really."

I knew my mother's tone and dipped my head, but Russ cleared his throat and spoke.

"Well, don't be hard on them, Maeve. They were mistaken, that's all. However, I'm glad that Keira is here, because I have been carrying something in my other pocket."

My head shot up as the rest of the table gasped.

"Maeve, I know we haven't known each other for a lot of years, but we're not children. You've told me that these people are very important to you and I'd like them to be important to me, so it makes sense that I say this with them here. Most importantly Keira, with your permission, I'd like to ask your mother a question. Maeve, would you be my wife?"

He did indeed have a black velvet box, and in it rested a beautiful emerald ring surrounded by diamonds.

My mother's eyes, as emerald as the jewel, sparkled as she looked from the ring to Russ. I hadn't seen her as lovely as at that moment for a long time.

"Of course!"

They embraced and kissed to cheers from our table.

Russ turned to me and took my hand.

"I plan to make your mother as happy as she makes me, Keira. I hope you know that."

"Oh, I know." And I did. At least I think I did.

The level of chatter was raised as Russ ordered a bottle of champagne to celebrate. My mother was amazingly animated, but broke off when she realized that we were missing Damian and Juliet and asked where they were.

"Damian is attending to pastoral duties," I said, "and I assumed that Juliet was in this restaurant. She was on a date."

"What, with that young man from last night?"

I nodded. "Apparently they hit it off. She said they were coming either to this restaurant or the Italian one."

"Well, I think I want to meet him," said Mrs. D'Ag.

"Ma, do you think that he really needs to go through the wringer? I mean they just went to dinner." Even as he said it, Anthony knew that his words were wasted.

"Yes. Exactly," she said. "What do we know about him? We need to look out for her since her parents aren't here."

"How about we focus on the good news at the table, Ma?" Alex attempted to deflect her.

This topic brought Alex's mother back.

"Maeve, of course! I don't want to take away from your wonderful news," she said. "Shall we start planning?"

"Angela!" Mr. D'Ag shook his head. "She barely has the ring on her finger. Let's not start baking the wedding cookies just yet!"

My mother laughed.

"That's fine, Marco. Every bride enjoys the planning period. That's what makes life worthwhile, right Keira?"

"What?" I was confused. Was she hinting that I was taking too long to get engaged or something?

"She means that's what puts money in your bank account. Keira Graham Events, remember?" Alex kicked me under the table. She knew me well enough to know that I was still processing the engagement and that I had a tendency to slip back into myself when I processed thoughts.

"Of course that's what I meant." My mother scanned my face. She knew me even better.

I had to pull myself back to reality.

"Well, I know one thing. If *this* wedding can't get the full Keira Graham Events treatment, I don't know what can." I hugged my mother and winked. "I'll even give you the family discount."

"Well, that's big of you," Alex said dryly. "I'm sure you'll try to work her in somewhere between the Mandelbaum bar mitzvah and the next dog birthday."

"Dog birthday?" Mr. D'Ag questioned.

"Oh, Pop, you didn't know that Keira was the premier planner of pooch parties in Denver, did you?"

He looked at me quizzically.

"Thanks, Alexandria." I punched her shoulder. "Papa D., it was the mayor, and ..."

I explained the mayor's one-of-a-kind dog birthday party to barely concealed mirth. After enduring an unending stream of puns, I caught a glimpse of my watch.

"Yikes! I need to scoot if I'm going to get ready for that parade."

"Yes," said Alex, "you don't want to be in the DOGHOUSE."

Anthony continued, "Will you PAWS when you pass by us?"

"Har-har." I shook my head. "A joke never dies in this family, does it?"

"Unfortunately, no," sighed Celia, but allowed, "That's why you love us!"

"Mother, Russ, I leave you to fend for yourselves." I stood to leave. "I'll see you on the Promenade Deck."

"Will we know when to look for you, dear?" my mother asked.

"Oh, don't worry, you'll see me." With that, I left.

"Keir! Keir!"

Juliet's voice caught up with me as I crossed the deck. She was hard to miss in a fuchsia ensemble with her curls even more springy than usual. She was on the arm of the dashing Langston, decked in his own smart casual outfit of cream linen trousers and olive linen sports jacket. They looked like they were ready to pose for a magazine cover.

"If I were you, I'd avoid walking past the Steakhouse at just this minute," I warned as they came up beside me.

"Why?"

"The whole family is seated near the window, and if they see the two of you, Langston will not escape an inquisition."

Langston laughed. "Ah, remember, I come from a large family myself and am quite prepared for the ethnic gauntlet."

I looked at them. He seemed quite comfortable with Jules, and there was an air of sincerity about him. Goodness! Was my mother correct in our conversation back home when she said that romance was just waiting on the deck of a cruise ship? And that reminded me of her romantic news. Was everyone around me destined for love in the moonlight except me? Well, I guess Damian wasn't out for a shipboard romance either. Great. I was comparing my single situation with my friend the priest.

"Well, walk into the fire at your own risk," I said.

Come to think of it, it was probably best that their romance be tested by the family. They would be able to spot if Langston was too good to be true.

"I'm off to get glammed up for the parade," I said.

"Will we know where to look for you?" Juliet echoed nearly the same question my mother had asked.

"Oh, don't worry, you'll see me," I answered once again and continued on my way.

"Where are the rest of the angels?" Bryce, the redheaded crew member dressed as an unquestionably recognizable disco cop, snuck up behind me as I caught a last glimpse of myself in the full-length mirror in the crew quarters. The parade was about to begin.

"I'd think you were too young to remember that program," I smiled at him in the mirror.

"Program?"

"You know, *Charlie's Angels*?"

"Ah, no," he winked. "I meant the other angels who fell to earth with you when you fell from heaven."

"Bryce! Is that the best cheesy line you can come up with?" Neil groaned as she came toward us. Bryce winked, blew us both a kiss, and went to find the rest of the Village People.

"Keira! You really look flash! I knew that dress would work for you, but I didn't know how well," Neil smiled and adjusted her oversized orange afro wig.

"You don't think it's too ..." I couldn't finish the sentence.

"Too what? Too spot on? Too sexy? Yes and yes, and I think you should be happy that it is."

I turned back to the mirror. The shimmering dress hugged my every curve, and the sweetheart neckline was cut perfectly. Makeup guru Magda had managed to re-create the '70s look and had even added eyelashes and improbably green eye shadow that made my own green eyes stand out even more. She helped me flip the sides of my hair out to achieve the iconic "wings." If I didn't know better, I'd say I had been transported to 1979.

The music began, and I heard Brennan's voice as he entered the room to round us up.

"All right, kiddoes, the time has come. Let's—" His pep talk stopped abruptly as he scanned my side of the room and caught my eye.

"Let's what, Brennan?" Bryce shouted.

Brennan regrouped and continued, picking up steam. "Right ... um ... let's give our guests a night to remember. Let us go forth and 'ease on down the road'!"

The crew shouted and catcalled. Brennan adjusted his Village People full-feathered headdress, staring at me all the while, then turned to lead the merry group out for the parade.

CHAPTER SIXTEEN

The Promenade Deck was packed to the hilt as we danced and strutted through the crowds to the beat of high-energy disco hits. I was close enough to the front to see Brennan lead not only the rest of the Village People but also the entire parade with enthusiasm and gusto. The cruisers cheered and whistled—most of them had cleverly concocted '70s looks from their own wardrobes. The crew distributed oversized neon sunglasses, boas, and beads along the route, to add to the festive air.

I didn't need to wonder whether I would find my friends and family. They were clustered in front of the Promenade Cafe with a prime view not only of the route, but also of the overhead bridge where Brennan was holding court since he'd reached the end of the parade.

"Farrah! Farrah!" shouted Alex.

"Where's Charlie?" yelled Cam as he and Anthony struck the Angels' famous back-to-back pose pointing imaginary guns at imaginary bad guys.

I caught my mother's eye as she smiled and blew a kiss my way.

It was impossible not to step up my game and twirl and prance a bit more, and I dashed over to join them.

"We knew you had that in you!"

I started to answer Alex, but the music switched to a familiar beat, and all eyes turned to the bridge spanning the Promenade Deck as the Village People broke into the popular YMCA dance. I couldn't help but stare at Brennan as the Indian Chief. He absolutely stood out, not only for his moves but because of his unmistakable charisma and those darn dimples!

"Your man Brennan is sure having a good time!" said Alex as we both joined in the dance.

"He's not my man," I had to shout over the revelers.

"Whatever you say," said Alex, her eyes on the bridge, "but wow, what a body!"

I looked back up where he was. I had to admit, in the bare-chested costume, he did look less Cruise Director and more Cover Model.

The high-energy dance ended as the crowd continued its rhythmic clapping, and the man himself bounded down the bridge stairs onto the deck in time for the music to change to a slower beat. I soon recognized the unmistakable strains of "How Deep Is Your Love" from *Saturday Night Fever*.

"Don't look now, but I think you are going to be asked to dance," Alex nudged me.

"What?" I looked at her, then looked out to the floor in time to see Brennan McAllister coming toward me with one hand outstretched.

"Shall we?"

I could barely hear him over the music.

Why not?

I took his hand, and we began to dance.

You know those fantastic moments in the movies where suddenly everything comes together and all else just fades away and it's just the two characters and the music swells and a magical light sparkles on them and they both figure out that they are meant to be?

Get serious.

This was just a dance. And with my friends and family in the background whooping and catcalling, I'm pretty sure Brennan would not have been interested anyway.

My face must have turned all shades of red, so I kept my head tilted down. This guy already had a strange opinion of me, and now what must he think!

He led me expertly through the John Travolta moves—well, sure, he did this at every parade every week, right? The music changed, but he didn't let me go.

"Keira?"

His voice was so quiet I almost couldn't hear him.

"Keira, look at me."

I lifted my head. Oh.

His eyes were bright, and his face was somehow different. In place of his usual cocky grin was a more sincere smile.

"Brennan?" I searched his face.

He led me to a more secluded area, and he scraped the outrageous Indian Chief headdress off and laid it on a nearby table. His normally perfect hair was matted down, and, without thinking, I reached up and ran my hand through it, then pulled back quickly.

"Sorry," I said softly and turned away.

He placed his hands on either side of my face and pulled it up so that he could look into my eyes.

"For what?"

I shrugged.

He shook his head.

"Don't be sorry. Do you think I'll be sorry for this?"

He leaned down and kissed me tenderly.

I blinked and whispered, "I guess not."

"Or this?" His next kiss was decidedly more forceful, and I reached my arms to entwine them around his neck.

We eventually broke apart, but he moved his arms to encircle my waist. I left my arms resting on his shoulders.

"Nice."

For an articulate girl, sometimes I could be at such a loss for words.

Brennan threw his head back and laughed.

"Just nice? Not as good as advertised?"

I pulled my arms away.

"What, you'd like to think that all women are clamoring after you?"

"Well, sure," he began playfully, but saw my face. "No, Keira. I don't know why you think that of me."

"Seriously? You don't practice that smile? You haven't seen those sapphire eyes?"

"Come on." He shook his head and grabbed my shoulders.

"Right." My skepticism was ruining the mood, but I didn't care.

"Keira, you have to believe me," he started.

"Sure." I was on a roll now. "Aren't I just the girl of the cruise?"

"No, no, no," his voice became insistent. "You don't recognize me, Graham Cracker?"

Graham Cracker? I hadn't heard that nickname in forever—since I was in college, in fact. I stopped, looked at him, examined his face a little closer. My eyes widened. Oh no! No! It couldn't be!

I ran off to find Alexandria as the music blaring through the Promenade Deck changed to ABBA's "Dancing Queen."

Years Earlier

> "Ali, why do you insist on singing that ABBA song over and over? I keep hearing it on the radio, too," I asked my roommate as we crossed the Notre Dame campus on a crisp fall day of senior year.

"It's a contest. I entered it hoping to win tickets to the show that is coming to town that's based on their music." She returned to her singing.

"Oh, Mamma Mia? It's all based on their music from the '70s, right?" I asked. "Are you expecting me to go with you?"

"Uh, yeah," she said, her pixie hair bobbing up and down as she nodded. "Who else?"

"I thought maybe you'd talk one of your admirers into taking you and buying you dinner."

"Ha! I want to wear a boa and dance in the aisle. Frat boys generally are not into boas outside of keg parties."

I rolled my eyes. Ever since freshman year, when we had been randomly matched as roommates, Alex had not allowed me to remain in my introverted comfort zone but dragged me to numerous activities. I had accompanied her on enough visits to her family back East to know that she came by her exuberance naturally, so I didn't stand a chance as her best friend to be left behind.

"Fine, I'll go." I secretly hoped she didn't win the tickets.

"Cool beans. What's on your agenda today, Keir?"

"Probability and Statistics, Abstract Algebra, then my turn in the computer lab."

She frowned.

"What, Alex?"

"Well, I didn't want to say anything."

"But obviously you're thinking it, so go ahead." I stopped short.

"It's just ..."

I could tell she was trying to be diplomatic.

"Just what?" My tone must have been impatient.

"Well, Keira, you're so ... organized."

"That's it? I'm organized? Oh, the humanity! The world will end because someone has the audacity to be organized!"

"Are you finished?" She tapped her foot.

"Yes."

"What I mean is, that you make everyone fill out all this paperwork to work in the lab, and it just seems so—"

"Organized?"

"Unnecessary."

"Unnecessary!"

Alex pulled herself up to her full five foot two inches.

"Yes. Unnecessary. Come on, Keira, we know that you don't make the math majors or your fellow computer geeks—"

"Hey!"

"Come on, face it. Your computer department is full of geeks. And you don't make them do it."

"Well, your marketing people are not as ORGANIZED as my people."

She waved me off.

"I know, I know. You've explained it all before. But it seems a little ... prejudiced. They have a nickname for you, you know."

"I know, I know, ever since freshman year. Ice Princess."

"Oh, yeah, sure, that one. But you have one just for the computer lab."

I was afraid to hear it.

"Graham Cracker."

"Graham Cracker?" I plopped down on a nearby bench.

"Yes, because you always crack down on people for no reason. And the guys say you also crack their—"

"I get it, I get it." I stopped her before she explained the more vulgar definition.

I plopped my elbows on my knees and rested my chin on my fists.

"I wouldn't worry about it if I were you." Alex sat beside me and encircled my shoulders in a hug.

"You would say that, Miss Popularity."

"What! You are popular, too!"

"I thought I was a geek!"

"Uh, with those killer eyes and your hair and your body? You could never be a geek. I've been around when guys fall all over themselves to get next to you."

I leaned my head on her shoulder.

"Oh, they're just comparing me to you and making the obvious choice."

She hopped up.

"Hey!"

"Sorry." The mischief spread from my smile to the rest of my face. "You gave me the opening, and I had to take it."

"Glad to see you rebounded so quickly."

I sighed. "No. Not so much."

"Come on, seriously, don't worry about this lab thing."

"Oh, I'm not changing the process. But, well—"

"I know. It's hard to be the only one in the world who is right," she said with sarcasm.

I hopped up.

"Do you not have some sort of class to study for?"

"Nope. I get by on my looks." She grinned and skipped off. "See you in the student union after your lab. I signed us up for a pinochle tournament."

"Pinochle? Alexandria! I don't know how to play pinochle!" I called after her, but she was long gone.

I entered the lab after my classes to take over my shift from Marlon, the grad student who had managed it for the early part of the day.

"No takers on your shift?" I looked around at the empty room.

"Oh, no," he said, as he gathered his books and backpack to leave. "All the machines were taken, but they seemed to leave at the same time."

Now I was paranoid. Did they all leave because it was my shift? Impossible. Alex could not know everything.

I pulled my own books from my backpack and began to study. Time passed before I heard the distinctive click and swish of the door opening. I glanced up to see one of the regulars.

Tall, with scruffy hair and a beard, he wore the horn-rimmed glasses that seemed to be on all the undergraduate boys that semester. He pulled a sign-in sheet from the stack and took his normal place at a computer near my desk. His fraternity had complained about my sign-in process to the head of the computer department just enough that they could now sign in with the frat name and their frat nickname. I suppose that counted as successfully rebelling.

This shambling freshman was "Capone," and he had explained to me that he earned his nickname because he played violin. His frat brothers apparently could only associate the violin case with gangster movies, hence the nickname. It was a serviceable, if oddly generated, nickname, I suppose. And I certainly had heard worse in the fraternity circles.

Capone was soon joined by two sprightly coeds who I usually couldn't tell apart because they looked and dressed almost as twins in the most up-to-the-minute trends. Their names didn't help: Mariah and Marissa. They were chatty, and I often had to walk over to them and shush them if anyone else was in the room. They could have easily reminded me of my best friend except for the fact that Alexandria had a whole different level of work ethic and an amazing intellect behind her vivacious personality.

They became especially chatty when a football player nicknamed Real Deal walked in the room. He rarely came in on my shift, but when he did, Mariah and Marissa quickly sat up and took notice. Frankly, it was hard not to take notice. He was tall with a dazzling smile and dazzling eyes. He was in the same fraternity as Capone, and everyone on campus, if not the country, was awed by his prowess on the gridiron.

"Keira!" He grinned as he swept through the door.

I shook my head, placed my finger to my lips, and gestured to the other students in the room.

Undeterred, he clapped Capone on the shoulder and sat next to him with a hearty "Capone!"

His frat brother shrugged him off and pointed to his screen to indicate that he was working.

"Oh, sorry," Real Deal said in barely hushed tones. "Oops."

He strolled to my desk to pick up a sign-in sheet.

In similar tones, he said, "By the way, we're having a kegger at the house tonight. Think you can make it? We'd love to have you there."

I put my finger to my lips again and whispered, "My roommate and I are in the pinochle tournament. Sorry."

"Bring her! We'll still be partying after the card game, won't we, Capone?"

Capone glanced over and shrugged.

"I guess."

"There! You can't let Capone, down. He'll be looking for you particularly!"

I looked at his frat brother, whose cheeks flushed. Great, Real Deal, pick on the freshman. I felt Capone's pain because I knew all too well what it's like to be shy.

Before Real Deal had a chance to make more of a scene, and since I saw more people entering the lab, I said, "Sure, we'll try to make it. How about you get back to your machine ... quietly."

His face split into a bigger grin, and he strolled to his computer, prepared, I was sure, to dazzle Mariah/Marissa and the other entranced female marketing majors who had entered the room.

"Wow, Keir, a personal invite from the star running back." Alex fluffed out her short hair and took a last look in the mirror before we left our dorm room.

"I think they think they're going to get special privileges in the lab if they're nice to me, don't you?"

"Maybe. Doesn't mean they'll get them, if I know you."

"Got that right. Besides I just felt bad for him picking on his pledge brother in the room."

"Who was it?"

"Some freshman they call Capone. You know the type: shy, bookish."

She threw her brush at me.

"Uh, yeah. I came into my freshman dorm room three years ago and met her."

I picked up her discarded brush and brushed my own hair out and prepared to pull it back in a ponytail.

"Maybe he was just pulling him out of his shell. Leave it," said Alex.

"Leave what?"

"Your hair, Rapunzel. Leave it out of its prison tonight. It looks good."

I looked in the mirror and shrugged.

"Sure, it's not like I'm going on a date or anything."

We left our dorm to head toward fraternity row.

"You know, you should have worn your hair down to hide your eyes during the card tournament," Alex said. "We might not have been eliminated so quickly."

"I TOLD you I didn't know how to play pinochle."

"But you didn't tell me you didn't know how to have a poker face."

"Wouldn't it be a pinochle face?"

"Must you correct everything?"

"Must you correct my corrections?"

I punched her in the shoulder, and we laughed as we continued toward the party. As we got closer, the music and laughter got louder, and we began to see more people heading the same way we were.

Once there, we were each handed a flower lei by the behemoth guarding the front door.

"I wasn't told this was a Hawaiian theme party," I shouted over the music into his ear.

"It isn't," he shouted back.

"Oh. Okay."

Alex and I looked at one another, laughed, and put the leis on.

Navigating through the front room, the kitchen, and into the backyard was no small feat. Along the way, Alex was stopped by numerous people she knew from her marketing classes.

"Needless to say, not a lot of computer 'geeks' here," I noted.

"I knew I shouldn't have told you that," she said.

I shook my head. "I'm just trying to give you grief."

We finally reached the crowded backyard where the food, drinks, and a DJ were. We each filled a red plastic cup with beer from the keg and stood to the side. Some sort of skit was about to take place.

Hawaiian music poured from the speakers and a line of young men in grass skirts with their backs to us filed onto a makeshift stage doing an awkward hula. The music sped up, and they turned around and revealed their coconut bras and leis as well as rather sketchy wigs with flowers entwined on their heads.

"Hey! I thought this wasn't supposed to be a Hawaiian party," Alex reached up to say.

"Aren't ya watching the dancing?" I answered. "It obviously isn't." We doubled over in laughter.

At that moment, the dancer on the end lost his wig, and I saw that it was none other than my most diligent computer lab attendee, Capone.

"That's Capone!" I yelled to Alex and pointed.

"That's Capone?" she yelled back. "He sure doesn't look shy to me!"

Grinning and kicking, he was dancing as if he were on Broadway. No, certainly not shy right now.

The music stopped, and the hula "girls" jumped down from the stage. I saw Real Deal grab Capone and pull him toward Alex and me. They continued laughing and gesturing until they reached us.

"So, what do you think of our dancer?"

Once Capone saw me, suddenly the shy computer lab personality I knew so well reappeared.

"Hey, um, Keira." His face turned red.

Alex took in this exchange.

"Aha! I see now."

"There is nothing to see, Alex!" I didn't want this freshman to be embarrassed by my best friend as well as his frat brother.

"No, of course," she backed off. But Real Deal was not as tactful.

"Well, say something to her, Capone. I got her here for you."

Capone wasn't wearing his glasses, and for the first time I could clearly see his eyes. They were such a beautiful shade of blue, but at that moment they were so mournful, looking from side to side as if searching for a way out of this situation.

Real Deal continued. "What do you think of our dancing king, Keira? Hey, that's it! They'll have to change that song that's been playing on the radio all week from 'Dancing Queen' to 'Dancing King'!"

Capone tore off through the crowd, but Real Deal kept singing behind him "Dancing King, you are the Dancing King!"

CHAPTER SEVENTEEN

The shipboard strains of ABBA had died down on the *Ocean's Essence* when I found Alex in front of the Promenade Cafe. I dragged her inside to a booth.

"It's him, Ali, it's him!"

"Who's him?"

"Capone!"

"The gangster?"

"No! From the university!"

"What! Where?"

"Brennan!"

"What?" Then she put it together.

"Noooooo!"

"Yes!"

"That's impossible. He was in my department. Wasn't he the big goof with that beard and all? How can you be sure?"

I shook my head. "I'm sure of it. You were a senior and he was a freshman, so you wouldn't have had classes together. And you really only saw him up close at that Hawaiian keg party that one time."

She leaned back.

"I'm not seeing it. You have to be mistaken."

"No, Alex, I'm sure of it. I saw him so often in the lab until he stopped coming on my shift after that kegger where that Neanderthal Real Deal embarrassed him."

"I still don't see it, Keir. I'm sorry."

"Look, Alex. Picture Capone without the beard and glasses. And obviously nicer clothes."

"But Brennan has those dimples and those eyes—"

"The beard covered the dimples, and I saw Capone's eyes at that kegger. You don't forget those eyes."

"Well, apparently, you did until about twenty minutes ago," she said dryly.

"Well, maybe, but here's the kicker. He called me Graham Cracker."

Alex shot straight up in her seat.

"Omigosh. THAT is too much of a coincidence. No one called you that except people from computer lab."

"I know, right?"

We both leaned back simultaneously.

"Well, what does this mean?" she asked.

"What do you mean 'what does this mean'?"

"I mean just what I asked, Keira. What does this mean?"

I shook my head.

"Come on, Keir. This is huge! A guy had a crush on you in college, and you don't see him for a million years—"

"A million?"

"Not the time for pinpoint accuracy, Keira, you know what I mean. A *number of years.* And wham! Here he is in your life. What does this mean?"

I leaned my head on my arms on the table.

"Alex, that's not all."

"What? Do you owe him money? Does he have compromising pictures of you?"

I sat up and turned my head to her. "Have you been reading mystery novels to pass the time? No." I dropped my head again and mumbled, "He kissed me."

"Say again?"

"He kissed me."

"Louder please."

"You know you heard me! He kissed me!" My head shot up.

"And?"

I leaned back and covered my eyes.

"And I kissed him back."

"Oh, honey, what's wrong with that?"

"What's wrong with that?" I groaned. "Don't you see?"

"I think it's sweet."

"Sweet. You think it's sweet?"

"Think about it. This guy had a crush on you in college. And you don't see him—"

"I know, I know, for a 'million' years—"

"For a number of years, and when he sees you, his feelings are rekindled. And your feelings are ... kindled. It's ... sweet."

I shook my head from side to side.

"No, no, no, it's not sweet. It's the opposite of sweet."

"Sour?"

I gave her a whap on the back of her head.

"No! It's illogical! He can't have had feelings all these years! We don't live in a romance novel, you drama queen! And I can't be falling for him after two days! It's just the ship ... and the sea ..."

"And destiny."

My head dropped to my chest. Of course Alexandria the Romantic would see it that way.

She grabbed my shoulders and turned me toward her.

"It all makes sense now!"

"Alex, nothing about this makes sense!"

"No, listen. He kind of knew who you were on the first day of the cruise when he was searching for you with Damian, remember?"

"What? No. He knew my name. That's it. He couldn't have assumed that the person with that name was me."

"I don't know. You said he mentioned your eyes and called you ice cool."

"He said someone described me to him. Besides, even my own mother would call me ice cool after the greeting I gave him, and my eyes aren't difficult to see. No, I seriously don't think he could have been pining away for me all these years. That doesn't make sense."

She shook her head.

At that moment, the rest of the family entered the cafe, laughing and talking.

"There you two are! I can't believe you are both back here when the fun is outside!" said Mrs. D'Ag.

"What's so serious?" Cam scooted in next to his wife as others crowded around us. Langston and Juliet had joined the crowd at some point and were with them, so apparently he had passed the family inquisition.

"Nothing." I gave Alex a warning glance.

"Oh, we just needed to fix Keira's glamorous eyelashes."

"Hmm." Russ looked from one to the other of us. "Good thing you could come in here. By the way, Keira, Brennan McAllister came over to speak with us and mentioned that he'd be out on this deck for a while. In case you need to know."

"Thanks, Russ." I hoped my face was not flushed.

Everyone grabbed sandwiches, pizzas, and drinks from the counter for a last-minute snack before bedtime. My fear of being discovered was blessedly lost in the laughter and rehash of the parade and dancing.

I thought about my conversation with Alex and remembered one other fact. I would have to cross paths with Brennan numerous times in the next few days on a professional level. I couldn't afford to act as if I were in high school and avoid him. I sighed and resolved to find him and get things back to normal. Sure, he might have once been "Capone," but I'd get him back on track with the reality of our current situation. The sooner the better.

"Hey guys, let me through. I need to get to my stateroom and get ready for tomorrow."

"Oh, come on! The night is young!" This was Langston, already comfortably part of the family.

"Jules, I'll see you in the morning?" My look told her that I needed the details about the meeting between her beau and the family.

"Got it." She said, seated cozily next to Langston with his arm draped around her.

I walked to the door that led out on the deck and looked left and right. When I saw the giant feathered headdress, I knew I was going in the right direction to find Brennan. As I got closer, I realized that he was not alone. Seriously not alone. Apparently he had given up on me and found a substitute. They were entwined in an embrace!

Stupid, stupid, stupid!

The word repeated in my head with every step as I swiveled and walked away from the couple.

All I could think of was how stupid I was to think that Brennan "Capone" McAllister would have kept a torch burning for me for all these years and that I would have to let HIM down gently.

Ha!

I would kill Alexandria when I saw her. Kill her dead with all of her romantic notions that got me swept up in some sort of *Love Boat* fantasy.

To avoid encountering the family, I took the most circuitous route possible to the sanctuary of my stateroom. Once there I yanked off the ridiculous dress and shoes, pulled off the garish eyelashes, and prepared to take a soothing shower to rid myself of this disastrous evening once and for all. Before I could get into the shower, I heard a slight tapping on my door.

"Sorry, not available," I answered as politely as possible, recalling that it could be one of the chefs with a problem.

"You are available to me," my mother's voice was distinctive. "I made you from scratch."

I pulled on my robe and cracked the door.

"Are you alone?"

"Yes. Open this door."

I walked back to my bed, flopped down, and closed my eyes as my mother entered and sat next to me delicately on the edge.

"You can fool the others with your need to 'get ready for tomorrow,' but I know better," she said.

"I'm fine, Mother." I didn't want to ruin her engagement night.

"It's no use, dear. I'm sitting here until you tell me what's wrong."

I cracked one eye open to see her perched with her hands crossed in her lap, prepared to wait me out. The hands of time swept backward, and I was a little girl again. I sat up and began to sob.

"Oh, Mommy, it's just all wrong."

She pulled my head down to her lap and began to stroke my hair.

"What's all wrong? You can tell me."

Then the tears poured forth along with a flurry of thoughts.

"I'm really happy for you ... you have to believe me, but I just miss Daddy ... and I don't recognize you with all the new things you're doing ... and it's going to hurt so much to not see my wisteria any more ... and Juliet found a nice guy ... and I opened my heart just a millimeter, and I got it smashed."

She let me cry for a moment, then pulled me up.

"Keira, that's quite a list! Shall we take them one at a time?"

Her eyes, a mirror image of my own, were so comforting, all I could do was nod.

"First, I miss your father, too, but you know he would want me to go on with my life. We've had this discussion several times, remember?"

"I know, but—"

"Shh. My turn to talk, sweetie."

"Russ is a good man. He is good to me, and I know he wants to know you better, if you'll let him."

I nodded.

"Are you really upset that I'm trying new things in my life?"

"It's your hair and clothes and zip lines!"

"Keira, do I embarrass you?"

I thought for a moment. I was actually proud of her for staying young.

"No, mother, I'm really proud of you. But you do understand how—"

"I know, dear, but you can't expect me to just sit in a rocker for the rest of my life and do crosswords and let my hair grow gray, do you?"

I pictured my mother as a sad sack. No. I knew I liked this other path she was taking.

"You're not really sad that Juliet might have found someone, are you?" she continued.

I shook my head.

"Good. I thought I knew you better than that. We met her young man, and he seems quite reputable. And you know Juliet well enough to know that she won't get swept away, right?"

I nodded again.

"And who on earth would be taking your wisteria?"

"No one. I just got afraid that you wouldn't have room for me in your life and I wouldn't be able to come visit it."

"You silly girl! It always has been, and always will be, Kee-wah's wist-ee-we-ah."

"Oh, Mother, I know. I was just overreacting," I crumpled backward again. "It's that Drama Queen Alex."

"Did she say something about the wisteria?" My mother was puzzled.

I reached for a tissue and blew my nose.

"No. She just talked about destiny and about Brennan."

"Ah. Brennan."

I sat up again.

"What do you mean 'Ah, Brennan'?"

"Well, you don't have to be overly perceptive to see the attraction there," she smiled.

"No, Mother, you don't understand. That's what I'm saying. And that's what Alex misunderstood, too. He's just a ... player."

"A player?"

"Yes, Mother, he just flirts with all the women. It's part of his job. You know, to make a cruise more enjoyable."

"So the fact that he jumped down off that bridge to find you and dance with you was all an act?"

"Yes."

"And when the two of you disappeared into the shadows? What part of the act was that?"

"Mother!" I blushed.

"We all saw it. You should know that it was because of Russ that the entire family didn't pounce on you with questions about it when we came into the cafe."

"What?"

"Russ insisted that no one bombard you with questions. He wanted to protect you."

I thought about that for a minute. I owed him a debt of gratitude. "That was really nice of him."

"Don't sound so surprised."

"No, no, not that. Just the whole Brennan thing is confusing to me."

"Tell me about it."

I lay my head back down on her lap and recounted the whole history of Capone at college and how I recognized Brennan as him this evening.

Mother took a deep breath.

"Well, what are you going to do?"

"What can I do? He obviously just wanted a little harmless flirtation in the shadows. It couldn't have meant much to him if he could move on from me to his next victim so quickly, could it?"

"Hmm."

"That's all you have? Hmmm?"

I jumped up from the bed and walked over to the wide window that overlooked The Commons Deck. It was late enough that not many people were out strolling. If I squinted, I could imagine that I was really in an apartment overlooking a city park.

My mother came over to stand behind me.

"Keira, I think you are really tired. It's been a long day. A nice hot shower is in order and then to bed."

I leaned my cheek backward on her hand on my shoulder. She was right.

"I need some time to think, that's all."

"Shall I pick you up for Mass in the morning?"

I nodded.

"Good. You'll see. It will all look different with a good night's sleep.

She hugged me, gave me a kiss, and walked to the door.

"Mother." I turned before she could walk out. "You know I truly am happy for you."

"I know you are, dear."

After I showered and washed myself clear of the make-up and hairspray, I braided my hair on either side of my head and felt like myself again. I saw the light on my phone flash, so I picked up the message.

"Call my room phone the minute you get this" came Juliet's voice.

Worried about any number of tragedies, I called and she answered.

"I'll be over."

Curious.

I opened my door to allow her in. She had obviously not been back in the room long because she was still dressed in her evening clothes.

"Is my mother still awake? Is there a problem?"

"She's fast asleep, and I grabbed the phone on the first ring to not disturb her. And why must you always think there's a problem?"

"I'm an event planner. There usually IS a problem."

She sat on the small desk chair, kicked off her sandals, and propped her bare feet up on my bed.

"So?" She knew I was referring to her situation with Langston, so she dove into the status.

"Well, you saw that the family didn't take a restraining order out on him, so he passed their test."

"I assumed so when I saw that Mr. and Mrs. D'Ag didn't seat themselves on either side of you as protection."

"Oh, they're good at subtle questioning. They remind me a lot of my family."

"You're not upset are you?"

"Not at all." She shook her head. "I mean, as you pointed out, I just met him."

"Well, good." I had to tread more lightly with the next question. "What about you? How are you feeling about him?"

She took a moment.

"Keira, I know it sounds odd. Doesn't it seem weird? I mean we really have only known each other in actuality for a total of hours."

I sighed but kept my silence. After all, who was I to give advice on matters of the heart with people who knew each other a short time? Luckily, Juliet didn't notice my sigh but continued with her own thought.

"Anyway, I think I'll just see how this plays out for the next couple of days before I pack my bags and move to Canada, eh?"

"True. True."

"Hey, you seem distant. Is something going on with you?"

Was it possible that Juliet had missed my whole mini-drama? Maybe so, since she didn't join the family until at least after Brennan and I had made our exit into the shadows. I decided it was better not to open that discussion.

"I'm just tired, Jules. It was a long day."

"Wow! You? Tired?"

She looked pensive for a moment, then grabbed my iPad from the desk and scanned the schedule for the next day.

"Okay. Here's the deal. Look at the schedule for tomorrow. The first two demos in the morning are repeats from the last two days. So, the way I see it, I think you should take the morning off."

"What? I can't take the morning off!"

"Don't you trust me?"

"Of course I do, but I can't take advantage of you like that."

She shook her head.

"No, didn't you hear me? They're repeats: Louisiana Annie and Joe. We had to double-book demos for them because they're so popular. Everything went well the first day, so there is no reason to think they won't go well again. You take a couple of hours and go into Cozumel and, oh I don't know, just walk around."

"That hardly seems fair."

"You can let me have an hour in the afternoon if you feel it would make things fair."

I took the iPad from her hands. She was right. If any two demos could run on autopilot, it was Annie's and Joe's. The afternoon demos were smaller, and even though they were new, I could handle an hour by myself.

I looked up from the notes.

"See? It could work," Juliet said.

I thought for another minute before I agreed. "Okay. But I'm not going to go far into town, and I'm taking my phone since I can get service while we're docked. So you call me the MINUTE anything goes haywire, right?"

She stood with her hands on her hips.

"Please. I've got this. Now get to sleep. And your mother said don't forget about Mass in the morning.

I laughed.

"Tell her I'll be ready before she will!"

CHAPTER EIGHTEEN

The next morning, I heard light tapping on my door a nanosecond before I was about to walk out and surprise my mother by knocking on hers.

"I'm ready, Mother." I opened the door not to my mother, but to her fiancé.

"Oh! Sorry!" I didn't know what I was sorry for exactly.

"No, Keira, I should apologize. I know you were expecting your mother, but I asked her if I could escort you up to Mass."

"Is she not going?" I looked out into the hallway.

"We're meeting her there, but I wanted a moment with you to see if you were okay this morning."

I looked at him with his tentative smile. This was the man who not only loved but was loved by my mother.

I owed him common courtesy, especially since I knew that he had been my "protector" last night.

"Thank you. A good night's sleep does wonders. Hold on a minute."

I looked back in the room, decided that I didn't need anything more than my room card key, then joined him in the hall to make the journey to the ship's chapel.

"This is so nice of you," I said.

"Well, I have an alternative motive, I guess," he said as we reached the elevator and he pressed the button, being careful not to look directly at me.

"Oh?"

"Well. We don't know each other very well. The situation with your mother and myself has come as quite a shock to you—"

I tried to politely disagree, but he smiled and shook his head.

"Oh, let's be candid, Keira. This situation isn't exactly what you would have planned, is it?"

I had to be honest.

"No. No, Russ, it isn't."

"Well, I propose that after Mass, the two of us have a quiet breakfast and chat. Would that work for you?"

"What about Mother?"

"I think your mother has enough people to find a breakfast companion, don't you?"

We reached the chapel and paused before entering.

Why not? I thought.

"It would make me really happy, Russ."

"Great!" He took my arm, and we entered the chapel. We found my mother and Alex's parents and joined them to await Damian and celebrate the daily Mass.

"So, we're going to the buffet this morning," said Mrs. D'Ag as we exited the chapel. "How about the rest of you?"

"I'll join you, Angela," said my mother.

"Russ?"

"I think Keira and I will have breakfast together," he answered.

"Good, good," Mrs. D'Ag nodded without a question and turned to Damian as he came out. "And you, my favorite child?"

"Well, I know that Tonio and Ali must not be around if you are calling me that!" Damian grinned.

"I'm sure I don't know what you're implying." She pinched his cheek.

"How could I miss breakfast with you, then, Ma, if I'm the favorite?" He winked at me, then asked, "Keir, I have an errand to run in Cozumel. Do you want to come on a walk with me afterward?"

"How do you know I have time to go ... never mind." I was sure that the chain of communication was too complicated. "But where are the others?"

"Already gone on an excursion to see Mayan ruins," he said.

I would have loved that, but it was an all-day excursion.

"What are the chances that Juliet's new friend is on this one as well?" I laughed.

"Uh, pretty good, since he signed up for it last night when he found out that's what they were doing."

"Wow! He really must like Juliet if he wants to risk having us all around him this much!"

"Oh, I don't know," Russ said. "I think the best thing for him to do is get to know the people she's close to. Every suitor wants the family's approval. I know I would." He winked at me.

Right. Our breakfast.

"Anyway, Damian, meet us in the park in about an hour?" I looked at Russ questioningly. Damian nodded.

"We'll all meet there. The rest of us signed up for an excursion as well—not as exuberant as the others, but we don't want to miss ours."

We broke and left for our respective morning meals.

The Commons Cafe felt as charming as usual, and the table that Russ and I managed to snag was secluded and cozy.

"So, Keira, let's talk," said Russ.

"Weren't we already?" Oh sure. About the plants, the weather, the bagels, the coffee—really deep conversation.

He laughed.

"I see so much of your mother in you."

"It's the green eyes, I guess." I continued to try to skirt any deep conversation.

"No, Keira, I've watched you manage this project this week, and I see so much of Maeve in your organization skills. But you have her charm and elegance as well."

"Catholic school," I smiled.

"Well, remember I went to Catholic school, too. There's only so much the nuns can do if they don't have much to work with. No, you have incredible innate intelligence."

"Hey, you're going to make me blush. Remember, we learned humility, too."

"Some of us needed more lessons than others," he pointed to himself.

I laughed, picturing a young Russ attempting yet failing to rebel.

"But Keira," he became serious once more. "One of the things I see in both of you is an incredible vulnerability that you take great pains to hide."

"My mother? Vulnerable? She's the strongest woman I know!"

He took a careful sip of his coffee, put his cup down, and leaned back in his chair.

"She exhibits a great deal of strength, that's true."

"Are you trying to tell me my mother is weak?" I didn't like the turn this conversation was taking.

"Just the opposite, Keira. I'm saying that because she has a natural vulnerability, she has learned how to stand up for herself when she needs to but also to reach out for help when she needs to."

I thought about that for a moment. I tried to see Maeve Graham through his eyes rather than my own. I was so used to seeing my mother as the stalwart society matron that I forgot that she was a ... person. With feelings and desires.

Russ sat with his hands crossed in his lap, calmly waiting for me to respond. I tried to see him as my mother saw him. Not as a "replacement" for my father, but as a partner in the next phase in her life's journey. Sure, he was younger than her, but he had a calm intelligence about him that erased those years. In addition, I could see that with his encouragement, she wasn't "going wild" with her new hairstyle, clothes, and newfound ability to try things like zip lines. She was just breaking out of her shell to exhibit what must always have been the real her.

It wasn't as if he gave her confidence, exactly; more like he let her know that he was there to accept and encourage her choices.

"You know what's odd, Russ," I finally said.

He tilted his head wordlessly.

"I was so worried about the fact that you were younger and thinking that you were 'corrupting' my mother that it never occurred to me that you are actually a stabilizing influence."

"You're making me sound like a fuddy-duddy now, Keira! How did I go from being a boy toy to curmudgeon?"

"Boy toy?"

"Well, you were worried that your mother was going to be perceived as a cougar, weren't you?"

My cheeks flushed.

"I apologize for that. It was just a knee-jerk reaction."

He laughed.

"I figured as much. But please, you can't have moved me all the way to the other end of the scale. I mean would a curmudgeon be seen in these shoes?"

He lifted his leg to display a foot that was shod in the latest style from Aldo.

"Well, I have to admit, I thought that if my mother would ever date someone again, he would be a little more Burberry and a little less Armani Exchange."

"Armani? On my salary?"

"You need to become better friends with Cam. He knows a guy—"

"Keira, much as I'd like to continue this fashion discussion, I want to get back to the other reason I wanted to talk with you privately."

Rats.

"We're good now, Russ," I tried. "If you can accept my apology, I promise I'll be a less petulant grown-up daughter."

He took both my hands in his.

"I appreciate that. I never saw you as petulant, just concerned for your mother. I would have been more concerned if you weren't."

I looked around, hoping that the others would arrive soon.

"You don't need to be afraid. I'm not going to pull a fatherly lecture on you."

"It's not that. I'm just in the middle of this project, and my mother can surely tell you, I tend to get a little hyper in situations like that, and—"

"And this situation with Brennan McAllister isn't helping, is it?"

I wanted to answer in so many ways, but I just took a deep breath and sighed, "Yes."

"I thought so," he nodded.

"Does the whole family know how foolish I was?" I asked.

"By the way he came searching for you after the dancing, they could tell something had happened. But no one knows the whole story."

"Did Mother tell you the whole story?"

He nodded.

"She told me last night."

"And?"

"Well, I know you feel badly, but I don't think you're foolish. You're a beautiful woman. He's a charming man. You're not the first couple to be swept away by music and moonlight for a kiss or two."

"Then Mother didn't really tell you the whole story. I mean about us knowing each other in college?"

"She said that you realized he was a college classmate and that he apparently recognized you as well—"

"No, no, no," I interrupted him, shaking my head from side to side. "That's not all. I had the mistaken thought that he carried some sort of torch for me, but apparently he just used the fact that we knew each other as an opening gambit after all these years. I'm just lucky I didn't fall for his line."

My heart quickened at the recollection of him bending over that anonymous female last night, with the moonlight glinting on the feathers of that ridiculous headdress.

"Keira, sweetheart, that doesn't make YOU foolish. That just makes you human."

I sighed once more.

"But, as I said, you remind me of your mother. I know that you won't let this vulnerable moment overcome you. You are capable and strong. And if you need to be reminded of that, I know you have a great support system in your mother and this delightful adopted family. And, well, I want you to know that you now have me as well."

My eyes were glistening. I reached over to give him a hug.

"Russ, I am so sorry I underestimated you."

"It's no problem. We won't speak of it anymore, all right, Kee?" His use of my father's pet name for me should have upset me, but instead it gave me comfort.

I sat back on my chair and grabbed a napkin to dry my eyes.

"Oh, Russ, I really am happy for you and my mother. You have to believe me."

"I do." His tone became more brisk. "Now. What would you like me to do about this McAllister fellow? I know I'm not your father, but I'm happy to give him a stern talking to if you want."

I blew my nose and laughed.

"Oh, I'll be okay as long as I can keep my meetings with him professional and with others around."

"That shouldn't be a problem. You travel with your own entourage after all," he said. "Speaking of which ..."

Across the deck came my mother, Mr. and Mrs. D'Ag, and Damian.

"Russ."

"Keira?"

"Thank you for this. Thank you for coming into our lives."

"Thank you for allowing me in."

"Well, I think we all need a walk after that breakfast," said Mrs. D'Ag. "That buffet is huge!"

"Mama D.," I laughed, "I never thought I'd hear you say there was too much food."

"Oh, not too much food, sweetheart," she patted my cheek, "just quite a bit."

She changed subjects easily.

"So, did you two have a nice visit?"

"Very nice." I smiled at Russ and took his hand.

"Good," she nodded. "Then we start out for our excursion, no?"

We stood to leave, and I realized that I had only brought my room key with me. I needed to go back to get my bag and other supplies for a morning walk.

"We'll wait for you to come back so we can all leave the ship together," said my mother.

"That's silly. I don't want to make you late for your excursion. You guys go ahead and leave. And you," I turned to Damian, "you don't have to come all the way up to my stateroom. Stay here and be comfortable. I'll be right back."

"When will we see you, love?" asked my mother.

"I'll catch you at the pool? Before dinner?" I hugged each of them, with a special hug for Russ, then moved off briskly toward my stateroom. I hadn't gotten twenty feet from the secluded alcove when I spun around to go back to remind them that the evening was formal—and crashed into someone.

"Keira," Brennan McAllister spun me around with his hands on my shoulders and searched my eyes. "I went up to the demo room to find you, and Juliet said you had gone into Cozumel."

"I did. I am. I will." I backed up. "Look, Damian is waiting for me to get my things. I need to go."

"Wait. I need to talk to you." I saw less Brennan and more Capone in his eyes.

"No time." I hurried off, and could tell that he would have followed me if Mr. D'Ag hadn't come up to him at that moment and pulled him by the sleeve of his jacket.

"Well, there's the man himself! I was just telling Russ here that we could take a tour of these beautiful plants on this deck. Now when was that again?"

I glanced backward and caught his eye just before he pulled himself back into full Brennan McAllister mode.

"Absolutely!" he grinned. "As a matter of fact, I'll be happy to arrange a private tour for you. It is my job to make everyone on this ship happy."

Hmm. Maybe the female passengers more so.

CHAPTER NINETEEN

I ducked into my stateroom and ran over to my balcony, went out, and leaned over the rail to see if Brennan was still there with my family. I saw Damian sitting alone, so I could only assume that the family had gone and that Brennan had left to perform his other duties. I grabbed my bag, dashed out, and quickly made for the elevator to descend and join Damian. I must have looked like a B-rated actress as I approached him, glancing over my shoulder looking for a follower.

"Psst," Damian whispered broadly. "The coast is clear, Mugsy."

"Har-har."

He stood and draped his arm across my shoulder, pushing me toward the elevators.

"Come on, before the 1940s music starts playing and Humphrey Bogart appears in a trench coat offering you a cigarette."

"Not funny, Damian. I would just prefer to get to our walk uninterrupted, that's all."

"Okay. Sure."

We continued in companionable silence until we reached the queue to leave the ship.

"Keira!" called out Neil, who was stationed at the kiosk offering bottled water to passengers leaving for the day. "Or should I say Farrah?"

"Great outfit last night!" chimed in her crewmate Gino, who had been costumed as the construction worker in the Village People. "Bellisima!"

"Thank you! And thank you for letting me participate."

"Oh, love, you're one of us!" Neil clapped me on the shoulder.

We walked through the security lines. The machines scanned our keycards and registered each of us as we checked out of the ship, and we heard a distinctive "bong" as each person's keycard was scanned. We would follow the same process in reverse when we returned to the ship.

When I reached the front of the line, Bryce grinned broadly from his position as keycard checker.

"Ah, Keira me darlin', there you are. Out for a spin in Cozumel. And with the good father, I see," he tipped his imaginary hat.

"Good to see you this morning, Bryce. We missed you at Mass," said Damian.

"He got in a little late last night, Padre," pointed out his roommate Winston.

Bryce colored.

"Well, good to know you were having fun," Damian smiled.

"Something like that," countered Winston.

"Enough, Winston!"

Damian laughed.

"We'll see you later, fellows!"

"What's up with that, Damian? I glanced at him sidewise as we walked down the gangway, along the dock.

"Well, he's been to Mass every morning."

"What! Bryce the Irish Rover?"

"Mm-hmm. Apparently he promised his 'dear Mam'." Damian approximated an Irish accent. "This has been quite an experience for me to meet so many crew members who are happy to have a priest on board."

We walked on silently for a moment.

"You know," I said, "I never thought about the fact that you are working on this trip. We just assume you're vacationing like the rest of us. I'm sorry. Plus I was the one who invited you!"

"Keira, this is what I signed on to do years ago, remember? I don't technically 'vacation' in my profession."

"I bet you've been busy at times this week when we haven't even realized it."

"Sure, but I love serving people this way."

I put my arm through his.

"You're pretty cool, you know that?"

"Well, you're pretty cool yourself. And I notice that you've developed somewhat of a fan club among the crew back there!"

"Oh, that's just because I was made up to look like Farrah Fawcett." I leaned on his shoulder as we walked along.

He pulled a small piece of paper out of his pocket, and I peeked at it.

"What's that address?"

"The Church of San Miguel."

"Why do you need to visit a church?"

"We have already run out of Communion wafers for daily Mass since so many people have been coming. I'm going to see"—he looked down at the slip—"Father Juan Pablo, who is restocking my supply."

"Wow, Damian. How did you figure out where you could go for supplies? Do you have some sort of app on your smartphone?"

He laughed. "No, but I should invent that. No, Brennan arranged it."

At the sound of his name, I jumped a little. "Oh."

"What?"

"Nothing. I guess that would be something that the cruise director would do."

Hmm. I guessed Brennan sure could pull the good boy act to the hilt.

I decided that I had talked about Brennan McAllister enough for one morning, so I switched topics.

"So, Damian, are you coming to Alex's cooking demo tomorrow morning?"

"Of course. Do you think anyone in the family would miss it? Is heckling allowed?"

"As much as I'd like to see that, no please." I smiled imagining Alex matching wits with her brothers in the audience. "Remember, my reputation is on the line here, too."

"I wouldn't worry so much, Keir. I've run into a lot of people who are taking the seminars, and I've heard so many good things about this whole event. I can't imagine that you get anything but great reviews."

"Mmm." I could only be noncommittal.

"Seriously, Keira, you can't be worried. This is a great success."

"I hope so, Damian. I want my business to take off, and this would be a great reference."

"Well, like Nonna used to say, '*Que sera sera.*'"

"I think that was Doris Day."

"Are you sure she didn't get that from Nonna?" He tilted his head quizzically.

"I wouldn't be surprised," I laughed, then looked down the next street. "Here we are, I think."

We turned down the pleasantly shady street, and after a few minutes reached the large church. In a moment worthy of a movie, the bell tolled just as we knocked on the door to the rectory. The door opened, and the smiling face of a spry white-haired priest appeared.

"Ah, you must be Father Damiano!" he said heartily in accented English.

"Pleased to meet you," said Damian, then pointed to me. "This is my sister's best friend, Keira. Well, she is also like a sister to me."

I smiled up at him.

"Lovely to meet you!" Father Juan Pablo said, shaking my hand. "Come, come!"

We followed him around to the front of the church, ascended the steps, and entered through the carved door. The interior was beautifully appointed. We walked down the side aisle alongside the pews.

"I think I'll stay here and light a candle." I indicated the rows and rows of flickering red votives.

"No problem. We'll be back in a moment," said Father Juan Pablo. He and Damian continued on to the working sacristy, where items were kept to prepare for services.

I lit the candle and moved to a nearby pew to wait for them to return. I found a peace and calm in the cool, dark church, and I welcomed the time to myself. Soon they were back, and we walked outside into the bright sunshine.

"So," said the cheerful priest, "that should last you until the end of the voyage."

"Thank you, Father," said Damian. "Can I pay you to replenish your supply?"

The elderly priest waved his hand. "It's taken care of. Brennan McAllister has made all the arrangements."

"Do you know Mr. McAllister?" I felt compelled to ask.

"Ah, yes! He used to come to Mass. And he would visit when he had a day off while was attached to a different ship as a crew member, before he was promoted. Fine, upstanding young man."

"We appreciate his efforts, don't we, Keira?" Damian nudged me.

"Uh, absolutely, Father." Were there other virtues I missed seeing in Brennan McAllister?

The priest clapped his hands together. "Can we return to the rectory, and will you let me offer you a beverage or a snack?"

I looked at my watch.

"Unfortunately, I need to get back to the ship. Damian, if you want to stay—"

"No, I'll escort you back."

"I understand. But you both come back to visit us when you have more time." The priest shook our hands, and we said our good-byes and began the short walk back to our floating home.

"That was nice," I said after a few moments of walking. "I'm glad you asked me to come with you."

"Well, I sensed that you needed a break."

"It seems like we've been on the ship a lot longer than three days."

"You've been really busy. So, I know that things are going well in general, but tell me, is it what you expected?"

"Well, the key to events like this is the planning."

He laughed.

"Well, yes, Damian, I know it's baked into the title 'event planner,' but not everyone can plan, you know."

"I'm just curious, Keir. If this is what you always wanted to do, why didn't you major in marketing like Alex? It seems like this career is in the marketing arena."

"It does, doesn't it? But this is really a hybrid field. It's marketing, of course, but requires lots of the project management principles that I studied in college."

"What about all that math that you studied?"

"Project management relies on math. But don't tell that to the event planners who came in through the marketing path—they'd run screaming." I smiled thinking of some of the marketing majors I'd supervised in the computer lab.

"Marketing majors like Alex?"

"Oh, you know your sister. She was a whiz at whatever she studied. There were others who never thought they'd need to do math after college."

"Anyone in particular?"

I stopped.

"If you think you're going to get me to talk about Brennan, you can save your breath, thank you. I've had discussions about him with Mother and Russ, and I'm ready to put him to bed—I mean THAT SUBJECT to bed."

"No problem, Keira." He barely hid a smile. "I was just reminiscing your college days with you. Why so touchy?"

"You weren't IN college with me, Damian. I think at that point you were in the seminary."

"Yes, but you came to visit a lot. And when you weren't there, it was 'Keira this' and 'Keira that.' Even on the phone."

"What?"

"You didn't know that you were Alex's hero?"

"Alex? Our Alex? The most confident person on earth?" I tried to reconcile this with the memory of the self-assured Alex who had pulled me out of my shell freshman year.

"Keira," he pulled me over to a quiet bench situated under a fragrant, overgrown bush. "When we sent her out there, she was the big fish in the little pond of our hometown. And you know what happens to small town big fish at the big bad university: they usually get swallowed whole. Well, who does she get matched up with for a roommate? A beauty queen with brains and a heart."

"You're making me sound like some character out of *The Wizard of Oz*."

"Well, keep that metaphor. She saw that you didn't have the courage. But she had that in spades! She looked up to you in so many ways and knew that all you needed was a nudge every now and then."

"Every now and then? We never sat still!"

"Exactly. You were the perfect partner in crime for her. The Romy to her Michele. The Ethel to her Lucy. The Thelma to her Louise—"

"Seriously? Thelma and Louise? Can you really see us going off a cliff?"

"I can't, because you would be the sensible one to put a stop to it."

"True. But hey, why am I Ethel and not Lucy?"

"You're kidding, right?" His eyes widened. "Alex is the very definition of Lucy!"

"All right, all right. But that still doesn't explain why you think she looked up to me, other than the fact that she's shorter than I am."

"Because she could count on you. You were and still are honest, true, loyal—"

"So I've gone from being the Cowardly Lion to Toto?"

Damian grabbed me around the shoulder with one arm, pulled me off the bench, and knuckled the top of my head with his other hand.

"Ow, ow, ow!" I pushed his hand away and rubbed the top of my head as we continued our walk. "One thing is for sure. When you and Anthony said you had adopted me as your little sister, you really meant it."

He grinned broadly.

"Too late. Once Nonna said you were in, you were in."

We both smiled nostalgically at the thought of Nonna's high standards.

"Anyway, SIS, the point of this discussion—"

"You mean sermon?"

"DISCUSSION ... is to let you know that we ALL know you are honest, loyal, and true. And we're thrilled with your success. But more than that, we all know how special you are and how much you deserve to find the right guy who deserves you. Don't be too quick to be discouraged. You'll know when it's right. Okay?"

I wiped my eyes with the back of my hand. "Did you all have a meeting this morning to see who could make me cry the most? First Russ, now you? I swear if your dad wants to sit down and talk with me—"

"Oh, you don't have to worry about that. Dad will be more likely to hand you a piece of gum and lecture you on the evils of makeup and nail polish."

"Well, that would be just as sweet and would make me cry just as much," I laughed. The church bell tolled once more.

"Goodness! I'm going to be late, and I don't want to leave Jules in the lurch!"

"We're not that far from the dock, so we're fine. Let's get you back to work. Is there anything else I can do for you?"

I hugged him tightly.

"You can find me a long lost brother that you might have or one that Cam might have. I just don't think I'm going to find anyone to bring into the family who deserves all of you!"

"Oh, keep your eyes open. You'd be surprised at who would fit in with this crazy crew!"

CHAPTER TWENTY

I had just enough time to return to my stateroom, change into my Keira Graham Events uniform, grab the necessities for the day, and dash to the demo room. I joined Jules for the end of the second day of Joe's demo, "Dip, Dip, Hooray."

"How's it going?" I whispered to Jules as I slipped into the chair next to hers at the back of the room.

"Perfect, but did you doubt it?"

"Nope."

"Louisiana Annie was a smash again, and Joe is taking them by storm. Both rooms have been packed. Not to mention—"

"Do the attractive ladies in the back have a question?" Joe shouted from the front of the room as he ostentatiously paused his demo. Heads whipped around.

"Could I substitute Greek yogurt in that particular dip?" I tilted my head sidewise and pursed my lips.

Joe's face split into a grin. "Why yes, that would work out fine. I was just about to recommend that."

The crowd returned their attention to Joe.

"How did you know that the question you asked would fit in with what he was saying at that exact moment?" Juliet whispered.

"I have amazing deductive powers." I stuck my tongue out at Joe behind the heads of the crowd, and he responded a friendly wink. "Plus I was in this demo the other day, remember? I knew where he was."

Juliet reached over for a fist bump.

I motioned for her to follow me outside. I could feel Joe's eyes follow us in amusement.

"So, Jules, do you want to take time off this afternoon?"

"No, I'm looking forward to the demos." She paused and pulled a small envelope from her pocket. "Brennan stopped by to leave this for you."

"Oh. Fine." I took the envelope and slipped it into my own pocket without opening it. "So, we're good to go for the next round?"

"Yes. Um, Keir," she paused.

I pulled my ponytail tighter.

"Yes?" Maybe that came out a bit more impatient than I wanted.

"Nothing, nothing. Let's get back inside. I hear the applause. That means Joe is done."

"Thanks for almost showing up, Keira," Joe snickered as I reached the stage following the end of his demo.

"Did you need anything that Jules couldn't provide for you?"

"I might have."

"Get over yourself, and don't think you can pull that pouty act with me, buddy."

His face split into a grin, and he pulled me down onto his lap. "I can't fool you!"

"Hey!" I jumped up. "You want me to lose my professional image?"

"Seriously?" He pulled his face sidewise. "I saw you and the Indian Chief last night, and you were anything but professional, sister."

"What?" I colored.

"Don't worry. I don't think many people saw you off in the shadows. It is easy for me to be stealthy. You know how most people ignore a poor crippled boy in a wheelchair."

"Poor crippled boy, my eye. Who were you with in the shadows? Besides, mine was just a moment of madness."

"Sure, sure, but how about that second time? That was sure more than a moment—what?" He must have seen my face fall because his teasing nature stopped.

"Um." I smoothed my hair and straightened my collar. "Yeah. That wasn't me."

"What?"

"Yeah, well." I blew out a breath. "You know."

Joe grabbed my arm.

"Hey, Keir, we've known each other a long time. You tell me if you need me to kick his butt, okay? Remember, I'm a trained soldier."

I looked at his wheelchair pointedly.

"Well," he popped a wheelie, "no one expects the wheelchair stealth daredevil."

"I think I'm good for now, but I'll let you know." I laughed as I began to walk away.

"I'm serious, Keir!" Joe called after me.

"I know you are. That's what scares me!" I walked away and felt the envelope from Brennan weighing heavily in my pocket.

I grabbed my materials and walked into the adjacent room to prepare for the next demo. It was quiet and empty except for the chairs and the stage, so I went to the furthest corner and sat alone. My hand shook as I pulled the envelope from my pocket and read my name on the front, written in impeccable cursive. I recognized the influence of private school education.

Slipping the single sheet of paper out, I unfolded it to find a hastily written note in the same cursive:

Keira,

I know you recognize me now and you must understand why I did what I did. We have so much to discuss.

Brennan

"Are you ready?" Juliet came upon me, just as I'd started to ponder what the note could mean. "You see that Aaron is here, don't you?"

I hastily refolded the note, replaced it in the envelope, and shoved it back in my pocket.

"I do, I do." I quickly gathered myself together. "I'm glad he ordered extra buns since the crowd is going to go crazy for this demo." I looked up to see that Aaron Lorton, the chef—who had come into the room and bypassed me somehow—was up on stage, uncovering his materials, and directing his crew.

A jovial crowd began to stream in for the demo, "Red, White, and Bun." Aaron was featuring the best hot dog recipes from the wildly popular blog "Red, White, and Bun: 50 Hot Dogs from 50 States." He had traveled around the country sampling hot dog stands, joints, and restaurants in each state and had documented his journey.

"Hi ladies," said Aaron's twin brother, Karl, as he walked toward us before the demo began. He slid buns piled high with Chicago Dog fixings on the table in front of us, then took the chair next to mine. The brothers were from the Windy City and took pride in educating people on the exact method of constructing a Chicago Dog.

"Yum." I took a giant bite.

"Whoa, slow down, girl. We have a couple more demos," Juliet said.

"I know, I know." I wiped the corners of my mouth. "But I didn't really eat breakfast." I turned to Karl. "How have you been?"

"Red hot," he said with a wink.

"Ha. Can you ever make a statement without using some sort of hot dog reference?"

"You do realize that hot dogs are how we make a living."

"Luckily for the two of you, you can switch off in presentations."

"Not so lucky." He made a grand gesture of smoothing his eyebrow with his thumb. "I am the better looking and more popular."

"You're identical twins, you goof." Juliet leaned behind me to flick him on the shoulder.

"To the untrained eye," he sniffed.

"Stop it, children," I laughed. "Karl, this dog is awesome. Just for my own benefit, are you two finally compiling the recipes and your journey into a book?"

"It's with the editor as we speak," he said, nodding. "After this gig, our publicist will start planning the book tour."

"And?" I looked at him expectantly.

"And what?" he asked.

"Aaron and I have already talked about an event in Denver, Keir," said Juliet. "He told me this morning about the book tour. I couldn't let an opportunity pass to pitch planning an event for them."

"Good girl." I smiled.

"Wow, you guys are always on top of it, aren't you?" Karl said.

"Never lose the opportunity to market, Karl," I said.

He nodded his head as he stood up. "Oh, I hear that. Can I get you another dog? We're moving on to West Virginia Dogs after the Chicago Dogs."

"Mmm. Those are with that special chili, aren't they?"

"It's West Virginia style, Keira. The sauce is specifically hot dog sauce, not chili."

"I shouldn't, but ..."

He grinned and took off down the aisle as Aaron began the demo.

"Bring me two!" Jules whispered loudly and turned to me, her look daring me to comment.

I looked down at my paper, smiling.

"Yes, Keira?"

"Nothing, Jules. I heard Canadian men don't mind their ladies a bit larger."

"Ha." We watched the demo for a while, then Jules tapped my shoulder and whispered. "Can I ask you a question?"

"Wasn't that a question?"

She rapped her fingers on the table, attempting to ignore my humor. I gestured for her to join me in the hall.

"What up, Jules?"

"Would you ever consider a long-distance relationship?"

"Why? Are you still thinking about getting serious with your Canadian doctor?" I had to tiptoe around the subject since we had almost argued about it yesterday.

"I don't know," she shrugged.

"Juliet, do I have to remind you again that you just—"

"Met him." She finished my sentence. "I know. But there's something about him that makes me want to explore this a bit more."

"Love at first sight is for the movies."

"This wasn't 'love at first sight,' Keira," she said. "It was at least second or third."

"Your argument is getting pretty thin."

"Well, I didn't say I wanted to marry him. I just said I wanted to pursue getting to know him better. Besides, after he gets back from the cruise, he's going on another round of Doctors Without Borders, so it wouldn't be any different than if he were from Denver and going away for a while."

"What! That's your justification? You're going to start a relationship with a guy who not only lives in another country, but is going to yet another country!"

"Well, when you say it out loud, it doesn't sound like it makes much sense."

"MUCH? Try ANY."

Luckily, we were in the hallway so the crowd couldn't hear my outburst. Karl joined us with our hot dogs.

"Here you go, ladies. Whoa. I sense some tension."

"No tension." I forced a smile. No need to draw him into our drama. "We were just wondering when you were going to get back with those dogs."

"I feel like I've been roasted on a spit," he pulled his hands to his chest.

We both groaned at his attempt at hot dog humor as he turned to go back to the stage. We quietly munched on our dogs, neither one wanting to return to the topic. Finally, I began.

"Look, Jules, I think if you want to get to know this guy—"

"Langston. He has a name."

"Okay. If you want to get to know Langston, by all means keep visiting with him for the next couple of days. But my advice would be not to put too much hope into anything here on the ship. These romances have an expiration date, and they always fade when the ship goes into dock."

"Ouch. Could you be more negative? Remind me not to ever come to you for comforting if I lose my cat or I get a bad manicure or something."

Whoa. She had a point. Where was all this extreme negativity coming from? I was usually cautiously optimistic. And I had started the day with such a nice visit with Russ, then a lovely walk with Damian.

I brushed the crumbs from my lap and felt the crinkle of paper in my pocket. Oh. Right. Brennan McAllister.

"See you at the pool? I could use a swim and some afternoon sun." I stretched my arms over my head after the end of the final demo of the afternoon.

"Langston is meeting me at the gym. Will you join us?"

I shook my head.

"I don't want to interrupt."

"Come on, Keir. Don't be like that. Haven't we already hashed this out?"

"No, no, I sincerely think you need to visit with him alone if you're going to get to know him better."

"But I want your opinion. I can't think about this in a vacuum."

"Do you honestly think you'll be making a decision in a vacuum? He went off with Alex, Cam, Anthony, and Celia all day today. You could have a full report in triplicate if you wanted it."

We laughed and began to make our way to our staterooms.

"Speaking of reports," Juliet said, "aren't you going to do the one for today's demonstrations before you go to the pool?"

"Rats. I forgot about it." Now I was sure that the report was just a flimsy gambit for Brennan, but I couldn't take a chance. "You're right. I'll finish it here and get to the pool as soon as I'm done."

"You need my help?"

"Go, go." I shooed her away. "I owe you this for the couple of hours this morning."

"I guess you do," she said and sprang away.

In the silence of the empty room, I pulled Brennan's note out of my pocket and reread it.

Keira,

I know you recognize me now and you must understand why I did what I did. We have so much to discuss.

Brennan

What the heck did any of that mean?

I know you recognize me now. Sure. Now. Because you didn't have the decency to introduce yourself when we met on the first day of the cruise.

You must understand why I did what I did. What do you mean "what I did"? Kiss me and how many other women? And what specifically did you say that I MUST understand?

We have so much to discuss. The way I see it, we have absolutely nothing to discuss, you playboy!

As lovely as the handwriting was, the note was so cryptic. And it was so generic it could easily have been a template that he kept ready to send at any minute (*Dear Keira, Susan, Meghan...*).

Aargh! How long was I going to dissect this stupid note from him? I glanced at my watch. The sun was going to set, and I was going to miss prime pool time!

I hastened to create a report for the day, sped to the purser's office to drop it off, and dashed to my stateroom to change into pool gear. By the time I reached the pool, the rest of the family had taken up a corner and were laughing and joking.

I slowed my pace as I arrived.

"Keira!" shouted Cam, who was the first to see me approach.

"Hey," Alex's head shot up. "Here you stroll, calm and casual, as if you are the talent making her entrance for a photo shoot. How do you always manage to look like that?"

"Because I always am, darling." I flipped my hair over my shoulder.

"Sit with me, sweetie," she patted the space next to her on her lounge chair. Other than my mother, Alex was the only person who knew that my bravado was so often only an act.

"You're just in time, Keira. Speaking of photos, I have a plan," said Mrs. D'Ag. "Tonight is formal night, and everyone will be dressed up. I want to meet early on the way to dinner to have a group picture taken."

"Ma," groaned Anthony, "those photographers are everywhere trying to get everyone to get a group picture. It's a scam."

"Your mother wants a family photo, so we're doing it," said Mr. D'Ag with a decisive air.

"Your family will look lovely in a photo, Anthony," said my mother.

"Oh, no, Maeve, when I say 'group picture,' I mean everyone," said Mrs. D'Ag.

"Do you realize how many people that is, Angela?" asked Russ.

"Don't argue with her, Russ," laughed Damian. "She's a force of nature!"

"I mean EVERYONE, Russ," she responded. "And that means you. Now, if any of you want to take other pictures separately, that's your business, but I want one picture with all of us."

"I guess I'll tell the photographer to bring the extra-wide lens, Ma," Damian patted her on the knee.

"Why would he need that? For Anthony's ego?" asked Alex.

"What?" Anthony shot up, grabbed his sister, and jumped in the pool.

"Cam!" shrieked Alex as she surfaced and sputtered water out of her face. "Aren't you going to do something?"

"Why yes, I think I will," he said as he grabbed me and jumped in, ignoring my laughing shrieks.

"You kids be careful!" said Mr. D'Ag, but he was too late as we were joined in the water by Damian and Celia.

"And we thought it would have been rough if we'd brought the grandchildren," said Mrs. D'Ag.

"So what cotillion are you dressed for exactly, Juliet?" I whistled as she strolled over to join me at our meeting spot. She was wearing a one-shouldered mini covered in the type of iridescent beads that threw off millions of rainbow lights with every step she took. She had found a pair of shoes that matched perfectly and was as sparkly as a glass of champagne.

"You should talk," she said. "Although I don't suppose you would have worn that at your actual coming-out party."

"What, this?" I glanced down at my black silk number, which was high-necked and had sheer sleeves. "Perfectly respectable."

"Um, twirl around." She made the spin gesture with her finger. When I spun, you could see that the back was cut devastatingly low.

"Yeah. Respectable." Her sarcasm could not be hidden. "Right down to the pearls, worn backward and hanging down to your waist. My gosh, Keira, that dress is—"

"Killer." Langston finished her sentence. He had walked up to where Juliet and I were waiting for the rest of the family. His appraising eyes were not lost on me or Juliet.

"Langston, I thought you and Owen had plans with the rest of your traveling buddies and we were meeting after dinner?" she said, squinting at him viewing me. She needn't have worried, however; his appreciative glance was just that, a glance. When he turned to her, his face lit up from more than the reflection of the beads in her ensemble.

"Juliet, I saw you walk across the deck from the elevator, and I had to come over to say hello before the guys and I continued with our plans." He gestured toward his brother and a group of other young men across the deck, patiently waiting for him. "Remember to meet me after dinner for a walk?"

If I didn't know better, I'd say he was a smitten fifteen-year-old!

"Absolutely!" Juliet was attempting to hide it, but her inner high school sophomore was showing as well. Hmm.

A kiss later, and he was gone.

"My boyfriend is so dreamy," I teased in a whispery voice.

"Hush up!" She punched my arm. "I told you before, we're just getting to know one another!"

"First of all, ouch." I rubbed my arm. "And okay, whatever you say. But I have to tell you again, be careful."

She started to say something, but the rest of the family descended almost at once.

"Well, you two look amazing," said Celia, who was pretty dolled up herself in a black crepe sheath.

"All of our girls are pretty amazing," said Cam, hugging his own wife, who as usual had managed to be cutting edge in a black-and-white formal that had the appearance of being printed from newsprint.

"Are we ready for a picture?" asked Mrs. D'Ag, looking around at the photographers who were stationed around the Promenade Deck with various backdrops. She frowned and shook her head.

"I don't like any of those backdrops. I want to be on the stairs," she pointed at the ornate stairs that separated this deck from the next.

"But the photographers are all set up, and the traffic—" Juliet began, but Cam put his hand on her arm.

"Shh. Watch. You girls think YOU'RE assertive. Sit back and learn from the master."

Mrs. D'Ag marched over forcefully to the nearest photographer, and though we couldn't hear them, we caught the entire conversation in pantomime. Within five minutes, the photographer not only had taken down his setup, but had blocked the stairway from traffic and was ready to shoot.

"Let's go, kids," she motioned us over loudly.

"And that," Cam said, "is how it's done."

CHAPTER TWENTY-ONE

"I cannot possibly have dessert tonight!" Anthony rubbed his stomach.

"Well, my dress is so tight, I'm guaranteed not to have any," agreed Celia.

"I think that's the trick to formal night," said my mother. "We have to wear our girdles under our fancy dresses, so we don't eat as much on at least one night."

"Oh, Mother, no one wears girdles! We all wear Spanx now!" I laughed.

"All of us?" Russ asked. I shot him a glance but could see the teasing in his eyes. Honestly, it was so much better being friends with him than adversaries!

Mr. D'Ag waved his hands in the air.

"What the heck kind of conversation have we gotten ourselves to here at the dinner table? Why, I knew everything would go to pieces—"

"When you started letting me wear nail polish and makeup," Alex interjected. "We know, we know, Pop."

"What's for entertainment tonight?" Mrs. D'Ag changed the subject.

"Well, there's a Marriage Game in the ballroom if we want to go watch that," said Celia, looking at the daily *Lodestone*.

"What on earth is that?"

"Oh, Neil told me about that," I said. "They pull couples out of the audience that have been married for different lengths of time—newlywed, about twenty-five years, and about fifty years—and play the old-fashioned *Newlywed Game* where they see if they can match answers."

"Sounds like it could be fun," shrugged Alex. "Let's go. Too bad we don't fit a category, Cam. I bet we could clean up."

"Not that you're competitive or anything," I pointed out.

She just grinned.

"Nope. Come on! Let's go see if we can get the best seats."

I crossed my arms and tilted my head to one side. "I rest my case."

We did manage to get good seats near the front of the ballroom, despite not arriving until about ten minutes before the show was to begin. Energetic music blasted from the speakers, and an air of excitement was in the room.

"Have you seen this show before?" asked a fresh-faced gal who leaned up from the row behind me. "My husband and I are on our honeymoon. We're going to try to go up. Are you and your husband going to try to go up?" She indicated Damian, who was seated next to me with his arm draped around the back of my chair.

He and I looked at each other, and with his usual quickness, he had an answer.

"I would, but this is my wife's third marriage."

"Damian!" I turned to the young lady. "Don't let him tease you. He's a Catholic priest."

She looked befuddled.

"Wow. I didn't know priests could get married, much less to divorced women."

"He's just—" I started, but announcements were beginning on the stage, and I needed to turn around.

"Should have just left it as it was, Princess!" Damian smiled.

"Ha! You are such a troublemaker, Padre!"

I turned fully to the stage and caught the eye of the emcee. It was none other than our cruise director, Brennan McAllister.

"This is a tribute to the joys of fidelity and matrimony," he announced.

I wanted to leave, but Russ, who was seated on the other side of me, put his hand gently on my knee. I looked over to him, thankful for his strength, and patted his hand and leaned back in my chair. I was with the people I loved. Nothing could go wrong.

"So, we have our newest couple," Brennan was saying as he pointed to a couple not much different than the young woman and her husband behind me. And we have our most, ahem, mature couple. He pointed to another couple onstage. "Married sixty-seven years, ladies and gentlemen. How DID they do it?"

"He's deaf!" cracked a jokester from the balcony.

Brennan pulled a face.

"Now, how about a couple kind of in the middle, about twenty-five years?"

We all looked around, but no one volunteered.

"Ladies and gentlemen, that usually doesn't happen. How about thirty-five to forty years?"

Two couples stood up. Then to my disbelief, Alex pushed her own parents up.

"Right here! Right here!"

"Alexandria! What are you doing!" her father exclaimed.

"Come on, Pop! You can win this thing," she said.

The camera focused on Mr. and Mrs. D'Ag. And their faces popped up on the screens to either side of the stage. Soon the audience started chanting in unison: "Come on Pop! You can win this thing!"

Brennan, grinning from ear to ear, walked over to us and put his arm around Mr. D'Ag's shoulder.

"What do you say, Pop? You seem to have a fan club here. Do you think you can win this thing?"

Then Brennan looked straight at me, and his blue eyes bore into my green ones.

"What do you think?"

He put the mike up to my lips.

"I think he can win this thing," I said without blinking.

Mr. D'Ag looked at his wife and shrugged.

"Well, Angela, it can't hurt."

The audience erupted in a cheer as Alex's parents followed Brennan to the stage.

Brennan explained the game and seated the three couples back to back so that the partners could not view each other's answers. Then he gave them each a yellow legal pad on which to write. Bryce assisted him onstage, and they traded quips to the audience's joy.

I kept my eye on Brennan.

How did shy Capone evolve into this suave game-show host? He was asking questions and leaning over the contestants' shoulders as they wrote, all the while maintaining a playful glee and just the right amount of naughty innuendo.

More to the point, how had I not seen this side of him in college? He was in my computer lab day in and day out like a lot of the freshmen.

I sat straight up.

Freshman.

He's younger than me. Oh no. Even if—EVEN IF—there had been a possibility of something beginning, after all my hand-wringing about my mother and Russ, wouldn't that have been hypocritical?

"Hey," whispered Alex from the other side of Damian. "The big show is happening up there. Where on earth are you?"

"What?" I better get my head back to the game. It wasn't like I had to worry about it anyway, since not only had Capone evolved into suave Brennan, but he moved several steps beyond. I shook myself back to reality and focused on the stage just as the Newlywed husband was answering a question.

"What one thing would I change about my wife?" He tilted his head sideways, and his eyes moved in the classic thinking pose.

Oh no. Don't do it. Don't do it.

"Probably her cooking."

He did it. Groans from the audience and a whap on the head from her.

"Ooooh, no," Brennan said with an intake of breath. "Sorry, not the answer we were going for. Before we show her answer, how about we go to our 'Mid-Weds'?" That was Alex's parents.

"Me?" Mr. D'Ag said as he displayed his card. "Well, I wouldn't change a thing about Angela. She's perfect the way she is."

Cheers from the audience.

Brennan then showed Mrs. D'Ag's answer sheet, which read "nothing," and she reached backward and patted Mr. D'Ag lovingly on the shoulder.

"A few more years will give you that wisdom, son." Brennan walked back over to the newlywed and patted him on the head. "Bryce, what does our mature couple say?"

"Both of their sheets match, Bren," said Bryce, and he displayed two cards with "Nothing" written on them.

Brennan mugged the audience, raised his hands palms up, and shrugged his shoulders in a "whaddya know" gesture. He moved on to the next question.

Easy when you're reading from cue cards, you sly devil. How would you handle a relationship if you were ever in one?

Mr. and Mrs. D'Ag were tied with the mature couple. The newlywed couple had long proven that they knew nothing about one another and were no longer in the race. The final question was a nail-biter.

The mature couple got the answer wrong so Brennan moved to the D'Agostinos.

"Mrs. Mid-Wed." Brennan matched blue eye for blue eye with Alex's mother. "When and where was your first kiss with your husband?"

"This is so easy!" whispered Alex. "We've heard this story a million times. They started dating at their freshman dance. We've got this locked up."

"Calm down, Ally-Cat. It's not like they're going to win a trip around the world." Cam patted her knee.

"A win is a win, Cam," she answered.

"Well," Mrs. D'Ag looked out into the audience, took a big breath, and said, "It was in first grade in Sister Regina's classroom."

"What!!!" Alex and Anthony howled in unison. The crowd laughed.

"Whoa, whoa, whoa!" Brennan walked to the front of the stage and peered outward, making a broad gesture of shading his eyes. "It seems as if we have disagreement from someone in the crowd. Could it be that there is a dispute to the contrary?"

Our crew laughed hardest and pointed to Alex and Anthony.

"Well." Brennan walked back to Mr. D'Ag. "Let's just see what is on Mr. Mid-Wed's card, since that's the one that counts."

He looked at the card, then at Mr. D'ag, who sheepishly shrugged, then back out at the audience.

"It says right here, ladies and gents," Brennan paused for effect, "first grade in Sister Regina's classroom."

The audience exploded, and it took a few moments for Brennan to calm everyone down. He himself was doubled over in laughter. Finally he straightened up and motioned for everyone to stop as he wiped tears from his eyes. Alex, Anthony, and even Damian were more shocked than anything.

"All right, Mr. and Mrs. Mid-Wed, you owe everyone, especially your family apparently, an explanation."

It was Mr. D'Ag who answered.

"Well, we were assigned to clean the blackboards. And ever since the first day of first grade, I had always thought Angela was the prettiest girl. I just got up my courage and I kissed her, right there, on the cheek."

"My, my, on the cheek?" asked Brennan. "What happened next?"

Mr. D'Ag turned red.

"She punched me in the stomach and said she'd let me know when she was ready for kissing."

Laughs from the audience.

"And when was that?"

"Freshman year," added Mrs. D'Ag, "at the dance." She reached to grab her husband's hand and smiled prettily at the audience. "I was ready to kiss him then, and I've been kissing him ever since."

A chorus of "awwww" followed.

"Aww, indeed," said Brennan. "And with that, you are our winners! Bryce, bring out the prizes!"

Third prize was a pair of baseball caps with the ship's logo emblazoned. Second prize was a pair of logo'd umbrellas. But the winners received a gift basket holding many ship items as well as a bottle of champagne and two glasses. We whooped and hollered as the basket was presented to our couple.

Bryce and Brennan started to leave the stage with the couples, but Neil walked onto the stage and held the cruise director and his sidekick back.

"One moment, I need you to help me with another presentation."

"Ladies and gentlemen," she said, "we're celebrating love this evening, and we think it's only fair to celebrate for one of our own."

What on earth?

The screens changed from the Marriage Game logo to a photo that I would much rather not have seen.

It was the rear view of a man taken at the end of the '70s party. The photo was shot on deck, and you could tell that he was bent over a woman. What blocked most of the view was his unusual headgear.

He was wearing a full-feathered headdress from the Village People.

Oh, no. What fresh torture was this? Was I to sit here and watch some weird twisted celebration of Brennan and a girlfriend? Or worse, maybe a fiancée.

I looked from side to side. Trapped. If I left the row, seated in the center as I was, I would be so visible. I leaned back in my seat and tried to take deep breaths. My new friend Russ was on one side of me, and my sturdy support Damian was on the other side. Alex leaned forward on the other side of Damian and signaled her own support with her eyes.

"We interrupted a very important question, but at first the young man didn't realize we caught him on camera," continued Neil.

Wait. Why was Bryce turning red? And why did Brennan step off to the side of the stage?

The screens changed, and the same man in the new photo was at a different angle, turned toward us.

It was Bryce!

He held his hand toward the camera, and the young lady behind him peeked out over his shoulder. It was Jinette, another of the cruise staff, who at that moment Brennan was leading onto the stage.

"Bryce," Brennan continued for Neil, "I wondered where the crowning glory of my costume disappeared to last night until I saw these pictures. Now we know we interrupted you from asking Jinette a very important question that night. Would you like to share it with this group of your most intimate friends?" Brennan gestured toward the audience.

Bryce shot both Neil and Brennan a look and took a deep breath.

Shyly, he walked over to Jinette, fell to one knee, and took her hands in his. He began to speak.

"Can't hear you!" came from the resident jokester in the balcony.

Neil pushed her microphone into Bryce's face.

"Jinette ... will ye ... I mean, can ye see yerself ..."

His brogue became thick, and he barely choked out enough words to finish his question. The petite blonde Jinette pulled him up and nodded her head. They locked in an embrace, and Brennan spoke.

"Ladies and gentlemen, we didn't plan that as part of the cruise. But once we found out our own Bryce's plans, well, we knew you'd like to share in this joy. Please, continue the engagement celebration, as well as the celebration of our newly crowned game winners, in one of our many clubs and bars! Good night."

The music swelled, and the crowd stood to leave.

"Well, that was lovely!" my mother said. "Of course, my engagement was much classier, and I liked it better."

She looped her arm through Russ's and smiled up at him as they headed out along with the rest of the family.

I headed toward the aisle, and Alex pulled me back. She motioned to Cam to join the others and that we would be along soon.

"OMG! What did you think when you saw that picture up on the screen?" she asked.

"What did you think I thought?"

"I know!"

"But what does this mean now?"

"Nothing, Alex. It just means that it was a mistake when I thought I saw him on deck, that's all. So what, though? Just because that wasn't him I saw kissing a girl doesn't mean he and I would work out. There are way more complications than that."

"What can you possibly mean?"

I forgot that she hadn't seen Brennan's mysterious note. We both sat back down in seats in the empty theater and I pulled it from my evening bag. She shook her head after reading it silently then dramatically read it aloud:

I know you recognize me now and you must understand why I did what I did. We have so much to discuss.

She folded it back along its creases and used it to tap thoughtfully on the chair in front of her.

"You have to do something about this, Keir."

"Why?"

"Aren't you the least bit curious?"

I took the note back, returned it to my bag, and shook my head.

"You know what? I think he just wrote this without thinking. I bet he doesn't even remember it."

"Who would do that?"

"You! People like you! All hot-tempered and—" I stopped, noting the look in her eye.

"What I mean is, some of us are more logical and don't do irrational things—" Oops. Not much better. Breathe. Start over.

"Look, I'm pretty sure this was just a half-baked apology. I'll just deal with it like that. It can't be more. Besides I'll give you three good reasons why it wouldn't work anyway."

I raised my hand and counted each on individual fingers.

"One. He's bound to be a 'girl in every port' kind of guy. And I think it's a result of having been an ugly duckling in college. He blossomed, and now he probably just goes through women like paper.

"Two. He travels for a living. Remember? I live in Denver. Remember?

"Three. He was a freshman when I was a senior."

Alex dove right in, folding down each of my fingers as she refuted each argument.

"Whoa. One. I might have bought that first reason a little bit. But you have to admit that not every ugly duckling turns into a mean swan. As for number two, well, jobs change all the time. People can move. But three, uh, explain that one to me?"

"Alex, after all the grief I gave my mother about Russ being younger, how on earth could I possibly come along and start dating someone younger? How hypocritical."

"Three years, Keira! Not a lifetime. Three years! And even so, do I have to have this whole older-woman-younger-man-not-an-issue conversation with you AGAIN?" She whapped me on the back of the head.

"Ow!"

I crossed my arms on the seat in front of me and leaned my chin on them. Alex followed suit. We sighed in unison.

"Look," I said finally. "We're wasting time here. We should be celebrating that victory with your parents and getting to the bottom of that first-grade kiss story, and YOU should be getting to bed relatively early. Tomorrow is your cooking demonstration. You are the headliner, and you need to be 'on' for the people."

"What? When am I never 'on'?"

I pulled her up to her feet and laughed.

"Too true. But let's not risk it, shall we? Let's blow this popsicle joint."

Arm in arm, we walked up the aisle to leave the theater. As we reached the last row, we saw a figure in a shadowed seat.

"I figured if I waited long enough, you'd have to leave eventually."

Brennan's smiling, dimpled face appeared as he leaned forward into the light.

CHAPTER TWENTY-TWO

Alex and I glanced at one another, unsure of what to do.

"It's okay, Alexandria." He winked up at her. "Remember? 'Capone's not a threat. He wouldn't notice if you were buck naked.'"

She caught her breath. I rarely saw Alex speechless, but this was one for the books.

"Capone, I mean Brennan, it was a long time ago. We ... I ... never meant any harm."

"What's he talking about, Alex?"

"It was in Marketing 350, back in college. Beth Jordan and I ... You remember Beth? With the long red hair? Only dated Thetas? Always wore pink because she said it was her signature color—"

"Focus!" I poked her in the shoulder.

"Well, class was over late, and we needed to get to a party. We had our outfits, and, well, the room was empty, so instead of going to the ladies room, we ducked in the back corner to change. We were sort of not fully clothed, and *someone* came in the room." Her cheeks colored, and she looked at Brennan.

The facts quickly clicked into place in my brain.

"Ali! You didn't have the decency to cover yourselves when he"—I pointed to Brennan—"walked in the room?"

She nodded slowly.

"What were you thinking?"

"You remember what Capone—"

"Brennan," I corrected.

"Was like in school. He never paid attention to anything but his books. We didn't think he even saw or heard us."

"Ah," Brennan smiled, "but I did."

Alex's attitude changed rapidly from one of guilt to one of irritation.

"Why didn't you say something then, you Peeping Tom!"

"What, and miss the free show?"

Alex lunged, and I caught her just in time to avoid her pummeling him.

"Ali! It was years ago!" I pointed out.

"Look at him smirking away. I ought to ... oooh! You were probably just hiding behind that beard all along!"

Brennan shrugged.

I turned my best friend toward me and shook her by the shoulders.

"In about ten minutes, you are going to see how funny this is. I suggest you go find the family and tell the story with all the embellishments I know you will add."

"What! And leave you here?"

"I can deal with him. And if you doubt my abilities, remember, there are security cameras all over. Now go!"

I turned her around and scooted her toward the exit.

"Do you still have those neon-green undies?" Brennan shouted at her back.

Alex paused as if she were going to turn around, then thought better of it and continued on her way.

When I was sure she was gone, I turned back to Brennan, who by this time had left his seat and was walking toward me.

"And then there were two," he said softly.

I moved backward, but eventually my path was blocked by a large object. Oh. Right. A waist-high decorated box served as a table for brochures during plays and shows and as a receptacle for used bingo cards during bingo afternoons.

Brennan stood directly in front of me and placed one hand on either side of me on the box.

As he leaned toward me, his sapphire eyes seemed luminous in the small amount of light available, and his normally devilish grin seemed somehow less playboy and more schoolboy.

"Keira ..."

He leaned in closer, and I did the only thing I could do.

I punched him in the stomach.

"Oof!" He reeled backward and grabbed his midsection with both hands. "What did you do that for?" he choked out.

I moved quickly away from where I was cornered and stood in the middle of the aisle, my fists still clenched.

He kept one hand on his stomach and held the other out toward me in defense.

"Hey! Put down your dukes. Truce?"

I looked down at my boxer pose and burst out laughing.

"You're safe." I grinned and moved over to a seat in the back aisle.

"Thanks, champ." Then he mimicked limping over to the seat next to me.

"Of all the responses I thought I'd get, that certainly wasn't one of them," he shook his head and his rumpled curls fell into his eyes. I resisted the urge to push them back on his head.

"Well, if it was good enough for Mrs. D'Agostino, it's good enough for me," I said.

"Oh. Your friend's parents' story from first grade. Ha-ha."

We sat silently for a minute. When he reached over for my hand, I broke the silence.

"Brennan, you have to know that I have so many questions."

He nodded.

"You couldn't have expected me to just make out with you with all those questions on my mind?"

"A guy can try, can't he?" He tapped the side of my foot with his.

I turned sideways in my seat.

"Does this usually work for you when you pick up the ladies?"

"Well, sure."

If his hand hadn't been clasping mine, I would have leapt up.

His tone softened.

"No, no, come on. Can't you tell I'm kidding?"

I guess he could read my expression. He grabbed my other hand and turned me toward him.

"Keira! It's an act! The whole debonair playboy thing is an act!"

"What? For what purpose?"

He dropped my hands, leaned back on his chair, and scraped his hair back from his forehead.

"I don't know. At first, I did it because I was scared, and now it's just what people expect I guess." He paused. "You remember me in college. I was the invisible man. No one saw me or paid attention to me. Admit it, you wouldn't have known if I was in your lab sessions or not."

I felt guilty because what he said was true.

"It didn't help that I was so shy. People like you who aren't shy don't get how awful that is."

I wanted to jump in and tell him how wrong he was about me being shy, but I knew I needed to let him continue his story.

"Well, I was a marketing major, and I loved everything about marketing—planning, analyzing, preparing content, trade shows—you name it, I loved it. But eventually I realized that I wouldn't get anywhere if I couldn't even market myself. So I did a little competitive research and realized that, demographically speaking, I needed to present myself less like Capone and more like—"

"Real Deal." Of course. The star running back.

"Yep. I took him as my model. I started working out, got rid of my beard and glasses, and eventually instead of being overlooked, I was sought after."

"Obviously this was after I graduated. I would have remembered such a transformation!"

He laughed.

"Well, it wasn't overnight, but yes you were long gone from campus. But you never left here"—he tapped his head—"or here"—he tapped his heart.

"What!" My face turned blood red, and my hands flew to my cheeks.

"Keira, I fell hard for you during that freshman year. There you'd be in lab, the blonde princess with the IQ off the charts. I was just happy you didn't catch me sneaking peeks at you. But then, why would you? No one paid attention to Capone. One night at the frat house, I made the mistake of letting Real Deal know how I felt about you, and he came to the lab and invited you to a party we had. You probably don't remember."

"Oh, I remember," I nodded. "You did a Hawaiian dance with your fellow pledges, and he dragged you over to where I was, and then you ran away. Why did you run away?"

"Are you kidding me? What would you have done? Real Deal felt so proud of himself 'getting you there for me.' Auugh, I can still see the disgust in your eyes."

It was me who clasped his hands this time.

"It wasn't disgust. It was, oh I don't know, something else. I saw a different side of you. A fun, laughing side that I didn't know existed. And I saw your beautiful eyes. But then you ran off, you idiot! And you never came back to my lab hours. Didn't you ever think I was shy, too?"

"What! You and Alexandria were the belles of the ball in college. You two were everywhere constantly!"

"Uh, yeah. SHE and I. She's the only reason I ever got out of the dorm room in my four years. Otherwise I would have sat there and pined away for my parents and my home and my wisteria."

"Wisteria?" He seemed confused.

"It's a whole thing." I waved him off. "My dad planted wisteria on the side of our house for me because they're my favorite. Back to you. So you decided that you needed to turn into some sort of playboy to be successful?"

I looked away, fearful of his answer.

"Not turn into one," he shook his head. "Act like one. Inside I was always, still am, the same old same old Brennan, the same old Capone! It wasn't a problem, though. Everything was going along smoothly until—"

I looked up at him.

"Until you came on my ship on Sunday."

He continued. "I never thought I'd see you again. Why would I? You had graduated, and someone said you had gone on to a successful career in high-tech. How would our paths cross? Then I got the purser's list, and I saw the star next to your priest friend's name and saw that he was traveling with the Keira Graham party. Can you imagine how my heart jumped when I saw your name?"

I wanted to doubt his word, but one look in his eyes and I knew he was telling the truth. He continued his story.

"Then I walked up to you after the mustering, and I didn't even have to ask if I had the right person. That hair and eyes, burned into my memory forever. You were the one that no one could ever measure up to. I could tell you didn't recognize me. Who would? I knew I had to take a chance with you before you did recognize me and all you would ever see me as was goofy old Capone."

"You never were goofy to me, Brennan. Even hiding behind the beard and glasses."

He reached over and caressed my hair, and soon his caresses pulled me closer.

"You're not going to punch me again, are you?" he whispered as he kissed me delicately near my ear.

I shivered as I shook my head to indicate no.

"Good."

He gathered me toward him for a kiss, but the arm of the theater seat was in the way.

We both giggled as I moved to sit sideways on his lap on his own seat, and our kisses moved on to the type that Sister Regina might not have approved of.

Many exquisite moments were passed in this way before I broke slightly away.

"Brennan, can I ask a question?" I whispered.

"Mm-hmm," he moved to kissing my forehead.

"What's the deal with the reports?"

"What?" He seemed distracted by the pearls cascading down the exposed back of my dress.

"The reports. Every day after the cooking demos."

"Oh. I made that up."

"What!" I moved my head away.

"I made them up," he tried to pull me back to him. "I just wanted you to see what it was like having to fill out all that documentation back in school."

"Are you kidding me?" The mood was definitely broken now. "I didn't need to do them? Don't need to do them? You did that as some sort of revenge?"

"Not really revenge, Keira," he shrugged. Then he realized his mistake as he tried unsuccessfully to rationalize. "But come on, you remember what your nickname was. Everyone knew what a hardcase you were. I just wanted to give you a little taste of your own medicine, Graham Cracker."

"I can't believe it!" I began, then did the only thing I could do.

I punched him in the stomach, jumped up, and ran out of the theater.

"Here she is," my mother looked up and smiled when saw me approaching our family group sitting together in the cozy Champagne Bar. But then her eyes widened.

The others also looked at me, and I realized that I must look a sight with mussed-up hair and wild eyes.

Russ jumped in smoothly. "Is it windy on deck? Didn't you say that you were going to step out for a minute?"

I shot him a thankful glance.

"Oh, I decided to try a new look—disheveled chic. What do you think?" I threw one hand on my hip and the other behind my head.

"I'm not a fan," Alex said pointedly. "Since when have you ever been less than picture perfect?"

"Since when have you had the common sense to keep your lip buttoned?" I shot back as I sat next to Russ and pulled my hair back into a hasty braid.

Alex and I had a wordless conversation with our eyes in which she conveyed her curiosity about Brennan's whereabouts, and I let her know that I would fill her in later. How she managed to not blather about the fact that she had left me with Brennan was a mystery to me.

"Keira, maybe you can help us here," Anthony said with a strange look at me. "Cam and Ali are doing the dance contest tomorrow afternoon, and Celia doesn't want to do it."

"I didn't say that, Tonio," Celia shook her head. "I just said I didn't want to wear matching outfits."

Anthony looked at me with a "see?" expression and waited for my opinion.

"She's doing the contest, isn't she?" I asked.

He nodded.

"Then what does it matter what she wears?" I concluded.

"Thank you, Keira," Celia looked at Anthony with her own "see?" expression. "I knew I could count on Keira to be the voice of reason."

"Thanks, Keira," Anthony pouted. "Just once in this family I'd like to get my way."

The table exploded in laughter as he got pelted with cocktail peanuts.

Then, just as quickly, silence fell, and everyone looked over my shoulder. I turned to see Brennan standing there. My face flamed as I jumped up and pulled him away from our group.

"What are you doing here?" I hissed.

"You left your purse," he held out my evening bag. I could either take it from him politely or look like an idiot.

"Thank you." I looked over my shoulder. If I weren't so embarrassed, I would have laughed out loud at the family and their attempt to be nonchalant.

"Anything else?"

Oh, that infuriating smile. Those dimples and those bright blue eyes.

"No, no. Oh. You do know that your lipstick is smeared though, don't you?"

My hand reached to my mouth. So much for covering up where I had been! The family knew what I had been doing—and now they knew exactly who with.

I turned fully around to see their grins, then swiveled back to face Brennan.

He put his hands on my shoulders and whispered in my ear. "I need to watch my public image while in uniform in front of so many passengers. But meet me on the top deck in the morning." And with that, he kissed me delicately on the temple.

Out loud to the rest of the family, he said, "Good night all."

If I could have magically disappeared from the family's view—better yet, if they could have disappeared at that moment—oh how sweet life would have been. But no, no. I had to turn around and take it like a big girl.

Count to ten. Turn.

"Anything to share with the rest of the class?" I knew Alex would be the one to break the silence.

Resigned to a barrage of questions, I sat back down next to Russ. Fortunately, he put his arm around me and handed me a napkin to wipe my mouth. Unfortunately, he was the first one to ask a question.

"So, I take it that it wasn't the wind that mussed up your hair?"

"Ha-ha." I cleared the last of what was left of my lipstick.

"Well, I think he's a nice boy," said Mrs. D'Ag. "He's done nothing but treat us all nice since we've been here."

"That's his job, Ma," Alex said. "But I agree, he's really nice. Even if he's the one that peeked at me and Beth in college."

"That's the boy from the story you just told?" Mrs. D'Ag asked. "You said he was ugly. Brennan McAllister is anything but ugly, honey."

"That's the point, Ma," said Anthony. "He's become handsome now, and he wants to date our little Keira."

"Well, she deserves someone nice." Mrs. D'Ag turned to my mother. "You know, Maeve, I always wished I had another son for her or could find her a nice boy before it's too late."

"Hey!" I jumped in. "I'm right here!"

"Well, sure honey, but we all just want the best for you," said my mother. "Do you like Brennan? I thought you didn't."

"No! I mean yes! He's a nice enough person, but you guys are missing a big point, aren't you?"

Blank stares.

"I live in Denver! He travels the world! Don't you see a problem there?"

I looked to the one person I thought I could count on for sensibility.

"Celia?"

She shrugged her shoulders.

"Keira, I love you to death, but I think you're over-thinking this. Can't you just enjoy the moment?"

"Auuuughhh!" I jumped up. "I'm going to bed. In case you forgot, I'm working tomorrow." I looked at Alex. "And so are you, so you should follow pretty soon."

As I started to walk away, Juliet and Langston joined us.

"Hey guys? Did we miss anything?" she asked as they pulled up an ottoman.

I walked away as quickly as I could.

CHAPTER TWENTY-THREE

I tossed. I turned. I tossed and turned.

Sleep would not come. I relived those moments in the theater over and over and over. A hot shower didn't help. Turning the TV on and off didn't help. Eventually my clock sounded, and I jumped out of my tiny bed.

As much as I tried to avoid it, I was ready early. Darn my efficient morning routine!

Oh, who was I kidding, I wanted to see Brennan. Looking in the mirror, I made sure I was neat from head to toe, slipped out of my stateroom, and quietly made my way to the top deck, Brennan's morning hangout. My heart dropped a bit when I saw that he wasn't there.

The morning breeze was crisp and the sun was delicate, so I walked over to the rail to take in the clear waves of the ocean. Today was a day at sea, so we would be surrounded by this blue perfection all day.

"Hi," a soft voice whispered in my ear, and I turned around to look into the blue perfection of Brennan's eyes.

"Hi."

He was dressed much like the first day we had met on this deck, in a tattered T-shirt, random shorts, and a baseball cap flipped backward. This time the shirt was emblazoned with the logo of our alma mater, Notre Dame.

"Go Irish," I said as I wrapped my arms around his neck.

"Go Irish."

He pulled me closer to give me the most perfect good morning kiss.

"Keira, I need you to promise that you won't punch me."

I threw my head back and laughed.

"I promise."

"Good." He pulled me close for another heart-melting kiss.

"Brennan—" I began, but was interrupted.

"Oh my Gawd, Doreen, have you ever seen such a view?" cut through the morning silence. We turned to see that the colors of the outfit worn by the speaker were twice as loud as her braying voice.

"Yer right, Linda, it's gaw-geous!" Doreen apparently shopped at the same store as Linda, one that specialized in gigantic bright stripes.

Brennan whipped me around to face the ocean and he himself stood beside me facing outward, pulling his ball cap around and shoving sunglasses on his nose.

"What in the world?" I said.

"Shh. When I'm in uniform I'm on duty, but in civilian clothes I try not to be too accessible. Sometimes it can cause problems."

"What? Those ladies seem harmless enough." I turned slightly to the side to view Doreen and Linda on the other side of the deck taking endless photos of each other.

"You never know." He shook his head. "On my last ship, I tried to avoid being out in public except in uniform and the one time—ONE TIME—I was out in civvies, a nice young lady got the wrong idea and it turned into a whole issue.

"Ohhhh. That explains it."

"That explains what?"

"Well, Neil said you had a reputation for seducing passengers."

"What!" His head shot up, but he realized he was too loud and quieted himself. "Once. ONCE. A passenger made a thoroughly baseless accusation. Hmm. Nice to know that my own assistant has my back."

I turned around to lean the other way on the railing, keeping my eye on the neon twins who were now making a big show of selecting deck chairs.

"Well. I don't know. Look at what's happening with you and me."

He spun me around and faced me.

"Hey. I thought I explained to you that I have been over the moon for you since college. Do you think I'm just looking for a shipboard fling with you?"

"Well, you did say you built this playboy image—"

"Image, Keira, image. It's what people want to see, so it's the role I play. Can't you see where the professional image of me stops and the real me starts?"

I must have paused a moment too long.

"Wow. Now I'd almost rather you would have punched me in the stomach. This is worse."

He stalked off.

"Where are you going?" I shouted after him.

"To WORK."

Great. Just when I was halfway ready to take a chance on us, I messed it up and he pulled back.

"Hey blondie," Doreen and Linda's sandals flapped the deck loudly as they hurried over toward me. "Wasn't that the cruise director you were talking to?"

I looked toward where Brennan had walked.

"No, ma'am, I can't say I know WHO that was."

Alex's cooking demo was taking place in the same theater where we had seen *Grease*. I walked in to find her stage set on risers. We also arranged to have mirrors over the stage so that the audience in the back would be able to see her.

Up on stage, I saw my best friend organizing her tools with the precision of a surgeon. Because she was as perky as a cheerleader, I always forgot that Alex was a renowned chef with her own chain of restaurants and was truly accomplished at what she did.

I shook off my own issues and joined her on the stage, concentrating on my job and what I needed to do to make this demo a success.

Alex glanced up and saw me, and her face split into a wide grin.

"Hey, sister-friend! Are we ready for this thing or what?"

Alex. As filled with joy as I remembered her from that first day of freshman year.

"I don't know about you, but my part is ready. I got you an audience." I laughed. "Have you seen Juliet?"

"Isn't she with you? Where have you been?" She stopped polishing a knife and shrieked, "Noo! Were you somewhere with your Frat Boy?"

"My Frat Boy?"

"Well, what else would you call someone you met through a fraternity at college."

I stopped in my tracks.

"Technically, we met in a computer lab ... and—"

"Whatever, Keira." She waved the knife around dangerously. "Now that I know who he is, I can't shake the Frat Boy image."

Juliet bounced into the room, singing along to whatever tune was channeled through her iPhone to her ears.

"And where have you been, Jules?"

She pulled her earbuds out and pointed to me.

"I was at breakfast with YOUR mother, who wanted to know where YOU were."

"I was getting some fresh air."

"Oh, is that what you kids are calling it these days?" She grinned.

I opened my mouth to answer but knew I would be outgunned by both Alex and Juliet, so I changed the topic swiftly.

"Anyway, ladies, are we set?"

"Like I said, girlfriend, all is set up here." Alex glanced around her tables. Cam strode in from off-stage, tying an apron and nodding his head. He was acting as sous chef. The two of them made a striking couple.

"Just bring on the students," he said.

As if on cue, people started streaming in. Alex and Cam came down off the stage to greet people, and soon the theater was packed. The last guests to arrive were the family, and we ushered them to their seats just before the house lights went down and the stage lights went up. Our music keyed, Alex and Cam hopped to the front of the stage, and their spotlights hit. And so began the final and biggest demo of the cruise.

Alex and Cam had a smooth working relationship that mirrored their off-stage relationship. Their preparation of Chicken Vesuvio was peppered with laughter and anecdotes about their restaurants and their son.

"Shall I tell you about the first time we cooked together?" asked Cam at one point. "I had to save her during a wedding catering mishap!"

"Save me? You were lucky I let you wash the pans we cooked with!" Alex flipped him with a towel.

"They're good together," Juliet leaned over and said. "We should send them on the road."

"Nah. Alex likes running her restaurant too much," I said. "Oh sure, she's great in front of an audience at charity events and things, and likes doing the guest shots on the morning shows occasionally, but that's just her natural bubbly personality—drama all the way." I smiled as Alex bumped Cam out of the way with her hip. "And he's so dedicated to his job as VP of engineering, he'd never want to give that up."

"Hmm. I guess so," said Juliet. "It's just that they work so well together onstage."

"It's because THEY work so well together in general. It was a match made in heaven, even if it took Alex awhile to figure it out." I smiled inwardly remembering Alexandria's dating woes before she finally realized that Cam Grayson was her soul mate.

"Awesome," Juliet's tone was pensive.

"What is it, Juliet?"

"Well. If I tell you, you have to promise not to get upset."

Did I all of a sudden have a reputation for violence? Well, I guess I did punch Brennan. Twice.

"Come out into the hall," I said.

"Okay," she began when we were out of range, "there's no way to say this but to say it. I was wrong about Langston."

"What? Did he hurt you? If he did, I'll smack him." Whoa. Maybe I was developing a violent streak.

"No, no, no," she laughed. "Nothing like that. I was just wrong when I thought he could be someone who could sustain a serious relationship."

"How do you figure that?" I asked, bearing in mind that I was the one all along who said to proceed cautiously.

"Well, he never talks about anything other than the hospital and his charity work. I don't know how to say anything about that without seeming uncharitable myself, but I don't think he can ever be married to a woman so long as he is married to the job that he has. Am I making any sense?"

"Perfect sense." I SO wanted to say "I told you so."

Not the time, Keira, not the time.

"I think this trip has been a really necessary break for him, but I can tell he's ready to get back to work. He already has been going into the ship's library spending a lot of time online, checking in on his next project. I can see him drifting away."

I nodded without saying anything.

"I wouldn't be able to deal with someone who had that much devotion to their job. I think I could deal with someone who is serious about their work, but they need to make time for me, you know? And I wouldn't want to be the person who was responsible for him having to choose."

"I know. You see it in Cam and Alex. They have separate demanding careers, and they both are serious about them, but you see how much they love each other just in, well, how much they love each other. And in how much they make time for Marco. And I know it will be the same for any other kids they have."

"Exactly," she nodded. "Being around your extended family and seeing all these great relationships makes me realize that I need to hold out for one. I don't know. Whoever thought anyone could find Mr. Right in five days, anyway?"

I pulled her in for a hug.

"I hear you. Look, is there anything I can do for you?"

"No. Got it covered," she shook her curls and jangled her myriad bracelets. "He'll be history before everyone has their bags packed and out in the hall for the stewards to take away tonight."

I put my arm around her waist, and we walked into the theater.

Yep, I thought, and unfortunately, Brennan McAllister would be history in that same time frame as well.

As we had anticipated, Alex's cooking demo was not only the most popular, but also the one where we had the most difficulty getting the audience to leave. It was past noon before the last person was gone.

"Great job, baby sister," said Damian as he gave Alex a tight sideways hug.

"Alex, I think you should have your own TV show!" said my mother. She turned to Cam. "And you should be on it as well!"

"Us? We'd kill each other!" Cam laughed. "No, this was fun, but the world turns on its axis better when we each stay in our own specialties."

"Who's up for lunch and drinks by the pool?" Alex asked as she flipped her jaunty chef's cap off her head.

A chorus of "me" came from most of the family, while the two older couples chose to have a quiet lunch on the Boardwalk Deck.

"Pop, I love you, but you are showing your age!" said Alex.

"You get to the pool," said Mr. D'Ag. "We'll wait until the sun isn't as burning hot, then we'll join you."

"What's on for the rest of the afternoon if we don't meet at the pool?" asked Celia, the planner. "This is our last day on the ship, and it is flying by really quickly!"

"I think we have to defend our title as Trivia Champions, then there's the dance competition," said Anthony.

Juliet nodded her head. "Sounds good. If we get separated between now and then, we'll all regroup at the dance competition to see Anthony's moves."

"Hey!" he said. "You sound skeptical!"

"No, no," said Cam as he pushed Anthony toward the door. "She just wants to take some good footage to enter in America's Funniest Home Videos!"

I walked slowly, the last of the group.

"What's up, Keir?" asked Alex, who had returned to make sure I hadn't been left behind.

I hesitated to share the morning's encounter, but she was my best friend after all.

"Well, if you ask me," she said loyally after I told her, "he lost the better end of the deal. As Nonna would say, 'he no deserve-a you anyway, bella mia. Now have some more pasta'."

"Is that what she'd say?" I laughed.

"Well, something very much like that," she allowed. "Come on. Your project is over. You don't have any further appointments. You were successful. We've got the rest of the day on this beautiful ship. No mopin', sistah!"

Ah, that familiar phrase from our college days. I nodded my head decisively as we continued on our path toward our staterooms.

"You're right. No mopin', sistah!"

I took time to complete follow-up paperwork for myself in my stateroom before I left to join the others at the pool. As I stepped off the elevator, I heard a voice I recognized.

"There she is, Rose!"

The Grant sisters.

"Hello, ladies!" I said. "Did you enjoy your classes?"

"Absolutely divine," said Elizabeth. "Thank you again, dear, for helping us. We were just telling our friends here what an efficient young woman you are, and they agreed that this is one of the best events they've ever attended."

I looked around and saw that they were with several other senior citizens, still attired for the seminar with name badges on and notebooks in hand.

"It is my pleasure."

"Well, we appreciate it."

"As far as we can see, everything about this event has been very well organized," said one of the gentlemen in the group whose name tag identified him as Eli. "Do you just do this for the cruise ship?"

"Oh, no. This is my job on land as well." I pulled out and distributed some of my business cards from my pool bag. It was a joke that I even carried business cards into the shower, but my motto was "Never lose the opportunity to market."

"Good to know." Eli tapped my card with his finger. "Now it says here that you're in Denver. Would you consider doing an event in St. Louis? Say, a wedding? My granddaughter is getting married, and I'm footing the bill. Darn girl won't be happy unless it's an event for at least 350 people. I'd like to know that I'm getting what I paid for."

Would I consider it?

"Yes, sir. Let me get your information. With your permission, I'll give you a call when we get back on land."

"Take my information and give me a call, too, dear," said a woman whose name tag read Ida. "We have friends in Denver who are having an anniversary, and we'd like to have them talk to you."

"Absolutely. I'd be happy to."

All righty then! My step was decidedly light when I left this likable group and reached the others at the pool.

"Wonder what the kids are doing right now," Anthony said lazily from his lounge chair later in the afternoon.

Celia peered out from under her impossibly large sun hat at him. "Seriously, we've been gone for almost a week and you just now thought about them?"

"Stop making me sound like a bad father." He reached over with his foot and nudged her. "You know this isn't the first time they've come up in conversation."

"I suspect they haven't even noticed you're gone yet," I said, smiling from my own lounge chair.

"Hey!" defended Anthony.

"You know," I said, "I'd like to go visit your mother and be pampered for a week, Celia!"

We all laughed companionably.

"Speaking of parents, where are ours?" asked Alex. "They never came to join us after lunch. What time is it, anyway? I didn't pay attention after Damian left." She shaded her eyes and looked at the clock across the deck. "Omigosh, you guys, we've been sitting here forever! Didn't anyone notice the time?"

"Don't you qualify as 'anyone'?" asked Cam.

"Are you going to substitute for the comedian tonight?" she shot back. "We totally missed the Trivia Contest."

I sat up. I couldn't believe we had been sitting that long talking, laughing, eating, and enjoying cocktails.

"We can barely make it to the dance contest if we leave right now, and that's just to watch it," I said. "You can't enter all sweaty like you are."

As if on cue, the music on the speakers cut out, and I heard the one voice that so recently had the ability to make my heart catch.

"Ladies and gentlemen, if you are participating in the Dancing Like the Stars competition, you have exactly twenty minutes to get to the ballroom and sign in. Who are the stars? Why, of course, you are! Come on down to try to win fantastic prizes."

Brennan's practiced tones finished, and the music came back.

I looked at Cam, Alex, Anthony, and Celia.

"You guys go get changed really quickly, and Jules and I will go see if we can sign you in. How's that?" I said. "Everyone else will probably realize we've gone there and meet us."

Cam and Alex looked at one another.

"Worth a shot. Let's go!"

We split up and went our separate ways. I just hoped our parents and Damian made it in time to get good seats.

CHAPTER TWENTY-FOUR

Juliet and I skidded into the crowded ballroom and saw that we were safely far back in the line to sign up. Laughing and breathing heavily, we didn't notice when Damian tapped us on the shoulder.

"You two make an interesting couple," he said.

"Hush up. We're here by proxy to sign up for the others."

"Okay," he said. "Uh, did you happen to notice who the competition was?"

"I don't know, people from the ship," I said as I scanned people already on the floor coupled up, pinning numbers on each other's backs. Then my eyes lit on two particular couples.

"You're kidding me."

The two couples in the spotlight were my mother and Russ, and Alex's parents! When they saw me, they hurried over.

"Keira! Are you entering? But with whom? And where are the others?" asked my mother.

"Mother ... when did you decide ... how ...?"

"Well, darling, you kids don't think you invented dancing, do you?" she said. "It sounded like fun when everyone talked about it last night, so today at lunch we all decided what the heck? But aren't the others entering?" She still looked confused.

"They went to change out of their pool gear. We're here to enter for them by proxy," I said.

"Do you have a problem with us entering?" my mother asked, ready, I'm sure, for a negative response. I didn't blame her, given how childish I had acted earlier in the week.

"No, Mother," I laughed. "Exactly the opposite. I think it's great! I just worry for the rest of your competition!"

I hugged her and Russ, and pulled Mr. and Mrs. D'Ag over for a hug as well, then they stepped back to the middle of the floor to get ready. Damian and Jules went to snag seats for us on the perimeter of the floor, while I progressed in the line.

"Next couple." The perky young crew member named Lisa smiled up at me when I reached the front of the line.

"Well, that's the thing. They're on their way. I'm here to sign them in."

"Oh gosh," she said in her flat midwestern tone. "I can't let you do that. The rules clearly state—"

"Oh, I think Miss Graham probably knows the rules," came a voice behind Lisa. "She is a great fan of rules. She just thinks that others don't know how to follow them."

"Lisa." I pursed my lips in an attempt to hide a smile. Brennan at his best. "My friends are right behind me. They're entering the contest. Is there really *any* reason we can't sign them in and let me have their number to hold for them?"

"Hmm. Is there any reason? Lisa, can we think of any reason?" Brennan addressed Lisa, who at that moment probably wished she were assigned to any other task.

"I ... um ... it's written ..." she faltered.

"Come on, Lisa," I said as I avoided Brennan's eye. "You know you can do this. Don't punish them for something you think I did."

"Interesting, Lisa. Miss Graham thinks people shouldn't be punished for things others 'think' they did."

"But Brennan, we can't—" Lisa started again.

"Lisa," I began, "I don't think we should be unreasonably stubborn here—"

"Lisa, Miss Graham apparently knows that being stubborn for no reason is unreasonable. She apparently—"

"Look," Lisa broke in with more strength in her voice, "I don't know what's 'apparently' going on here, but it's just dancing, Brennan. Work out issues between the two of you on your own time and leave me out of it. I have registration to finish." She ostentatiously gave me a pair of numbers. She gave him a look that clearly indicated to back off.

"Thank you, Lisa." I grinned at both of them and turned to walk away, but unfortunately had to turn back. "Um, actually, I need another pair of numbers?"

"What? Oh, here!" she said.

I turned this time with the maximum amount of confidence—knowing full well that Brennan was following my every move—and walked away, hoping, hoping, hoping silently that those guys would arrive already!

"Here!" I shoved the numbers at my friends as they arrived, panting. "And, oh by the way, you're competing against the parents."

"What?" They looked around the floor and saw our parents waving at them.

I left them to deal with that and moved to the seat saved for me.

"What on earth was all of that at the sign-in table?" asked Juliet.

"The effects of too much moonlight."

"What?" She looked at me, then at Brennan, who by this time was in the center of the floor, ready to start the show.

"You're kidding!" she said. "I thought you guys weren't—"

"I don't know what we are or aren't."

At that moment, the musical fanfare began. Brennan stepped into the spotlight and explained how the contest would run. The announced dance styles would include common ballroom styles, and the couples would show their best moves. One by one, those who were tapped on the shoulder would be eliminated and asked to leave the floor. The last couple standing would be the grand prize winner. There would only be one break when the number of couples reached six.

Since the floor was so crowded, it was difficult to see the first sets of couples who were tapped out. Eventually it came down to a more manageable number, including all the couples representing our family!

"Do you think one of our couples can win?" Damian asked over the cheering and clapping.

"I don't know. Stranger things have happened!"

Soon the field was whittled to ten couples. Unfortunately Anthony and Celia were tripped by another couple and were eliminated. When it was time for the break, our three remaining couples were still in!

"Hey, Keira, me love! I see that your family is doing well," Bryce walked over to chat with me as we stood and stretched during the break.

"We'll see what happens here." I crossed my fingers. "How is it that you're not one of the judges?"

"Conflict of interest." He shook his head and pointed to one of the couples. "They're Jinette's cousins. When it comes to the passengers, Brennan won't let any of us cross a line that would make it look like we're playing favorites."

I pondered that for a moment, then took a chance and asked,

"Bryce, were you on the last ship where Brennan was cruise director?"

"I was."

"And you got transferred here at the same time?"

"A lot of us did. Loren, Anders, Jinette."

I had to push one more question.

"Do you know more about why Brennan was moved?"

Bryce looked closely at me.

"Keira, someone didn't tell you the rumor about the female passenger, did they? That gal was so aggressive. She made moves on all of us. We were just lucky that Brennan backed us all up!" He shook his head vigorously. "I just wish that story wouldn't have followed him. He's one of the most stand-up blokes I know. Why, he probably wouldn't even have let you or Juliet be judges either since you're considered part of the staff this week."

What? Oh. Right. I smacked myself inwardly. He made such an issue of referring to Juliet and me as staff. He wanted to protect me and make sure there was no possible appearance of staff/passenger conflict if he and I were ever seen together.

"Oops, the dancing is starting again. I need to get back and be ready to give out consolation prizes," Bryce said and loped off.

I sat down and thought carefully. I had so misjudged him. And now, whatever he possibly thought he felt was most assuredly gone. Worse, I probably wouldn't even have the opportunity to apologize since he would be busy this evening, then we would put into port tomorrow morning and I would set off for home. And Brennan would just turn around and set off on his next cruise. Oh well, I thought, maybe we would see each other in another decade or so.

"Hey, get your head back here," Juliet leaned over and practically had to yell over the crowd's cheering and clapping. "The competition is starting again!"

I took a deep breath as I stood and prepared to cheer for my friends and family. No time to feel sorry for my bad decisions now.

Six couples were left on the floor. The music resumed and so did the enthusiastic dancing.

Unfortunately, the first couple tapped out was Cam and Alex.

We groaned.

In what seemed like seconds, two other couples were eliminated.

"Are you kidding me? Do you see who's left?" I punched Damian in the shoulder as the competition came down to my mother and Russ, Alex's parents, and one other couple.

"They're really good!" Juliet cried.

My mother and Russ were soon tapped out, and it was down to Alex's parents and the other couple.

"Can you believe this?"

"I remember that Pop and Ma used to go to Knights of Columbus dances all the time, but who knew they were this good!" said Damian.

The music switched to a complicated swing tune, and the other couple just couldn't keep up. They were tapped out. Alex's parents were the winners!

The entire audience leapt to its feet.

Brennan walked over to Mr. and Mrs. D'Ag and signaled for the music to stop.

"Well, look here!" he said. "If it isn't the winners of our Marriage Game! Apparently you two are meant to be together on the dance floor as well as in life."

He held the microphone up to Mr. D'Ag, who was breathing heavily and had pulled his handkerchief out to mop his brow.

"I ... guess ... so."

The audience cheered.

"Well, Mr. and Mrs. Mid-Weds—or should we say Fred Astaire and Ginger Rogers—we have a lovely grand prize for you." Brennan indicated for Lisa to bring over a large basket with matching bathrobes, slippers, and yet another bottle of champagne and glasses.

"How about another round of applause!"

As the cheering died down, Brennan indicated to Lisa to escort the winners off to the side of the stage. The entire family ran to the D'Agostinos to circle and congratulate them.

Brennan began to speak again, and we all turned toward him.

"Ladies and gentlemen, it has been a pleasure to cruise with you this week. Have you had a good time?"

Cheers.

"How about that beautiful sunny day we provided for you today?"

Cheers.

"Well, I have a bit of an announcement for you. This cruise line has been my home, well, since I graduated from college. I started out on the crew, just like Lisa here and moved from wonderful ship to wonderful ship, all the way up to being cruise director of the *Ocean's Essence*."

Uh-oh, I thought, something's happening.

"It's time for me to move on."

Groans.

"I appreciate that you fine folks like my work. But it's time for me to move on to the next phase of my journey, and I want you folks to know about it. I'm going to be taking on the marketing responsibilities at a resort on land."

What? Was he moving on to a resort in Cozumel? Is that why he had visited there so often?

"As a matter of fact, I've been recruited to be the vice president of marketing at the resort. Now I know you'd think I would stay in the sunshine, but I'm moving to a snow resort."

Everyone—especially me—hung on his words.

"So I invite all of you next winter to come join me for skiing, snowboarding, and hot-tubbing in the mountains. I'll be in Breckenridge, Colorado."

Breckenridge? One hour from Denver? Breckenridge, where I had skied and snowboarded since I was a little girl? Breckenridge ... how is that possible?

"Keira. KEIRA! Did you hear what I just said?" Juliet shook me.

"No."

"I said, is this some sort of joke? Or did he tell you about this?"

Everyone else in the family was staring at me as he continued his speech. They waited for information they apparently thought I had. I couldn't take the attention, so I tried to dash away. I didn't get very far.

"Keira." A hand reached out to grab my arm.

Brennan had finished his speech and was blocking my exit.

"Keira, we have to have one conversation that won't end with someone running somewhere."

He pulled me behind the ballroom curtain, leaned backward on a wall, and pulled me close to him. I looked up into his eyes.

"Isn't this breaking some sort of 'rule'?" It was the only thing I could think of to say.

His eyes widened.

"Rule? Did you really just say that? Oh, you are so kidding me." It took less than a second for him to sweep me into a kiss.

I pulled away.

"Brennan, I thought you brought me back here for a conversation," I whispered.

"Who needs talk?" He attempted to pull me back, but I put my hands on his chest.

"Wait ... wait ... I need some answers!"

Although I knew it took an incredible amount of restraint for him, he put both hands up in a surrender gesture and said, "Fine. Ask."

I moved next to him, leaned on the same wall, and took a deep breath.

"First, did you really have a thing for me in college?"

"Of course. How many times do I need to tell you that?"

"And you didn't forget me?"

He reached over and pulled my hair out of its braid. "From your silken hair to your icy eyes to the tips of your toes. No, Keira, I never forgot you. Who could forget you? There never has been anyone like you."

"And you're really taking a position in Breckenridge? And you didn't tell me this week?"

"You never let me continue a conversation long enough for it to come up." He rubbed his stomach pointedly where I had punched him.

"Oh, you're right." I thought for a moment more. "Did you know you were moving there at the beginning of the cruise?"

"Yes. These decisions aren't made in a few days, you know."

"Did you know I lived in Denver?"

"Not at the beginning of this cruise. But when I found out ... well ..."

"Well?"

Even in the low lighting behind the curtain, I could tell that shades of the old Capone had crept into the coloring of his face.

"Well, I thought maybe I'd finally have a shot with you, since I would be living so close."

"Hmm."

"Hmm? What does that mean, Keira?"

I tried to process it. There really wasn't such a thing as love at first sight, was there? But did it actually count as love at first sight if I already knew him from years ago? And if he already had fallen for me? Was this why I couldn't connect with anyone all these years?

Then it hit me.

No more thoughts. No more questions. No more processing and analyzing. I reached over and pulled him to me by the lapels of his blazer and brought his lips down to mine. He put his hands on either side of my head as my arms slipped around his waist and our kiss deepened.

Minutes later, I asked, "Do you think you have a shot now?"

"I don't know." He smiled, with me held closely in his arms. "I guess I'll just have to do more research to make sure."

EPILOGUE

"Candles are all set, Keira," said Juliet.

"Great," I answered. "Is the limo outside?"

"This isn't my first event." I could hear the sarcasm through the earpiece.

"I didn't mean to imply that."

"Sure. Calm down or I'll come take that headset away from you."

"Are the groomsmen ready to come onto the altar?" I continued, ignoring her threat.

"I knew you couldn't help yourself," she laughed. "They're walking on right now. Wow, I said it once and I'll say it again. The groom has a lot of hot-looking fraternity brothers."

"Juliet. Remember, I told you to stay away—"

"I know, I know. Stay away from the NFL star. But just until after the reception, right?"

"Jules, you never change! How about the flowers?"

"Well, I think the bride might have something to say about one tiny little change."

"What! I've been in the dressing room with the bridal party, and you haven't let us know anything about any changes!"

"Chill out! You put me in charge of planning this wedding. Let it go!"

"You know I don't like last-minute changes that might make things go wrong."

"Really, wow, this is the first I ever heard of you not liking things going wrong."

"Hold on. Ring bearer and flower girl need something." I put my hand over the mouthpiece and confirmed how to do the step-close-step maneuver.

"I'm back. Okay. Are all the honored guests seated? Groom's parents, extended family, etc.?"

"It's a wedding, Keira, not a rocket launch."

"Remind me to whap you on the back of the head when I get out there."

"I'd like to see you try. The priest will probably catch you and stop you first."

"Damian has no respect. No respect. Hold on, now it's the maid of honor."

I turned to the ball of energy demanding my attention.

"I said"—a very pregnant Alex tried to maintain her patience—"I'm going down the aisle now, and then it's

Elisabetta and Marco with the flowers and the ring, then you. And earpiece out. It won't look good in the pictures."

She took my earpiece and tossed it aside and adjusted the small wreath of flowers that circled my head.

"I'm glad you're wearing your hair down, Princess," she whispered with a smile and turned to go through the door. The children followed her, earnest in their duties. Finally it was my turn.

I took my mother by the arm and took a deep breath.

"Ready, Kee?" said my stepfather Russ as he took my other arm.

I nodded and smiled. When the door opened for us, the first thing that caught my eye made me tear up. The church wasn't decorated with the elegant vases of calla lilies that I had chosen, but with a different flower. Pots and pots of wisteria blanketed the altar and lined the pews.

"Kee-wah's wist-ee-we-ah" I whispered to my mother.

"Brennan worked with Alex's father to scour every nursery in the land to make sure you had them on your day," she whispered back.

We started to walk, and my heart was full of love as I lifted my head and looked into the smiling azure eyes of my groom.

RECIPES

The recipes that follow either were passed to me from my beloved late mother, Teresa Oliverio; have been shared by a few generous friends; or are my versions of recipes collected from random sources over the years. Those that are not specifically attributed below are either my mother's or are significantly different from any original version that I have collected.

The chefs featured in this book are imaginary, and the titles of their books, blogs, and presentations are completely imaginary as well.

KEIRA'S FAVORITE BUTTERSCOTCH BROWNIES

¼ cup unsalted butter, melted
1 cup packed dark brown sugar
1 egg
1 teaspoon vanilla extract
¾ cup all-purpose flour
1 teaspoon baking powder
½ teaspoon salt
½ cup chopped walnuts
½ cup butterscotch chips

1. Preheat the oven to 350°F. Grease an 8″ x 8″ baking dish.

2. In a large bowl, combine the butter, sugar, egg, and vanilla and mix until completely incorporated.

3. Stir in the remaining ingredients. The mixture will be thick.

4. Spread in the baking dish. Bake 20 to 25 minutes. Cool completely and cut.

Makes 16 bars

BREAD PUDDING

(Courtesy of Lou and Cindy Phillips,
Highlands Ranch, Colorado)

1 loaf (10 ounces) French bread
4 eggs
4 cups milk
1 tablespoon vanilla extract
½ cup butter, melted
3¼ cups sugar
1 cup raisins
Vanilla ice cream

1. Slice the bread into 1" slices and let it get stale.
2. Preheat the oven to 350°F.
3. In a large bowl, beat the eggs with a whisk. Add the milk, vanilla, butter, and 3 cups of the sugar. Beat well.
4. Add the bread and raisins and mix well by hand until wet.
5. Pour into a 13" x 9" baking dish. Sprinkle with the remaining ¼ cup sugar. Bake for 1½ hours.
6. Serve hot and top with the ice cream. Enjoy!

HURRICANE

Juice of ½ lime
Ice
2 ounces light rum
2 ounces dark rum
2 ounces passion fruit juice
1 ounce orange juice
1 tablespoon simple syrup (½ sugar plus ½ water)
1 tablespoon grenadine
1 orange slice, for garnish
1 cherry, for garnish

1. Squeeze the lime juice into a cocktail shaker over ice.
2. Pour in the rums, juices, syrup, and grenadine. Shake well.
3. Strain into a hurricane glass.
4. Garnish with the cherry and orange.

Makes 1

SHRIMP PO BOY

Oil for frying (preferably peanut)
¾ cup panko
¾ cup all-purpose flour
1 tablespoon Cajun seasoning
1 teaspoon salt
2 eggs
1 pound medium shrimp, shelled, deveined, and tails removed
4 small sandwich rolls
Remoulade (see recipe below, or use prepared)
Shredded lettuce
2-3 tomatoes, sliced about ¼″ thick

1. Pour enough oil in a large frying pan to come up about ¼″. Set the pan over medium-high heat. When a small amount of flour sizzles immediately after you drop it in, the oil is ready.
2. Meanwhile, in a large bowl, mix the panko, flour, Cajun seasoning, and salt. In a medium bowl, beat the eggs.
3. Working with a few at a time, dredge the shrimp in the egg, then in the panko mixture. Shake off any excess, place in the pan, and fry until golden on both

SHRIMP PO BOY CONTINUED

sides, about 2 minutes total. Set the fried shrimp aside on paper towels to drain.

4. To assemble the sandwich, slice the sandwich rolls almost all the way through and smear remoulade on both the top and bottom. Lay down a layer of shredded lettuce on the bottom of the sandwich, then arrange the shrimp on top. Lay 3-4 slices of tomato on the shrimp and press the top of the bread down on the bottom, compressing the sandwich a little.

PO BOY REMOULADE

1¼ cups mayonnaise (not salad dressing)
¼ cup mustard
1 tablespoon sweet paprika
1 tablespoon Cajun seasoning
2 teaspoons prepared horseradish
1 teaspoon pickle juice
1 teaspoon hot sauce
1 large clove garlic, minced and smashed

Mix all the ingredients together in a medium bowl. Refrigerate for 1 to 2 hours before use.

NAN'S VEGGIE DIP

½ pound cream cheese, softened
2 tablespoons milk
2 tablespoons French or Dorothy Lynch salad dressing
1 tablespoon finely chopped onion
½ cup ketchup
Dash of salt

Mix all the ingredients together in a medium bowl and chill. Serve with cut-up veggies of your choice (carrots, celery, broccoli, etc.).

GREEN OLIVE CROSTADE SPREAD/DIP

Splash of olive oil
6-8 cloves garlic
1 jar (21 ounces) green olives with pimientos
Splash of balsamic vinegar
3 tablespoons chopped Italian flat-leaf parsley

1. In a blender or food processor, pulse the oil and garlic until the garlic is rough chopped.
2. Add the remaining ingredients and blend until smooth.
3. Refrigerate for at least 2 hours. Serve at room temperature as a dip or spread on small bread rounds.

TEX-MEX CORN SALSA/DIP

1 bag (12 ounces) frozen sweet yellow corn, defrosted and drained
¼ cup diced red bell peppers
2 medium-size jalapeño chile peppers, seeded and chopped (Note: if you like more heat, leave as many seeds as you wish)
½ onion, finely chopped (about 1/3 cup)
2 tablespoons fresh lime juice (about 2 limes)
½ teaspoon salt
½ teaspoon freshly ground black pepper

Combine all ingredients in a large bowl and mix well. Serve with corn chips or use as salsa on burritos or tacos.

MAMA'S STUFFED PEPPERS

5 green bell peppers
2 tablespoons olive oil
½ onion, chopped
1 pound ground beef
1 pound ground pork
2 eggs
1 cup grated Parmigiano or Romano cheese
½ cup chopped parsley
2 cups cooked rice, cooled
3-4 cups tomato-based pasta sauce, preferably homemade

1. Preheat the oven to 400°F. Spray a 13″ x 9″ baking dish with cooking oil or spread a few tablespoons of oil on the bottom.

2. Cut the stems from the peppers, cut each in half lengthwise, and scrape out the seeds and membranes. Place in the prepared baking dish.

3. Heat the olive oil in a small skillet over medium heat. Stir in the onions and cook until translucent.

4. Put the cooked onions in a mixing bowl and add the beef, pork, eggs, cheese, parsley, and rice. Stir together until evenly blended.

5. Divide the filling among the peppers.

MAMA'S STUFFED PEPPERS

6. Pour in enough of the pasta sauce to barely cover the peppers. Cover the dish with aluminum foil and bake until the peppers are tender and the filling is cooked through, about 40 to 45 minutes.

7. Remove the foil and let stand 5 to 10 minutes before serving.

TESSIE'S CABBAGE ROLLS

(In the style of Tessie Shevechuck,
Carolina, West Virginia)

Sauce:

2 tablespoons extra-virgin olive oil
2 cloves garlic, diced
1½ quarts crushed tomatoes
2 tablespoons white vinegar
1 tablespoon sugar
Salt and pepper

Filling and Cabbage:

2 tablespoons extra-virgin olive oil
1 medium onion, chopped
2 cloves garlic, minced
2 tablespoons tomato paste
1 pound ground beef
1 pound ground pork
1 large egg
2 tablespoons chopped parsley
2 cups cooked rice, cooled
Salt and pepper
1 large head green cabbage or enough for 18-20 leaves

TESSIE'S CABBAGE ROLLS CONTINUED

1. *To make the sauce*: Add the olive oil to a saucepan over medium heat. Add the garlic and sauté for 1 minute. Add the tomatoes and cook, stirring occasionally, for 5 minutes.

2. Add the vinegar and sugar and simmer, until the sauce thickens, about 5 minutes. Season with salt and pepper and remove from the heat.

3. *To make the filling*: Add the olive oil to a skillet over medium heat. Sauté the onion and garlic until soft, about 5 minutes.

4. Stir in the tomato paste plus ½ cup of the prepared sauce. Mix to incorporate, then take it off the heat.

5. In a large mixing bowl, combine the beef and pork. Add the egg, parsley, rice, and the onion mixture. Toss with your hands to combine. Season with salt and pepper.

6. Core the cabbage and place the cored side up in a deep bowl or saucepan. Cover with boiling water and let stand for 5 minutes to soften and loosen the leaves. Drain. Remove the largest 18-20 leaves and reserve. Place the remaining cabbage on a cutting board and slice. Place the sliced cabbage in the bottom of a buttered or sprayed baking 13" x 9" pan.

TESSIE'S CABBAGE ROLLS CONTINUED

7. *To assemble and bake*: Preheat the oven to 350°F.

8. Carefully cut out the center vein from the reserved cabbage leaves so they will be easier to roll up. Put about ½ cup of the filling in the center of the cabbage and, starting at what was the stem end, fold the sides in and roll up the cabbage to enclose the filling. Place the cabbage rolls, seam side down, side by side in rows on top of the sliced cabbage in the baking pan.

9. Pour the remaining sauce over the cabbage rolls. Cover the pan with foil.

10. Bake for 45 minutes. Remove the foil, then bake for an additional 15 minutes, until the meat is cooked.

WHAT'S SHAKIN' BACON FRIED RICE

½ pound bacon, cut in large dice
1 small onion, diced
3-4 cups cooked rice, cooled
1-2 cups frozen peas (amount is according to taste)
3 eggs, beaten

1. In a wok or a pan large enough to accommodate a lot of stirring during cooking, brown the bacon thoroughly over medium-high heat. Move bacon to the side of the pan and drain all but ½ cup of the grease.
2. Turn the heat to high. Add the onion and sauté briefly.
3. Add the rice to bacon and onions and stir to combine.
4. Add the peas and stir to combine.
5. Make a hole in the center of the rice mixture by pushing the mixture to the side.
6. Add the eggs in the center and cook, scrambling until mostly done. Mix the eggs into the rice mixture as it finishes cooking.
7. Remove from the heat and serve.

(Note: This is also good with bamboo shoots or leftover vegetables. If using, add immediately after sautéing the onions. If desired, use a frozen peas-carrots mix instead of just peas.)

DARBY'S CHICKEN SALAD

2 cups chopped apples
2 cups sliced red globe grapes
2 cups chicken cubes or shreds
1 cup finely chopped walnuts
About 1 cup Greek yogurt
About ½ cup sour cream
½ cup finely chopped onion
Salt
Freshly ground black pepper
About 1 tablespoon chicken fajita seasoning mix

In a large bowl, combine all the ingredients, adjusting the yogurt, sour cream, and seasonings to taste. Refrigerate for a minimum of 1 to 2 hours for best flavor.

AUNT LYDIA'S CHEESECAKE

Crust:

1½ cups finely ground graham cracker crumbs
1/3 cup butter, melted
1/3 cup sugar

Filling:

4 packages (8 ounces each) cream cheese, well-softened
2 cups sugar
7 eggs
Juice from 1 large lemon
2 teaspoons vanilla extract (or substitute almond extract)
2 tablespoons all-purpose flour
1 pint heavy whipping cream (don't substitute half-and-half)

1. *To make the crust*: In a large bowl, mix the graham cracker crumbs, butter, and sugar thoroughly. Press onto the bottom of a 9" springform pan.

2. *To make the filling*: Preheat oven to 350°F.

3. Add the cream cheese to the bowl of a mixer and cream on medium speed. Add the sugar, a little at a time.

AUNT LYDIA'S CHEESECAKE CONTINUED

4. Add the eggs one at a time, keeping the mixer on medium speed.

5. Add the lemon juice, vanilla, and flour.

6. Add whipping cream, mixing until just combined.

7. Pour over the graham cracker crust. Bake on the middle rack of the oven for 1 hour. Turn the oven off and, leaving the oven door closed, keep the cheesecake in the oven for another hour.

8. Remove from the oven and refrigerate. This is best if made one day before serving.

DELUXE LEMON BARS

1 cup all-purpose flour
1/3 cup plus 1 tablespoon confectioners' sugar
½ cup butter or margarine
4 large eggs
¾ cup granulated sugar
¾ cup bottled lemon juice (Important! Use bottled, not fresh)

1. Preheat the oven to 350°F.
2. Mix the flour and 1/3 cup confectioners' sugar in a medium bowl.
3. Cut in the butter until the mixture resembles small peas. (The mixture should be dry and crumbly.)
4. Press into the bottom of an ungreased 9" square baking pan. Bake for 15 minutes, or until lightly golden.
5. Meanwhile, beat the eggs with a mixer for about 3 minutes, until pale and thickened.
6. Gradually add the granulated sugar and continue beating for 1 minute longer until the mixture is thick. Stir in the lemon juice.
7. Pour onto the hot crust. Bake for 15 minutes, or until golden and a pick inserted in the center comes out clean.
8. Sprinkle with the remaining 1 tablespoon confectioners' sugar. Cool the pan on a rack. Cut into 16 bars.

PROMENADE BROWNIES

¾ cup cocoa powder
½ teaspoon baking powder
2/3 cup cooking oil
½ cup boiling water (measure accurately)
2 cups granulated sugar
2 eggs
1 1/3 cups all-purpose flour
1 teaspoon vanilla extract
1 tablespoon seedless raspberry jam
¼ teaspoon salt
Confectioners' sugar

1. Preheat the oven to 350°F. Lightly grease a 13″ x 9″ pan or two 8″ square pans.
2. In a large mixing bowl, stir together the cocoa and baking powder. Blend in 1/3 cup of the oil. Add the boiling water and stir until the mixture thickens.
3. Add the granulated sugar, eggs, and the remaining oil and stir until smooth.
4. Add the flour, vanilla, jam, and salt and blend thoroughly.
5. Pour into the prepared baking pan. Bake 35 to 40 minutes for the 13″ x 9″ pan, or 30-32 minutes for the 8″ pans.
6. Cool. Dust with confectioners' sugar before cutting into squares.

CHICAGO DOGS

(In honor of Wade, Nancy, and Andrew)

Cooked wiener
Bun (preferably poppy seed)
Mustard
Relish
Chopped onion
2 tomato wedges
1 dill pickle spear
2 sport peppers
Celery salt

The Chicago Dog is a Windy City classic. The ingredients must be piled onto the bun in the correct order. And whatever you do, don't ruin it with ketchup!

To assemble: Place the dog in the bun. Squirt mustard down the center. Add a dollop of relish and a spoon of onion. Put the tomato wedges between dog and bun on one side and the pickle spear between dog and bun on the other. Add the sport peppers and a generous dash of celery salt.

WEST VIRGINIA DOG

(In honor of my home state)

Bun
Cooked wiener
Sauce (see recipe below)
Mustard (optional)
Onions (optional)
Slaw (optional, if you are from the southern part of the state)

HOT DOG SAUCE

2 pounds ground beef
4 tablespoons chili powder
1 large onion, finely chopped
1½ teaspoons garlic salt or garlic powder
1 tablespoon cayenne (more if you like it hot!)
1 can (12 ounces) tomato paste
2 teaspoons salt

1. Place the beef in a large pot and add enough water to cover the beef. Bring to a boil. The color will be gray at this point, but this is right. It's important to not brown the beef.

2. After the water begins to boil, add the remaining ingredients. Turn down the heat and simmer for at least 1 hour.

Note: West Virginia hot dog sauce should never be confused with chili! It is simply "sauce," and many hot dog joints in the mountain state are known for their sauce. If you are traveling in northern West Virginia, put these hot dog eateries on your list: T&L, Hometown Hot Dogs, Lupo's, and the king of the hot dog, Yann's. Also, ketchup is NEVER an option.

CHICKEN VESUVIO A LA ALEXANDRIA

Olive oil, for browning
2 pounds russet potatoes, peeled and cut into lengthwise wedges
1 pound sweet Italian sausage, cut into 1″ pieces
4 pounds bone-in chicken (mix of thighs, breasts, legs, as desired), or 1 chicken cut into 14 pieces
Salt
5 tablespoons olive oil
6 cloves garlic, crushed
1 medium onion, peeled and rough-chopped in large pieces
1 cup dry white wine
1 cup chicken stock
2 red or green bell peppers, cut into thick slices
16 ounces frozen peas, thawed

1. Preheat the oven to 400°F.

2. Coat a skillet with olive oil and heat over medium heat. Add the potatoes and sausage and brown on all sides, about 8 minutes. When browned, transfer the mixture to a large roasting pan.

3. Season the chicken all over with salt. In the same skillet, brown the chicken on all sides in batches, about

CHICKEN VESUVIO A LA ALEXANDRIA CONTINUED

8 to 10 minutes per batch, transferring to the roasting pan as completed.

4. Add 3 tablespoons of the olive oil, the crushed garlic, and onions to the skillet.

5. Once the garlic begins to sizzle, deglaze with the wine. When the wine has reduced by half, add the chicken stock. Return to a boil, and then pour all the skillet contents into the roasting pan.

6. Add the bell pepper to the roasting pan. Sprinkle everything with salt, stir to mix, and drizzle with the remaining 2 tablespoons olive oil.

7. Place in the oven and roast for 20 minutes. Remove from the oven and scatter the peas over the mixture. Stir and return to the oven. Roast for 30 to 40 minutes longer, stirring occasionally.

Serves 6 to 8

AUTHOR'S NOTE

Regal Cruise Lines and the ship *Ocean's Essence* are a composite of any number of cruise lines and cruise ships that I have had the privilege of traveling on during many wonderful seagoing vacations. Any passing resemblance should be interpreted as a general cruise experience on most ships and not on any specific ship or itinerary. Some experiences were completely fabricated because they were necessary for the story and should not be interpreted as typical of cruising or of staff interaction.

ABOUT THE AUTHOR

Award-winning author Barbara Oliverio is the daughter of Italian immigrants and grew up with a love of books and a passion for learning. She and her husband keep their luggage readily available in their suburban Denver home for their own travel adventures by land, air and sea. This is her second novel.

For book club appearances or bulk purchases
please contact Barbara Oliverio directly at
barbara@scolapastapress.com